STRANGE DISAPPEARANCES

MARQUISE DE MAINTENON WHO FIGURED PROMINENTLY IN THE CASE OF
"THE VEILED SULTANA"
(Harper's Magazine 1852)

STRANGE DISAPPEARANCES

BY

ELLIOTT O'DONNELL

WITH EIGHT ILLUSTRATIONS

New Foreword by
LESLIE SHEPARD

CITADEL PRESS BOOK
Published by Carol Publishing Group

CONTENTS

LIST OF ILLUSTRATIONS

NEW FOREWORD

Some of the most thrilling stories ever invented by novelists have been about mysterious disappearances.

It is not difficult for fiction writers to invent convincing reasons for disappearance. Secret service—disputes over inheritance—criminal activities—jealous lovers—all these are stock plots, and at the end of the book everything is explained.

But the stories in *this* book are true. And most of them remain a mystery. They are not only strange—they are absolutely inexplicable.

In November, 1809, Mr. Benjamin Bathurst, representative of the British government, was in a small German town on his way back from a meeting in Vienna. In the presence of two persons he was checking the horses which would draw his coach on the way back to England. He walked around to the horses on the far side—and just vanished. He was never seen again.

What became of Count Philipp von Königsmarck, the handsome lover of Princess Sophia, wife of the prince of Hanover who became George I of England? On Sunday, July 1, 1694, Königsmarck was seen to enter the Electoral Palace. He never came out.

Who was the real Martin Guerre? One morning, in the 1550s, Martin walked out from his cottage in the Rieux district, France, and disappeared, leaving a wife and child behind. Eight years later he came back and was recognized by his wife, his four sisters, and his Uncle Peter. He resumed his married life, until one day another Martin Guerre turned up, this one with a wooden leg, the result of war service in Flanders. Now the first Martin was charged with impersonation, and even Uncle Peter changed his mind and said he was an impostor. One hundred and fifty witnesses were examined by the judge, and opinions were roughly divided until Martin's wife changed her mind and said the man with the wooden leg was the real Martin. The other was imprisoned and executed.

There are other exciting mysteries in this book, some of them cloak-and-dagger affairs of distant history, others as recent as the nineteenth century. The compiler was a writer who specialized in the weird, uncanny, and inexplicable.

ELLIOTT O'DONNELL (1872-1965) was the son of a clergyman. Born in England, he claimed descent from Irish chieftains of barbaric days, including Niall of the Nine Hostages (the King Arthur of Irish folklore) and Red Hugh, who fought the English in the days of the first Queen Elizabeth. O'Donnell was educated at Clifton College, Bristol, England, and Queen's Service Academy, Dublin, Ireland.

His first psychic experience was at the age of five, in a house where he saw a nude elemental figure covered with spots. Later, as a young man in Dublin, he was half strangled by a mysterious phantom. He must have had exceptionally strong nerves, for in his later life he deliberately became a ghost hunter. Before that he traveled all over America, worked on a ranch in Oregon, and was a policeman in the Chicago Railway Strike of 1894. Returning to England he worked as a schoolmaster and trained for the theater. He served in the British army in World War I, acted on the stage and in films. He wrote his first book in his spare time, a psychic thriller titled *For Satan's Sake*, and soon found his true profession as an author. He wrote several popular novels, and then specialized in true stories of ghosts and hauntings, producing over fifty books which were enormously popular. The titles were irresistible: *Ghosts with a Purpose—Fatal Kisses—Screaming Skulls—Famous Curses — Women Bluebeards — Strange Sea Mysteries — Haunted Britain — Werewolves — The Sorcery Club — Strange Cults and Secret Societies of London*. As an expert on the supernatural he achieved fame as a ghost-hunter. He lectured and broadcast on the subject in Britain and America, and appeared on television. In addition to his books he wrote scores of articles and stories for national newspapers and magazines. He once said: "I have investigated, sometimes alone, and sometimes with other people and the press, many cases of reputed hauntings. I believe in ghosts but am not a spiritualist."

In spite of his hazardous hobby, he lived to a ripe old age of ninety-three years. Like leading Irish families, the O'Donnells were reputed to have a Banshee—the wailing ghost that heralds a death. It is not recorded whether his own passing evoked this romantic phantom.

A word of warning about the present volume. O'Donnell had the great Irish gift of telling a good story, but the actor in him could not resist a little embroidery. Do not look for scholarly precision in these yarns, for O'Donnell's romantic flair has freely invented conversations that were never recorded, and the novelist in him cannot resist purple patches.

I think that he was often torn between fact and fiction, and this is reflected in his literary output, where his novels were as popular as his factual stories (some critics even suggested that it was difficult to tell the difference). O'Donnell was an incurable romantic, who announced his hobbies as "investigating queer cases, inventing queer games, and frightening crooks with the Law." I have never heard of any criminals being awed by O'Donnell!

But he was a born storyteller, and you may read these enthralling stories how you will. They are sheer entertainment by any standards. A *New York Herald Tribune* critic commented on this book: "Full of variety, and it is freshly written."

This collection of real-life stories reads as easily as any thriller.

1971   LESLIE SHEPARD

STRANGE DISAPPEARANCES

CHAPTER I

THE MYSTERY OF THE MASKED SULTANA

ONE of the most attractive women at the Court of Louis XIV during the régime of Madame de Montespan was Madame de Béthune. Even in a Court famous all the world over for its many beauties, she was conspicuously beautiful, and there was hardly a poet, wit or gallant in Paris who hadn't raved about her hair, her eyes and her many other physical attractions. Hence, of course, the deadly scandalmongers of those times did not spare her. Gossip associated her name with more than one love affair carried on clandestinely, behind the back of her chivalrous and trustful husband, and she was suspected of having almost as much influence over Louis as had Madame de Montespan herself. But, at length, a day came when the never ceasing tongue waggers wagged their tongues a little too freely, and M. de Béthune getting to know that one of them, a certain gentleman whose name history for some reason or another has failed to record, had been making very grave allegations regarding his wife's chastity, alluding to her as the mistress of more than one notorious Court roué, at once challenged him to a duel.

Apparently, particulars of the encounter were never made public, but, whether fairly or foully, Béthune was killed, and his charming wife, in consequence, left a widow. She seems, however, to have dried her tears, if indeed there had been any tears to dry, very soon, for the coffin containing the remains of her gallant and ill-fated spouse had scarcely been lowered into its grave, and the earth sprinkled over it, before she threw aside her mourning and plunged more unrestrainedly than ever into the gaieties and excesses of Court life. For some undiscovered reason she never married again, but continued to figure in endless scandals till the fleeting years began to diminish her attractions and younger and prettier Court belles, competing with her, gradually thrust her into the background. It was at this juncture that Madame de Montespan ceased to appear at Court, her place being taken by Madame de Maintenon, a lady of a very different character. Louis was growing old and Madame de Maintenon, who, although very much under priestly influence, seems to have had a genuine penchant for religion, gradually prevailed upon him to reflect seriously upon his anything but pious

past and to form resolutions, at least, of setting a
rather better example to his people than he had
done heretofore. Consequently, Louis, outwardly
at any rate, became a penitent, and princes of the
blood and noblemen actually accompanied Madame
and her train to Mass, while the belles of the Court
were forced to discard their disgracefully low-
necked dresses and to don others, more decorous
and decent.

Madame de Béthune laughed. The young ones
had robbed her of her popularity, and this was
their just punishment. For her own part, now that
she could no longer please, it mattered not a
tittle how she dressed, so she put on sombre
black and became a convert to the most ascetic
piety.

When she died, which she did not very long after
her retirement from the world—her extremely
religious mode of living apparently not suiting her
constitution—she bequeathed her entire fortune, a
pretty large one, together with her only child
Rosalie, to the Benedictine Convent of St. Rosalie,
which had been founded many years before by one
of her husband's ancestors. In the sixteenth century, when Calvinism first made its appearance
in France, the Béthunes, as well as the Rohans,
Madame de Béthune's ancestry, embraced the new
faith and for a considerable number of years fought

bravely enough in the ranks of the much persecuted Huguenots. Some time prior to Louis XIV's ascent to the throne, however, both families had waxed somewhat lukewarm, and Madame de Béthune, soon after the death of her husband (or shall we say murder? For there were grave suspicions at the time of foul play), became reconciled to the Roman Catholic Church, with which, as a matter of fact, for purely worldly reasons, advancement at the Court being very difficult for Huguenots, she was known to have been coquetting for a long time.

Rosalie therefore was brought up a Roman Catholic, and on her mother's death it was fully anticipated that, in accordance with a mandate expressed in the latter's will, she would become a nun. Greatly to the astonishment of all, however, Rosalie did no such thing. She was young, she argued, only nineteen, well favoured—she might, indeed, have said beautiful, for she was even more beautiful than her mother had been at the same age —and very fond of Court life. Why, then, should she be shut up for life in a convent and doomed to a career for which nature had rendered her totally unfit?

It was in vain that Madame de Maintenon and the late Madame de Béthune's priestly advisers remonstrated with her, pointing out the hollowness of life at Court, with its many dangers and temptations, and the advantages that would accrue to her were she to decide upon a life within the cloisters of St. Rosalie.

"Just think," they said, "what joy and peace would be yours, were you to join this sisterhood! Why, with your money and intellect you might soon become an Abbess. You would then be in supreme authority over a whole community of sisters, who would love and reverence you, respecting your every thought and wish. Think of that, the power you would have! Besides, it was your mother's dying wish. If you despise that, Heaven will undoubtedly punish you sooner or later."

But even this dire prospect made no impression upon Rosalie.

"I will take my chance," she said. "My life is my own to do what I like with, and no will or wish of my mother's shall determine it for me."

"Oh, but it must," the priest who was spokesman responded, "especially when that wish has the sanction and approval of the Church."

"Then, you mean to coerce me?" Rosalie retorted angrily.

"Coerce is not a very pleasant term to use, my child," the priest replied suavely, "we shall merely have recourse to persuasion. The power and influence of Holy Church is great, very great indeed," and so saying, he left her.

" Can you think of any reason for Rosalie de Béthune's obstinacy ? " this same priest said to Madame de Maintenon one day, when, with several of his colleagues, he was closeted alone with her " Is it, do you think, merely because being young and attractive her heart rebels against the idea of seclusion in a convent, or is there, do you suppose " —and here all the priests looked knowingly and anxiously at Madame de Maintenon—" some other cause ? Her father, you know, and her ancestors, on both sides, were heretics. Can it be possible, do you think, that Rosalie de Béthune has a leaning that way herself ? "

" No," Madame de Maintenon said shortly, " I'm sure she hasn't. She cares nothing for religion, Church, or Calvinism. It's far more likely she's in love."

" In love," the priests cried in chorus, opening their eyes wide and looking round at one another, " with whom ? "

" Ah, that's more than I can say," Madame de Maintenon replied, " but no girl, alone and unaided, could stand up against such pressure as you, and I, and others have brought to bear on Rosalie de Béthune. There's a man in the case, without any doubt."

"True," the priests again replied in chorus. "You understand your sex, of course, much better than we do. That is only natural. She must be watched."

"She shall be," Madame de Maintenon replied with asperity. "I will see to that, and as soon as Father Duroque returns from the country I will speak to him about her."

The conference then broke up.

Father Duroque, besides being the beautiful Madame de Maintenon's great friend, was the King's confessor and first cousin to the Abbess of St. Rosalie; consequently he was a person of great influence, and Madame de Maintenon had little doubt but that the rebellious Rosalie, when tackled by him, would soon be forced to submission. She would have preferred Rosalie entering the Convent of St. Cyr that she, Madame de Maintenon, had founded, but she did not wish to offend Father Duroque, who, apparently, had made up his mind that Rosalie de Béthune should retire, with all her wealth of course, to St. Rosalie. True to her word, the moment Father Duroque returned to Versailles, she approached him, and the two then laid their heads together to discover the real reason of Rosalie's objection to taking the veil. Rosalie, at this time, was living in her town house, where she kept a large retinue of servants.

These, together with her father confessor, were all " got at " ; and, as the result of a constant system of espionage, it was at length discovered that Rosalie de Béthune was corresponding a great deal with a certain Count d'Ambois, a young gentleman of very ancient lineage, whom the King, only a short while before, had made an officer of the bedchamber. This Count d'Ambois resided in Paris with his mother, who, it was soon ascertained by the spies of Father Duroque and Madame de Maintenon, was doing all she could to bring about a marriage between her son and Rosalie. She knew, of course, that the all powerful Madame de Maintenon would oppose any marriage on the part of Rosalie, no matter with whom, and so great was her dread of the intercourse between the two young people being discovered by Madame de Maintenon that she insisted upon Rosalie coming to the house —which she did, almost daily—in disguise.

The young Count, it must be stated, evidently admired Rosalie. He could scarcely fail to do that, but it was very obvious that he was far too vain and shallow to form any deep attachment to anyone, and what unquestionably attracted him most to Mlle. de Béthune was her fortune. Rosalie, on the other hand, though gay and, perhaps, in some respects thoughtless, possessed a passionate nature, and was undoubtedly fond of the Count, placing implicit faith in his constant avowals of undying affection.

" And you really love me," she was overheard by Duroque's paid eavesdroppers to say to the young Count, one night, in the conservatory of the latter's Paris home, " as much as all that, and promise to remain true to me no matter what our enemies may say or do ? "

" I promise on my honour," the Count replied, seizing her hands and smothering them with kisses.

" You will marry me despite all and everything ? "

" I will," he ejaculated. " It is only for you to name the day and hour."

" Then, let it be Sunday," Rosalie cried eagerly. " Sunday at noon," and a little later, disengaging herself from his ardent embraces, she crept softly away, Duroque's spies surreptitiously following her.

The next day, Madame de Maintenon and Father Duroque, together, called upon the Countess, who at the mere sight of them trembled all over as if she had had the ague, and informed her that the intrigue between her son and Rosalie de Béthune having been discovered it was essential that she should intervene and see that the affair was broken off at once. " It is not only that Mlle. de Béthune is destined for convent life, in accordance with the will of her much respected mother and our will too," they said, " but the taint of leprosy * as well as heresy is in her veins, and that alone, were your son to marry her, would bring down the wrath of Heaven on his head and yours."

The Countess, however, although by this time on the verge of fainting with fright, was inclined to demur, and her visitors, noting it, immediately threw aside their mask of religion and told her plainly that unless she did as they had told her to do, and that without delay, both she and her son would be sent to the Bastille, and subjected to all kinds of torture.

It was enough. The Countess, knowing that her visitors had it in their power to do all that they threatened, flung herself down on her knees before them, and with clasped hands promised to do all that was required of her, if only her life and that of her son might be spared. Madame de Maintenon looked at the holy father and smiled.

" That is good," she said, " rise, Madame, and carry out your promise. You won't find us ungrateful."

That same evening all the letters and parcels the Count had received from Rosalie de Béthune were

---

* It was said that one of Rosalie de Béthune's remote ancestors had suffered from this disease. (*Vide* " Chamber's Journal of Popular Literature," October 13th, 1860.)

returned to her, with a curt message in writing from the Count to say that all intercourse between the two was over, and that the engagement must be considered at an end. No explanation was given.

The Count did not wait for results. Knowing Rosalie's passionate and fiery nature, and fearing, as he may well have feared, that she would at least try to see him, and, also, terrified, almost out of his wits, by what his mother had told him regarding the Bastille, he left Paris post-haste, and that same night travelled, at what for him was a break neck speed, *en route* for Italy.

His apprehensions regarding Madame de Maintenon and Father Duroque, however, were quite groundless. Having achieved their purpose, namely the breaking off of his clandestine engagement to Rosalie de Béthune, they dismissed him from their thoughts, but in order to prove they were in the habit of keeping their word they sent the Countess d'Ambois a substantial sum of money.

The Countess anxious, in her turn, to ingratiate herself in their good books and, at the same time, gain favour with the Church, which she feared she might have alienated, presented a very remarkable gift to the Convent of St. Rosalie. It was a crucifix covered with precious stones and believed to have been fashioned out of a portion of the Cross on which our Lord had been crucified. Given centuries before to the d'Ambois family by the Doge Dandola, who had obtained it, together with other spoil, in the sacking of Constantinople, it was regarded as a mascot, and was popularly believed to preserve its possessor from any actual physical danger.

The Abbess of St. Rosalie was delighted with it, and, to show her gratitude to the donor, succeeded in obtaining for the Countess a royal pension, and for the young Count d'Ambois the position of Keeper of the King's Wardrobe.

But, in the meanwhile, how did it fare with Rosalie ?

Madame de Maintenon and Father Duroque had fully expected, now that her engagement to the young Count had been broken off, she would submit to their mandate and enter the Convent of St. Rosalie. Greatly, however, to their surprise and indignation she declined to do any such thing, and openly defying them continued to live, as sumptuously as ever, in her town house.

" It must be the heretic blood in her," Madame de Maintenon said to Father Duroque. " Only one resource is left open to us now, the Bastille. We must break her rebellious spirit." And the pair forthwith laid their heads together, in order to discover some pretext for having the fractious Mlle. de Béthune committed to the State Prison.

In the meanwhile, she was placed under an inter-
dict that forbade her attending Mass and places
of amusement, while no one, saving the clergy, was
allowed to visit her.

Thus, the conspiracy was progressing, when a remarkable incident occurred. On a certain winter's
day Mlle. de Béthune was sitting alone in one of
the big salons of her mansion, meditating upon her
fate. It was fast growing dark, but as yet no lamps
had been lighted, and the apartment was illuminated solely by the flickering flames of a log wood
fire.

Outside, in the large, gloomy hall, menials—all
paid spies of Father Duroque and Madame de
Maintenon—were collected together in groups
discussing in low voices, devoid of even a particle
of pity, the approaching arrest of their mistress,
whilst, outside in the grounds, three burly musketeers kept constant watch lest she should try to
escape, or lest anyone other than a priest, or who
had not Father Duroque's special permission to
visit the house, should gain access to it. Indeed,
Mlle. de Béthune could not have been more closely
watched and guarded. But to proceed. Five
o'clock had just sounded, when a monk, his hood
pulled low down over his eyes, entered the grounds
and, as the musketeers of the house had had orders to
admit priests, made his way to the front entrance,

unchallenged. Arriving there, he demanded to be shown into the presence of Mlle. de Béthune's father confessor, with so great an air of authority that the lackey he addressed obeyed him without any questioning. He, however, as well as several of his fellow servants, noticed that the stranger walked with a quite unusual briskness for one in holy orders, and one and all were much impressed by the litheness of his figure and his youthful carriage.

When the Father's quarters were reached, it was found that he was busily engaged upon a substantial repast of roast fowl and venison, which he was helping down with copious draughts of the choicest Burgundy, and that he did not appear to be too pleased at being disturbed. He glanced round angrily in fact, and was about to say something rude, when the stranger, stepping forward, threw aside his hood and for the first time disclosed his face. It was singularly arrestive. Though very pale, there was no sign of ill health about it, nor was it possible to derive from it an indication of the man's age. He might have been fifty, or, on the other hand, he might only have been in the early twenties, a middle-aged man or a mere youth. The expression was curious ; it was proud and corpse-like, notwithstanding the fact that the eyes, deep-set and fierce, and surmounted with shaggy eyebrows, were altogether so keen and penetrating that the father confessor, laying down his knife and fork and half rising from his chair, was strangely disconcerted, and could only stammer out :

" Who—who in the world are you ? "

" I am Father Cyprian of the Society of Jesus," the stranger said sternly, "and I am sent here by the vicar-general to hold a conversation in privacy, strict privacy," and he laid great emphasis on the word strict, favouring the holy father, at the same time, with such a glare that the latter felt his knees shake, "with Mlle. de Béthune. See, here is my mandate," and he handed the reverend father a letter, as he spoke.

The reverend father had seen communications from the vicar-general before, and this one certainly seemed to be in his handwriting. Moreover, it bore his well-known seal. Concluding therefore that all was in order, he merely bowed. He would have liked, of course, to have asked questions, but, according to the rules of the Society of Jesus, Father Cyprian was his superior, and, consequently, he dared not interrogate him.

" Come," Father Cyprian exclaimed impatiently, " I have no time to spare, not a minute. See that I am conducted into the presence of Mlle. de Béthune at once."

"Certainly, certainly," the father confessor stammered, " I will take you to her myself," and with a covert glance at the half consumed fowl, that was rapidly getting cold, he proceeded to escort Father Cyprian to the large salon previously referred to.

What actually took place between the Jesuit and Mlle. de Béthune was never known.

The maidservant, in other words spy, who, obeying the father confessor's whispered order, peeped through the key hole of the salon, could only see the two talking together, she could not catch a syllable of what they said, but from their earnest manner she concluded they were discussing something of the utmost importance. She told the father confessor afterwards that Mlle. de Béthune appeared to be very frightened at first, then thoughtful, and at last resolute ; she seemed, in fact, to have braced herself to do something that had, at first, appeared very distasteful to her. All the while they were talking, this same spy declared, the monk never relaxed his curiously set expression, and that whenever he looked at the door, which he did repeatedly, his eyes seemed to pierce right through it. The interview only lasted half an hour, at the end of which time Father Cyprian took his departure, abruptly quitting the premises without a word to anyone. Shortly afterwards

Mlle. de Béthune sent for the father confessor and informed him that, as a result of Father Cyprian's visit, she had determined to carry out her mother's dying wish and was ready to enter the Convent of St. Rosalie at once.

The father confessor was pleased of course, but also somewhat disappointed. He had been hoping that Mlle. de Béthune would decide to become a nun through his influence, so that his superiors would have to credit him with her conversion ; and, now that her change of mind was due to some one else, he felt aggrieved. His dejected looks, however, made no impressions upon Mlle. de Béthune. Hastily collecting a few of her most treasured possessions and packing them, with sundry articles of clothing, in a trunk, in a remarkably short space of time, she took her leave of him and set out. Her arrival at the convent and resolution to take the final veil created a great sensation in Paris, and the subject aroused all the more interest when it became known that the vicar-general had neither sent Father Cyprian nor anyone else to interview Mlle. de Béthune, and that the letter bearing the vicar-general's seal was a forgery.

The question of the monk's identity, of course, was freely discussed by everybody, and, owing to the stories told by those who had seen him of the strangeness of his eyes and expression, many

believed that he was not human at all but supernatural, and that Mlle. de Béthune had been
persuaded to enter the Convent of St. Rosalie by
divine intervention. The vicar-general himself
favoured this theory, and it certainly acquired
some semblance of probability from the fact that
strange happenings in connection with Sister
Rosalie, as she was now called, were continually
taking place in the convent. Also, it was obvious
that Rosalie Béthune's character had seemingly
undergone a complete change. Anxious, apparently,
to mortify the flesh, she passed whole nights in
succession without sleeping, and when, on rare
occasions, she did allow herself to lie down, it was
always on a flat tombstone ; and she did this, in
addition to scourging herself daily and performing
other severe penances, without flinching. Moreover, it was affirmed that ghostly lights burned in
her cell at night, and that, when she prayed there,
strange, unearthly voices were heard praying with
her.

But more wonderful still, perhaps, rumour stated
that all kinds of miracles were being performed by
Sister Rosalie. For instance, it was said that one
of the nuns, long bedridden, on being touched by
Sister Rosalie, at once got up and walked ; and that
a plant in the garden of the convent, that was dried
up and withered, became fresh and green again

soon after she had stroked it with her hands. In fact, owing to a widespread and growing belief in her supernatural powers, people soon began to flock to the convent from all parts of the country to be cured of their ills. All brought presents, the upper class money and jewels, the peasantry an abundance of food, and thus the convent speedily became one of the richest in the land.

When at the very zenith of its prosperity, however, a dreadful and altogether unlooked for calamity occurred. One warm, windy night, three hours prior to the ringing of the bell for matins, those living in the vicinity of the convent, who, for various reasons, happened to be up and about, were startled to see the sky suddenly become a fiery red. At first they thought it was an aurora bore-alis, but they soon discovered their mistake. The Convent of St. Rosalie was on fire, and, the interior of the building consisting largely of wood, the con-flagration had spread to all parts of it. Indeed, so rapidly did it burn that it was almost entirely de-molished before even the nearest neighbours could get to it, and when they did arrive upon the scene they were too late to be of any assistance.

Only a mere shell of the place was left standing, and the only apparent survivors were the port-ress and the woodcutter. Neither had the least idea how the fire started. They said they had been roused from their sleep by loud screams and, on rushing from their respective rooms to ascertain the cause, they had found their passage to the nuns' quarters barred by flames. It was impossible, they declared, to rescue any of the sisters, who, caught like rats in a trap, were literally roasted to death.

The provincial police were sent for, and, on the ruins being searched by them, a quantity of bones and ashes, presumably the remains of the Abbess and nuns, were found, but not a vestige of any of the convent treasures. Gold and silver plate, as well as jewels, had completely disappeared. The portress and woodcutter were searched by the police, but nothing of any value was discovered on them, and though they were subjected to a severe examination by the bishops and priests, they never departed from their first avowal, namely, that they knew nothing. And the origin of the fire has consequently remained a mystery.

Some curious stories in connection with it, however, soon got afloat. For instance, a shepherd, who, on the night of the fire, was watching his flock in a field not very far away from the convent, declared that, directly after the conflagration began, two mounted travellers, enveloped in cloaks and carrying enormous saddlebags, stopped him and inquired the nearest route to the sea. Their faces, he said, could not be seen in the darkness—it was a very dark night—because they wore their hats pressed very low down over them.

Now, although much significance was attached to this story, especially when the peasants began to discover that the miracles supposed to have been wrought by Sister Rosalie were no miracles at all but bare-faced impostures, every effort made by the local authorities (and they made many) to trace the two travellers was fruitless ; they had apparently vanished in the night, without leaving the slightest clue as to their whereabouts or their identity.

Hence the authorities, both temporal and spiritual, finding themselves unable to solve the mystery either of the fire or of the two travellers, decided to let the matter drop, and it was publicly announced that Sister Rosalie had perished with the other nuns when the convent was destroyed.

The peasants, however, living in the vicinity of the convent, regarded the whole affair as one of a most sinister nature and, still believing in its association with the supernatural, took care to give the blackened ruins a very wide berth after dark.

Several years passed. Count d'Ambois was still Keeper of the King's Wardrobe, the post he had got through giving up Rosalie de Béthune, and his mother still enjoyed the State pension she had acquired in a similar manner, but, somehow or

other, both mother and son had become very
unpopular at Court. People regarded them as,
in some degree, responsible for the tragic
ending of Rosalie de Béthune, whose youth and
beauty had gained her many sympathizers, and they
were largely shunned in consequence. The King,
too, seemed to share in the general feeling of repugnance towards them, and in order to get rid of
them, at least for a period, he appointed the Count
an attaché to his Embassy at Berlin, and suggested,
in other words commanded, that the Countess, in
the capacity of hostess (the Count being still un-
married) should accompany him. We must now
follow them to Berlin.

The Coronation of the Elector of Brandenburg,
as the first King of Prussia, drew to Berlin, where
the ceremony was about to take place, people from
all parts of Europe. Never had Berlin, or, indeed,
any city in Germany witnessed such festivities.
Entertainments on a princely scale took place
every night, and the climax was reached when the
newly crowned King gave a masked ball at the
Royal Palace and invited all who cared to don
fancy dress to attend. Never was there such a
vast gathering in the Palace before, and never,
perhaps, has there been since.

Knights in armour, ladies in mediæval costumes,
Court jesters, clowns, harlequins, columbines and

legion other characters displaying every degree of histrionic art filed into the great, gaily illuminated building in endless procession. The vast salons were filled to overflowing, the halls and staircases were crowded, and it was computed that the company numbered at least three or four thousand.

Of course the young Count d'Ambois and his mother were present on this occasion, the former clad as a monk and the latter as a nun, but as they had few friends amongst the guests—indeed, they seemed to be just as unpopular in Berlin as they had been in Paris—and found the noise of the numerous bands and the crush of people wearisome, it was not long before they began to talk of going home. They were, in fact, crossing the vestibule on their way out, when a Sultana, wearing a black velvet mask, in addition to a veil, who had been watching them closely for some time, intercepted them and, with no little show of authority and condescension, immediately engaged the Count in conversation.

The magnificent attire of the lady, her aristocratic and haughty manner, and the extreme beauty of her bejewelled hands, which she took care to display to the best advantage, made a deep impression on both the Count and Countess. Both felt convinced that the Sultana was a person of considerable importance, most probably some

German princess or rich titled lady, and the Countess opined that, in all probability, she had been attracted by her son's good looks and somewhat distinguished bearing. Hoping therefore that her son would follow up this conquest, and desirous of giving him every opportunity of doing so, the Countess drew aside, but continued to keep an eye on the pair from a discreet distance.

For some minutes they remained where she left them, and she remarked with no little satisfaction that the Sultana, having evidently descended from her pedestal, was now talking and laughing unrestrainedly, and every now and then tapping the young Count playfully on the shoulder with her fan. She was barely within earshot, but presently she heard the Sultana say, half seriously and half jocularly:

"Sir Monk, I have a confession to make to you. Let us go where it is quiet;" and they moved away.

The Countess then watched them pass through a small side doorway, hung with handsome drapery, leading to an ante-room, in which the King sometimes held interviews with court officials or members of his private household.

Time passed, the guests left in batches, and the great salons at last began to get very empty. Still the Countess watched and waited, and still no sign

of the Monk and the Sultana. Four, five, six
o'clock passed, but the truant pair still continued
in their place of retirement. Wondering if there
could be another means of egress from the ante-
room, unknown to her, through which the couple
might have surreptitiously beat a retreat, the
Countess searched around everywhere, but could
discover none. Then, at last, weary and impatient,
she determined to invade the room itself. A deathlike silence greeted her as she crossed the threshold.

Though the dawn had long broken and the cold
grey light of a fine early morning had dissipated
the last straggling shadows of night, a lamp, suspended from the centre of the ceiling, still burned.
Flowers were in evidence everywhere, the air was
thick and heavy with their scent, and reclining at
full length on a richly upholstered and flower
festooned divan was the Monk, his coarse garments
drawn tightly round him. Believing him to be
asleep and wondering what had become of his
companion, the Countess stole up softly to his side,
and was in the act of bending over him to arouse
him, when she felt something splash on to her foot,
and looking down in astonishment, saw to her
horror it was blood. The Count d'Ambois had been
murdered. A dagger had been driven into his chest,
and its hilt, a crucifix wrought in gold and set with
jewels, with the arms and quarterings of the

d'Ambois family on its reverse side, was immediately recognized by the Countess ; it was the rare and costly crucifix that she had given to the Abbess, the Abbess of the Convent of St. Rosalie.

A hue and cry was instantly raised for the Sultana, but though Berlin was searched from one end to the other, and a large sum offered for her apprehension, not a trace of her could be found. Nor was she, in fact, ever heard of again.

Later on various gold and silver articles and jewels found in several shops in Prussia were identified as having belonged to the Convent of St. Rosalie, and, on being questioned, the proprietors of these shops declared that they had purchased them, soon after the burning of the convent, from two travellers whom they had never seen before and had never seen since.

Now, supposing the shopkeepers' story of the two travellers to be true, and one may presume, I think, that it was true, since it corresponded with the story told by the shepherd, who could the travellers have been ?

One of them assuredly possessed the mascot of the d'Ambois, the jewelled crucifix heretofore mentioned, and, that being so, might not that one have been the Sultana, and the Sultana—Rosalie de

Béthune ? Obviously the masked lady at the ball
had not killed the Count for money, and surely no
other woman saving Rosalie de Béthune would
have killed him, thus, for vengeance. Hence,
perhaps, the identity of one of the " two travellers " is solved—but who was the other ?

CHAPTER II

THE SKELETON IN THE CELLAR

IN August, 1789, a certain M. de Bougainville, an inveterate gamester, staked his last franc at a gaming table in Paris, lost, and in a frenzy of despair killed himself.* The attention of all Paris being concentrated just then on affairs of the greatest national moment, this suicide of a comparatively unknown gamester passed almost unnoticed, and, but for certain strange and startling incidents arising from it, would doubtless soon have been forgotten. What these incidents were, we shall very shortly see. M. de Bougainville had only one child, a girl named Julie, who at the time of her father's death was in her seventeenth year.

She was left absolutely destitute, that is to say literally possessing nothing but the clothes on her back, and these, far from being of any value, were both ill-fitting and shabby. Had she been brought up to do anything, or been at all clever with her needle, or merely pretty, she might have

* " Undiscovered Crimes," by " Waters." Published 1862.

stood some chance of earning a livelihood, but she had been taught nothing of a practical nature, and being plain and sickly had positively no recommendations, saving her disposition, which seems to have been fairly amiable. Her position therefore was desperate, and she was contemplating following the example set by her father, when an aged priest, Father Étienne Lafont, who had known her parents, learning of her plight, prevailed upon the Sisters of the Ursuline Convent, which he still visited regularly as confessor, to offer her shelter. And so Julie, seeing no alternative but suicide, became a nun. However, Julie had an uncle, Alexis de Bougainville, her father's brother. He was in Brazil, and occasionally sent her presents, and his stepson, Alphonse Bertin, his first wife's only child by her first husband, was in Paris, articled to M. Dupré, a notary of some standing.

Alphonse, although he might, perhaps, be termed a relative, was not in a position to render Julie financial aid, and probably, if he had been, he would not have done so, as he lavished all the money he could save upon a pretty *modiste* named Josephine Ramon, with whom he was desperately in love. Now Josephine had many admirers, and it so happened that Alphonse Bertin's cousin, Eugene Le Gros, the first Madame de Bougainville's sister's only son, was one of them; but, although she encouraged him and bestowed her favour upon others, it was generally supposed that she favoured Alphonse Bertin most of all. Alphonse, in fact, seems to have been a general favourite, and certain it is that he was highly esteemed by M. Dupré, who, however, did not approve of his friendship with Josephine Ramon and never liked Eugene Le Gros.

This was actually the state of affairs when Julie went into the convent. About twelve months later, M. Dupré received a letter from Alexis de Bougainville's lawyers in Brazil to say that he was dead and giving particulars as to the contents of his will. His second wife, and the two children he had by her, having predeceased him, he had left the bulk of his money, namely £24,000, to Julie, and eight hundred pounds, only, to be divided equally between his stepson, Alphonse Bertin, and his nephew by marriage, Eugene Le Gros. Should Julie, however, die without issue, the £24,000, to be invested in French bonds, was to go to Alphonse, with the exception of thirty thousand francs, which was to be given to Eugene. If Alphonse died childless, then the entire fortune was to revert to Eugene, who would be the general and unfettered legatee.

This was the gist of the matter contained in the missive M. Dupré received, and as soon as he had recovered from the astonishment it caused him, and had thoroughly digested its smallest details, he sought Alphonse, and communicated everything to him, asking him at the same time to say nothing about it for the present to anyone, and least of all to Julie. He then went on to explain his reason for not wishing Alphonse to say anything about the will for the present, especially to Julie. He was, he said, most anxious to bring about a match between Julie and Alphonse, and he feared that if Julie knew she was an heiress, she might think Alphonse was merely wanting her money and consequently refuse to marry him.

"But I don't care for Julie," Alphonse expostulated. "At least, not enough to marry her. I am in love with some one else."

"You mean you fancy you are," M. Dupré laughed, "but believe me, my dear Alphonse, it's only infatuation. I have lived too long, not to know the difference between love and infatuation. A youth with your education and breeding could never be really in love with such a vulgar, designing young person as Mlle. Josephine Ramon."

"Sir!" Alphonse ejaculated, his cheeks flushing, and he seemed on the verge of making some angry observation, when he suddenly curbed himself and remained silent.

"Tut, tut!" M. Dupré exclaimed good-naturedly,

"don't frown. It's only your own welfare I'm thinking of. That *modiste* girl is not good enough for you. Do be guided by me, my boy, give her up and fix your affections on your amiable cousin instead."

He argued so plausibly, and pleaded so earnestly with Alphonse, that the latter at length said he would think the matter over.

"Do," M. Dupré replied with an air of great relief, "think it well over, and let me have your decision, say, in a fortnight's time. A fortnight to-day."

" I will," Alphonse responded rather slowly, as if it cost him some effort, " and I'm sure I'm very grateful to you, sir, for the interest you take in my affairs. I appreciate it very much."

" Tut, tut ! " M. Dupré again exclaimed, laughing good-humouredly. " You see, having no children of my own it's only natural I should take an interest in those of other people. And I have known Mademoiselle Julie and you ever since you were so high," and he indicated with his hand a distance from the floor, corresponding to their height. " How are you off for money, ready cash, Alphonse ? "

Alphonse flushed. " I'm in rather low water, sir," he stammered, " indeed, I was thinking of asking if you could advance me a little."

"I will, with pleasure," M. Dupré said genially, "for I'm convinced by your manner that you intend doing as I wish and breaking off your acquaintance with Mlle. Ramon immediately."

He eyed Alphonse keenly as he spoke, but the latter did not wince; whatever he may have thought, his expression remained unaltered.

"I will let you know all about it, sir," he repeated, "in a fortnight's time."

M. Dupré then advanced him some money, and no further reference was made to the subject under discussion that day.

Two days later, as M. Dupré was about to retire to rest, at a rather late hour, there was a violent knocking at the front door of his house, and, on his opening it, Alphonse staggered past him into the hall and leaned against the wall. His face was scratched and covered with blood, his clothes were torn and muddy, and he was out of breath and trembling all over.

"*Mille tonnerres*," M. Dupré ejaculated, aghast with dismay and astonishment, "Alphonse! And in such a state! What on earth has happened?"

"I've been robbed and nearly killed," Alphonse panted, and he proceeded to tell M. Dupré that he had received a note from Josephine Ramon, asking him to meet her at a certain quiet and unfrequented spot, and that when he had arrived there he had been violently assaulted by a man and woman, who had beaten him about the face and body, and robbed him of his watch and purse. M. Dupré asked him if he could describe the locality where the attacks had been made and the people who had assaulted him, but to this he replied somewhat evasively, evincing much confusion, and stammering out something about the place being as far as he could remember, in his present dazed condition, somewhere in the vicinity of a cabaret called " Le Lion d'Or," where he had spent the evening. He had no very vivid recollection of his assailants, not sufficiently, at least, to enable him to identify them. He could only say they were dressed in black, and that he did not recollect ever having seen them before.

M. Dupré, attributing his confusion and agitation to the effects of the assault, ceased interrogating him, and, after giving him some brandy, saw him safely to his lodgings.

By the following morning he had apparently quite recovered, and, on coming to the office at the usual time, he informed M. Dupré that he had decided to give up Josephine Ramon, who, he felt, was in some way associated with the attack made on him the previous evening, and to marry his cousin, Julie, provided, of course, that he could persuade her to accept his addresses.

M. Dupré was delighted. " Excellent ! " he exclaimed. " *C'est trés bon.* I will go at once to the convent and interview Mademoiselle Julie." Julie, of course, had not taken the veil ; she was still only a novice. " Why, what's the matter ? " Alphonse had turned deadly pale and seemed on the verge of fainting.

M. Dupré stayed with him till he had apparently quite recovered, and then, patting him on the back in the most friendly and fatherly fashion, hastened off on his errand.

On arriving at the convent, he told the porter, an unprepossessing looking man, called Jules Bart, that he had come to see Mlle. de Bougainville, and asked to be taken to her quarters at once.

" That's not possible," Jules replied with an insolent grin. " You'll have to be content with the Mother Superior."

" I'll report you to her for your abominable rudeness," M. Dupré said angrily, " lead me to Mlle. de Bougainville directly."

Jules bowed with mock humility, and preceding M. Dupré escorted him to a large room on the ground floor, almost facing the entrance. M. Dupré was about to seat himself, when the door of the room opened, and the Mother Superior appeared in a great state of agitation.

" You have come to Mlle. de Bougainville," she cried. " Alas, she is not here."

" Not here ! " M. Dupré exclaimed, staring at her in utter astonishment. " Why, why, where " —he was about to add " the devil " but checked himself, such language would not do in so holy a place, so he merely said—" where in the world is she ? "

" We do not know," the Mother Superior replied, wringing her hands, " she left here surreptitiously last night, and we have not heard of her since."

M. Dupré was about to make some comment, when the door of the room opened, and the Commissary of the local police entered. Without wasting words he at once explained his mission. He had come about Mlle. de Bougainville, who, he had been given to understand, had been an inmate of the convent. Her body had been found in a ditch a mile or so away, and from its condition there was no doubt whatever she had been brutally murdered.

The Mother Superior and M. Dupré were appalled. They looked at one another aghast. Troublesome as the times were, for the Great Revolution had just begun and deeds of violence were already far from uncommon, they were not prepared for news like this. Julie de Bougainville, a young and innocent girl, a mere child, living a holy life, too, to be foully done to death. It was incredible, horrible, monstrous !

"Who has done it ? " M. Dupré gasped, as soon as he had recovered his equanimity sufficiently to speak. "The mob, I suppose ? "

"I don't think so, monsieur," the Commissary replied. "See here," and he held up, as he spoke, a small piece of frayed cloth. "We found this clenched in the fingers of Mlle's de Bougainville's right hand, and in one of the pockets of her dress this letter," and he handed the Mother Superior a dirty, crumpled sheet of paper. "Read it," he said.

The Mother Superior did so. It was addressed to Mlle. de Bougainville, and in it Mlle. de Bougainville was told that there was a shameful plot on foot between the Mother Superior, M. Dupré, and Alphonse Bertin, to deprive her of a fortune left her by her Uncle Alexis ; and that she was either to be forced into marrying Bertin or into taking the final veil, in either of which cases, eventually, the vast wealth she had inherited would pass into Bertin's hands. Finally, the writer of the letter, asserting that she was a friend of Julie's father, bade Julie come that night to the Château D'Aix, where she would find a young man in a green blouse and soft glazed hat, waiting to conduct her into the presence of the said writer, her father's friend, who was in a position to tell her a great more. The epistle, which was obviously in a disguised handwriting, was signed " Marie Coulanges."

" Do you know anyone named Coulanges ? " the Commissary said, as soon as the Mother Superior had finished reading.

" Yes," she replied. " I knew Marie Coulanges, the person this letter purports to be from, but she died over a year ago. Some villain has forged her name."

" So I thought," the Commissary said significantly. " Do you recognize this ? " And he handed M. Dupré the piece of torn cloth.

M. Dupré looked at it closely and turned deadly pale. It was similar in texture and colour to the coat Alphonse Bertin was wearing the previous evening. He recognized it at once.

" Well," the Commissary said abruptly, " what is your reply ? "

M. Dupré cleared his throat and, with a great effort, spoke.

" I have seen a coat similar to that," he stammered.

" So I thought," the Commissary grunted, " and I'm going to interview him at once."

M. Dupré groaned, and the Commissary, turning on his heels, left the room with a curt " good morning."

Events then followed on each other with dramatic swiftness. The Commissary, proceeding to Alphonse's lodgings—Alphonse was out at the time—searched his wardrobe, and found a muddy, blood-stained coat, with a piece torn out of it. It matched in colour and texture the fragment of cloth found in the dead woman's hand. The Commissary then comparing some specimens of Alphonse's handwriting with that of the letter discovered on the murdered woman, and coming to the conclusion they were all penned by the same person, namely Bertin himself, at once went in search of Alphonse and, on finding him in a semi-intoxicated condition in a neighbouring café, arrested him on the charge of murdering Mlle. Julie de Bougainville.

At the ensuing trial, Alphonse pleaded not guilty. The testimony against him, however, was very strong. Several persons professing to be experts in caligraphy, together with the police and M. Dupré, all declared that, in their opinion, the writing in the letter found on Mlle. de Bougainville was that of the prisoner. Jules Bart also declared that, early on the day of the murder, a man styling himself M. Maillard had called at the convent and offered him two louis d'or to give the note signed " Marie Coulanges " to Mlle. de Bougainville. He said he knew the man at once, having seen him, at least, on one occasion before. He was the prisoner, Alphonse Bertin. Next M. Dupré, with obvious reluctance, testified to the prisoner coming to his house late on the night of the murder, bleeding and dishevelled, stating that, in consequence of a letter he had received from Josephine Ramon, he had gone to a certain spot, expecting to meet her there, but had, instead, found two people, complete strangers to him, who had at once attacked and robbed him. He had, however, neither been able to describe the spot nor his assailants.

Josephine Ramon, the next witness, denied ever having written such a letter to the prisoner. She said that on the day of the murder he had come to her house and had made proposals to her of such an improper nature that she had at once ordered him out of the place. He had gone, and she had not set eyes on him again till now, when she saw him in the dock. After she had given her evidence, the police described their finding of the body, with the note of assignation penned in Alphonse Bertin's writing clutched in its right hand, and near it a fragment of the prisoner's coat.

This practically concluded the evidence against the prisoner. Alphonse in his defence denied all knowledge of the letter signed " Marie Coulanges." He admitted that the piece of garment found near the body of the murdered woman was torn from his coat, but persisted in his story of the attack on him, the night of the crime. He maintained that Josephine Ramon was the only person to whom he had mentioned the will of Alexis de Bougainville (at this there was a loud cry of " Liar " from Josephine Ramon. " You never said a word about it to me "), and that the letter he had received asking him to meet her near the Château D'Aise the night of the murder was in her handwriting (here there was another cry of "Liar! You know I never wrote to you "). He declared that in the scuffle with his assailants a piece of his coat had been deliberately torn off by one of them.

Asked, however, by the judge if he could produce Josephine Ramon's letter, he was obliged to admit he could not, and said he believed it had been stolen from him during his struggle with his assailants.

That concluded his examination. No more questions were put to him, and, as had been anticipated by everyone in court, a verdict of guilty was returned, and he was sentenced to be guillotined.

There was one person, however, who believed in his innocence, and that was Father Étienne Lafont, confessor at the Ursuline Convent, which had given shelter to Julie de Bougainville. He declared the writing in the letter signed " Marie Coulanges " was not that of Alphonse Bertin but merely a clumsy imitation of it. He also discredited the testimony both of Jules Bart and Josephine Ramon. The former, he said, and he had every opportunity of knowing, since he was brought in contact with him daily, was an habitual liar, while the latter, according to the testimony of more than one person of repute, was a scheming, thoroughly unscrupulous girl, who would stick at nothing to achieve her own ends.

He believed they were in league, and that it was all a plot against the unfortunate Alphonse Bertin. Dismayed at the idea of an innocent man being executed, he exerted all his wits and influence to get him off. The Revolutionaries were in power then, and at the risk of his own life, for the priests were very unpopular with the mob, he had constant interviews with various of the Ministers and prison authorities. In Eugene Le Gros, who said he was away at the time of the murder, he found a useful ally. Though Le Gros would never commit himself to saying whether he thought Alphonse was really guilty or not, he certainly appeared to render Father Lafont all the assistance that lay in his power, often accompanying him on his missions, and seconding him in his interviews. And in the end Alphonse's sentence was commuted.

Instead of being guillotined he was sent to the galleys for life.

Some months later, those who had taken an interest in the case were greatly surprised to hear that Eugene Le Gros and Josephine Ramon were married. The news of their marriage, indeed, created no little sensation ; and to Father Lafont especially it was of considerable significance. He was still of the opinion that Alphonse Bertin was the victim of a dastardly plot, and he meant to do all he could to procure his release, and bring about the conviction of the guilty parties. He knew intuitively he had made an enemy of Josephine Ramon, and that some one, who it was he could not say for certain, was closely watching all his movements. That he was not deceived by his intuitions was proved in a very unexpected manner. Jules Bart was suddenly taken seriously ill. Now Father Lafont had always felt that Bart knew more about the murder of Julie de Bougainville than he had cared to admit, and consequently he went often to the sick man's bedside, in the hope that he would eventually prevail upon him to confess. And in this he was not disappointed. Jules Bart *DID* confess one morning, but what he actually said regarding the murder of Julie de Bougainville Father Lafont, presumably, never had the chance to divulge. Coming out of the sick man's room, looking very thoughtful and troubled, he told one of the officials of the convent that he had just been listening to a very painful confession, and that he was now going to Notre-Dame, but would have to be very careful, as he had been warned that certain evilly disposed people were watching for an opportunity to do him harm. He then wished the official good morning and quitted the convent. After that he was never seen nor heard of again.

The heads of the convent and various of his friends prosecuted inquiries, but with no result, and it was generally concluded that he had fallen into the hands of the mob, which was just then unusually bitter against the Church, and so perished.

In the meantime, Jules Bart died, and just before he drew his last breath he was heard by those standing near him to be cursing some one, the name of the cursed one sounding very like Eugene. Also, when his body was being prepared for burial, the letters T.F. were found branded on his left shoulder, a discovery that proved what Father Lafont had always suspected, namely, that Jules Bart was an escaped felon.

A year passed by, and still the mob ruled Paris ; ever cutting off heads, and ever looking around for fresh victims. Having annihilated the nobility and all who were generally regarded as aristocrats, it next took to butchering the professional classes and more wealthy of the business people, and among those whom it now slaughtered was Eugene Le Gros.

He and his wife were arrested the same day, and would have shared the same fate, had not some of Josephine's relatives chancing to see her being borne away in the tumbrel to the place of execution, peremptorily demanded her release, on the grounds that she was a genuine hard working *modiste ;* and, the mob taking her side, her captors had no other alternative but to set her free.

But while fate was thus kind to Josephine, it certainly did not favour her spouse, for some of the onlookers, recognizing Eugene as a former officer in the hated Royalist Army, immediately raised a loud cry of " Traitor, assassin," in consequence of which he was torn from his guards, and, there and then, hanged to the nearest lamp-post. His death cries, in fact, must have been heard by Josephine, as she was being hurried away from the scene, dazed and half demented, by her friends and relatives, and, the shock of having, perhaps, narrowly escaped being served in a similar manner proving too much for her, a virulent fever set in, and she soon became seriously ill. A Dr. Petit was called in to attend her, and to him her relatives confided that they were very upset and worried by her delirium, as, in her ravings, she was continually referring to some struggle, the struggle of some one, battling for his life with mysterious assassins, and of stealthy, muffled footsteps coming up to her room from the cellar.

" It is enough to freeze anyone's blood to listen to her," they said to the doctor, " she seems to have something on her mind, and if we only knew of a priest we would send for one, but they have all been killed."

" I think I can help you there," the doctor responded thoughtfully, " I'll tell the Abbé Delmar, and, doubtless, he'll come along."

The Abbé came. When he entered Josephine's room, she was apparently dozing, but, as he crossed the floor to her side, she awoke and catching sight of him gave a wild scream of terror.

However, after he had said a few words to her, in his usual firm but quiet and benevolent way, she grew calm, and after gazing at him intently for some minutes, without speaking, suddenly exclaimed :

" I recognize you now. You are the priest who once lodged in my house. I thought at first," but, instead of going on, she suddenly stopped short and, with a face full of the most abject terror, caught hold of the Abbé by the arm. " There, there," she whispered, and in such horror-stricken tones that the Abbé, used as he was to death bed scenes, felt his blood run cold. " Hush, do you hear that ? It's *HIM*. He's come out of the cellar, and

he's coming up the stairs. Those stealthy steps
follow me everywhere. I can even hear them
in my sleep. Oh, save me from him, Father, save
me," and she fell back on her pillow, shaking in
every limb.

The Abbé could hear no steps, but he did his
best to soothe her, and implored her to tell him if
she had anything to confess.

She did not answer, but burying her face in the
pillow burst out crying, and continued thus for
two or three minutes. Then, suddenly sitting up,
she again seized the Abbé by the arm and whispered:

"Listen, he is going back to the cellar. The
steps grow fainter and fainter. But he will return,
when you are gone. Oh, say you won't leave me,
you won't, will you, Father," and flinging her arms
round the Abbé's neck she again burst out crying.
In a few seconds, however, she stopped and looking
earnestly at the Abbé, said, "Father, do you believe
the dead can come out of their graves and pass
through locked and bolted doors ?"

"If they could in scriptural days, my daughter,"
the Abbé responded slowly, "they assuredly can
now."

"I know they can, Father," Josephine replied,
"I know they can, for *HE* does. He comes right
up here, although the door of the cellar is both
bolted and locked, I saw to that myself. Promise

me, Father, that you will go down into the cellar
and sprinkle his grave with holy water, perhaps that
will keep him quiet."

"To whom do you allude, my daughter," the
Abbé said quietly. "Who is this *HE* you talk
about ? "

"I can't say, I can't say," Josephine replied,
shivering violently. "No one, nothing," and falling back again on the bed, she lay, as before, her
face buried in the pillow, moaning and crying
alternately.

The Abbé Delmar, finding his efforts to calm
her fruitless, at length rose to go ; whereupon she
hung on to him frantically crying out :

"Oh, don't go, don't go. He'll come again, he'll
come again. Save me, oh, save me."

But the Abbé gently disengaged himself, and
after exhorting her to trust in God and solicit the
mercy of Heaven, quietly left the room. Strongly
suspecting that some evil deed, probably murder,
had taken place in the house, and that Madame Le
Gros knew all about it, the Abbé, after conferring
with Dr. Petit, went with him to the local Police
Station, and told the Commissary there all that had
happened.

The Commissary listened with interest. He
remembered the murder of Julie de Bougainville
and the subsequent disappearance of Father

Lafont perfectly well, indeed, he had had the handling of both cases, and in his opinion it was as clear as daylight that the ravings of Madame Le Gros bore upon one of these cases, if not on both.

" You say," he said thoughtfully, " she continually cries out about a cellar, presumably the cellar of the house she is in, and of some mysterious being, who keeps coming out of it to frighten her. That might be delirium and nothing more, mightn't it, doctor ? "

Dr. Petit shook his head. " No," he said, " I don't think it is all delirium. Madame Le Gros is, doubtless, very ill, indeed, it is quite possible she won't last through the day, but her brain keeps wonderfully clear. I can't help thinking with the Abbé that there is a mystery at the back of it."

" Then, in that case," the Commissary said, with a glance round for his hat, " I had better go to the house at once." He quickly summoned two of his subordinates, and the two started immediately for Madame Le Gros's.

On the way, they were delayed for some considerable time by vast throngs of people waiting in the streets to see Robespierre pass by, and when they reached their destination Madame Le Gros was dead. No one was with her, they were

informed, when she died, and if she had had anything to tell she died without telling it.

All the same, the police at once made their way
into the cellar and commenced digging. For some
time they worked in vain, but at last, just as they
were beginning to despair of finding anything, the
spade of one of them laid bare a head. It is un-
necessary to refer at length to what followed. The
same sickening details invariably accompany a
gruesome discovery of this kind, and it is sufficient
to say that human remains, pronounced by Dr.
Petit, who had arrived upon the scene, to be those
of an old man, were gradually brought to light.
In this case, however, they were unrecognizable
owing to the action of quick lime, and therefore
identification was impossible

And for the same reason it was quite impossible
to ascertain the cause of death. Dr. Petit, the
Abbé, and the police were all of the opinion that
the mysterious "he" Madame Le Gros had so
continually referred to in her ravings, was, in very
truth, the dead man they had now unearthed, but
the question of his identity baffled them. Was he,
or was he not, Father Lafont?

The fortune of Alexis de Bougainville that had
brought in its wake so much misery and crime,
after sentence of death had been passed upon

Alphonse Bertin, went to Eugene Le Gros, and on the death of his wife it was divided between their respective nearest of kin. These people had considerable influence in Paris at the time, and much significance may be derived from the fact that they wrote to Dr. Petit, the Abbé Delmar, and the Commissary of the Police warning each of them in the very strongest terms possible, that if they did not cease meddling in the mystery surrounding the murder of Julie de Bougainville and the disappearance of Father Lafont, and refrain from seeking to elucidate it, they had better look out for their own safety; and the times being still very disturbed and troublesome the hint was taken, and the matter dropped.

It is interesting to note, perhaps, that Alphonse Bertin, whether through the connivance of his friends or not, it is impossible to say, escaped from the Bagne and fled to America, where guilty or not guilty, as a peaceful and law-abiding citizen, he spent the remainder of his strangely chequered career.

CHAPTER III

BENJAMIN BATHURST, the third son of
Dr. Henry Bathurst, Bishop of Norwich, was
born on the 14th of March, 1784. He entered the
Diplomatic Service at an unusually early age, and
consequently as secretary to the British Legation,
first at one place and then at another, he had
acquired a considerable knowledge of foreign affairs
when still very young.

In May, 1805, he married Phillida,* daughter of
Sir John Call, Bart., of Whiteford, in Cornwall,
and four years later he was sent by his kinsman,
Earl Bathurst, Secretary of State for the Foreign
Department, as Envoy Extraordinary to the Court
of the Emperor Francis at Vienna. The mission
entrusted to Benjamin Bathurst was of the greatest
importance, and for this reason. Austria just then
was in a very critical state. It had recently
raised (by conscription) a Landwehr, or Militia,
numbering nearly half a million men, and Napoleon,

* Called Phillida in the Diary of her brother, George Cotsford
Call, and Philadelphia in her father's will.

RIGHT HONBLE. HENRY, EARL BATHURST
(1762-1834)
(From " Brit. a 1" 1822)

assuming this step to be a covert act of hostility towards himself—indeed, in the circumstances he could scarcely have done otherwise—had demanded an explanation. Both Russia and Prussia had declined to assist Austria in the event of a rupture with France, and Napoleon, in the meanwhile, had concentrated armies under the respective commands of Davoust, Massena, Oudinot and Bernadotte at various points near the Austrian frontier. Hence, the Emperor Francis realized that he was in somewhat of a tight corner It was at this juncture that England intervened and sent Benjamin Bathurst to Vienna, with injunctions to do his utmost to persuade Austria to declare war against France, her reason for doing so being that she was about to send an expedition to the Peninsula, where an insurrection against the French had already commenced, and was desirous that an attack should be made on the French in the East, in order that Napoleon's attention might be diverted from the West.

Now Bathurst found it no easy task to convince Francis that England had the men and money and generalship necessary for an expedition that was at all likely to prove successful. Francis knew the capabilities of the French, he had already suffered at their hands ; their vast armies now lay at his very doors ; and defeat at their hands would mean absolute ruin. Of what use could an ally like England be to him ? Her Navy, powerful though it was, could be of little material assistance, and her Army he had hitherto been led to suppose was far too small to be at all effective against a great Continental Power such as France. He was really in a serious quandary. For senti-mental reasons mostly perhaps, he did not want to offend England, and he knew only too well the consequences of offending France. Fortunately, for the success of his mission, Bathurst was of an exceptionally enthusiastic and sanguine disposi-tion ; also, for one so young, he was extraordinarily tactful and, at the same time, persistent ; and Francis, though firm at the outset, at last began to waver, and finally gave in. Austrian armies, then, crossed the French frontier ; but at various places, in fact everywhere, they met with defeat ; and, as a result, a Peace, in every way advantageous to France, was concluded at Schön-brunn.

This occurred in October, 1809. Bathurst, who remained in Austria throughout the campaign and until the Peace was concluded, now that there was no longer anything for him to do in Vienna, made immediate preparations for his return to England. Instead, however, of selecting the shortest way home, which would have led him through part of France, he decided to return via Berlin, North Germany and Sweden,* stating, as his reason for doing so, that he believed Napoleon to be inspired with a bitter animosity against him, and to be looking out for an opportunity to have him assassinated.

Whether Bathurst had any positive grounds for such a belief, or whether it was merely due to his imagination, has never been known for certain. Anyhow, so sure was he that his life was threatened by Napoleon, that he not only chose a roundabout route to London, but he stepped into his carriage at the outset disguised as a German commercial traveller and calling himself Mr. Koch. In addition to the driver and postilion, he was accompanied by a man named Krause † (variously described as his " Secretary " and a " King's Messenger," but about whom Bathurst apparently knew very little, and who was travelling for additional safety, at Bathurst's request, under the name of Fisher), and his servant, Nicholas Hilbert. As far as is known to the contrary, no one saw them depart from Vienna, saving the hotel servants. Arriving at Budapest they stayed there at least long enough for Bathurst to attend to his correspondence and

* He mentions this route in a letter to his sister written at Budapest on October 14th, 1809. (*Vide* " Memoirs and Correspondence of Dr. Henry Bathurst," by Mrs. Thistlethwayte.)

† Spelt also Krouse and Kraus.

write to his wife * and a Mr. Williams ; and afterwards, continuing their journey, they arrived, in
due course, at Berlin.   Here Bathurst got into communication with Baron Wissenberg, the Austrian
Minister, and according to one authority was put
on his guard against Krause, of whom already he
appears to have been somewhat suspicious. When
he left Berlin he took the precaution of arming
himself with two pistols, while he kept another pair
close beside him in the carriage. Proceeding on
the journey he arrived with his companion at
Perleberg about noon, November 25th, 1809.

Perleberg, which is on the river Stepnitz, a
tributary of the Elbe, was at that date quite a
small town, walled in like Launceston.† Being on
the high road, however, it boasted several fair-
sized inns ; and close to the post-house, where
Bathurst pulled up, and which was kept by a man
named Schmitz, was a rather more pretentious
looking building, known as the " White Swan,"
and kept by a man named Leger. Both inn and

* The letter he wrote to her was dated October 14th, 1809.   In
it he refers to the route he has decided to travel by, viz., Colberg
and Sweden. (*Vide* " Memoirs and Correspondence of Dr. Henry
Bathurst.") Regarding the time Krause actually joined Bathurst
there would seem to be again a diversion of opinion.   Some
authorities would lead one to suppose the two did not travel together
till after Berlin.

† *Vide* " The Search for the lost Mr. Bathurst," in the " Westminster Review," Vol. CXXXIV.

post-house stood close to the Parchemer Gate of the town, beyond which lay a small suburb, that is to say a few small houses and cottages, the high road by which the travellers had come continuing past the post-house and " White Swan," through this Parchemer Gate and the suburb to Hamburg.

Having got out of his carriage at the post-house, Bathurst, after informing the ostler that he should not be continuing his journey till he had dined, went off to the " White Swan " and ordered his meal. He was then seen to be wearing a pair of grey trousers, a grey frogged coat, a diamond pin in his scarf, a very costly looking sable overcoat lined with purple velvet, and a fur cap. From the moment he sat down to his midday dinner at the " White Swan," his movements are uncertain.* It would seem to be generally agreed, however, that soon after dinner he left the inn and crossing the market place of the town called at Captain Klitzing's, who was in command of the local garrison,† and, without disclosing his identity, asked for military protection at the post-house, on the grounds that he feared the French were plotting against his life. He was so agitated when he

---

* The testimony of witnesses subsequently interrogated re the same is very confusing and conflicting.

† Termed also the Military Governor of the town.

said this, that a lady, presumably Captain Klitzing's housekeeper, who was giving him tea, noticed that his hand trembled violently as he took the cup from her.* He told Captain Klitzing that something had occurred that had alarmed him very much, but he did not say what that something was. At the same time he repeatedly alluded to his fear of foul play at the hands of French spies, whereat, apparently, Klitzing only laughed and told him that he thought his sense of danger from that quarter quite unwarrantably exaggerated. He, nevertheless, promised to send two cuirassiers to the post-house at once, and after a little more conversation Bathurst took his departure.

On leaving Klitzing, Bathurst, it would seem, went direct to the post-house and ordered his carriage for nine o'clock that evening instead of seven, which was the hour he had apparently previously arranged to set out. He then, it appears, proceeded to the " White Swan," where he remained some hours in a small room looking over his

---

* This lady subsequently married a local doctor called Kestern. She was alive in 1852 and told Mrs. Thistlethwayte, who interviewed her, that she had vivid recollections of Mr. Bathurst's visit to Captain Klitzing. Her evidence would not appear, however, to have been very reliable, as she first of all denied Bathurst had presented her with money on leaving, and then contradicted herself. She did not explain what the money was for, nor did Mrs. Thistlethwayte apparently interrogate her on that point. (See " Memoirs and Correspondence of Dr. Henry Bathurst.")

correspondence, burning certain letters and writing others ; and by the time he had finished, close on seven o'clock, it was, of course, quite dark.

It is therefore astounding to find, according to one account,* that now, just when one would have expected his dread of foul play to have increased, he actually dismissed the cuirassiers, sending them back to Captain Klitzing. Now, if this story be true, and he really did act thus inconsistently, how can such conduct be explained ? This is a question to which no one, so far as I am able to ascertain, has ever ventured to suggest an answer. Moreover, according to another account, in addition to this inconsistency, he seems to have displayed a spirit of folly and recklessness utterly at variance with his former reticence and caution, inasmuch as he subsequently went to the post-house and stood there before a fire, in the midst of ostlers and others, shunning no one, and carelessly taking out his watch, a very costly one, and displaying a purse full of gold. An explanation for this undoubted act of folly might, perhaps, be found in his youth— remember he was only twenty-five years of age— but how the eyes of the ostlers, none too well paid you may be sure, and other dependents must have glittered at the sight of so much apparently little valued wealth !

* See " Memoirs and Correspondence of Dr. Henry Bathurst."

At a few minutes to nine o'clock Bathurst, it is stated, went into the road in front of the post-house and watched the horses being put to. No one, however, would seem to have watched his movements very closely, though it was asserted afterwards by some of those present that he stood by the horses' heads, where the feeble glare from the ostler's lamp fell full on him. After that no one has ever testified to seeing him. He vanished suddenly, noiselessly and wholly inexplicably.

His disappearance was not discovered, however, till the carriage had been in readiness some time. Accounts vary very much as to those who were actually present when the carriage stood waiting. One writer * asserts that, when the search for Mr. Bathurst commenced, the landlord was standing in the doorway of the inn (presumably he meant the post-house) chatting to Krause, the postilion was mounted, ready to start, and Nicholas Hilbert was at the carriage door, holding it open for his master. Then, one or other of them, tired of waiting, commented on Mr. Bathurst's non-appearance, and the search for him began.

According to another account,† Mrs. Schmitz had taken her stand by the horses' heads as soon

* See account of disappearance in the " Cornhill Magazine," January–June, 1887.
† See " Memoirs and Correspondence of Dr. Henry Bathurst."

as the equipage was ready to start, but getting tired of the job (or possibly having other duties to attend to) she had entrusted it to her son, Augustus, a thorough ne'er-do-weel and the associate of some of the most disreputable people in the town, and her daughter. These two, it was stated, stood at their post for just as long as it suited them, and then called to Elizabeth Nagel, a servant in the employ of their parents, who, besides doing domestic work, often officiated as post-woman in Perleberg, to take it from them; and she, according to this same authority, must have been actually with the horses when Bathurst's absence was first noticed. Nothing untoward, however, was anticipated, it being supposed that Bathurst was either engaged in one of the rooms of the post-house or inn, or had gone for a stroll, till those who had started to look for him came back and reported that he was neither in the post-house nor at the "White Swan." A more thorough search was then organized, and when that, too, failed, some one suggested that Captain Klitzing should be informed of what happened. Hilbert then set off and reported the occurrence to the military commander. Klitzing acted with most commendable promptitude. He at once sent some cuirassiers to the post-house to take possession of Bathurst's carriage and effects. He then went to the " White

Swan," ordered a carriage, and had Krause and Hilbert put in and sent under military escort to another inn, the " Crown," where they were assigned quarters and kept under military observation. Opinions, as to how strict that observation was, vary. According to some,* it was very lax, while, according to others, it was the reverse.

Indeed, the subject formed a matter of dispute between Klitzing and the civil authorities at Perleberg, who, not being at the best of terms with Klitzing, apparently, were only too glad to seize any pretext for a quarrel. Hence, from that time onward, perpetual wranglings between the military and civil authorities added considerably to the difficulty of solving the mystery of Mr. Bathurst's disappearance. Indeed, what with Klitzing saying one thing, the local magistrates, another, and the local press chipping in and complaining of both, the case, deviating from its proper course, began to look like a burlesque in which every one separately suspected every one else.

To return, however, to the night in question, that of Saturday, November 25th. The news of Bathurst's disappearance speedily spread, and four magistrates, Pfuetzen-Reuter, Wendt, Schulze and Teltou, being told of the affair after they had re-

* See " Memoirs and Correspondence of Dr. Henry Bathurst," and the " Cornhill Magazine."

tired for the night, rose from their beds and went
to join in the search for the missing man. They
searched the " White Swan," the post-house, their
immediate vicinity, and all parts of the town, but
in vain ; and, at last, baffled and exhausted, they
regained the Crown Inn, where a ball was still in
course of progress and where, according to some
accounts, they found Klitzing, refreshing himself
with punch and participating in the revels. In the
morning the search for Bathurst, in which every
one joined—peasants, citizens, magistrates, game-
keepers and soldiers, as motley a crowd as had ever
collected together in Perleberg—was renewed with
unabated vigour. The river was dragged, the adjoining wood, ditches, marshes and hedges scoured,
outhouses were searched, as were also all houses
and places of doubtful repute, but without avail.
Not the slightest trace of Bathurst could be found.
Klitzing rode over at noon to his superior officer,
Colonel Bismark, at Kyritz, and returned with full
authority from that individual to investigate the
case.

About this time a discovery was made. Krause
informed either Klitzing or the civil authorities,
it is not clear which, that his overcoat was missing.
He had had it at the post-house, and, when he had
last seen it, it was there with Bathurst's.

Upon receipt of this communication it appears that either Klitzing or one of the magistrates at once went to the post-house and demanded that the two overcoats should be given up, whereupon Mrs. Schmitz, after a good deal of hesitation, confessed that she had one overcoat, but only one ; and that, she said, Krause had told her, belonged to one of the two Jewish merchants who had arrived at the post-house from Lentzen shortly after Bathurst, and had left some hours prior to the time fixed for Bathurst to leave.

Not satisfied, apparently, with this explanation, the civil authorities had Nagel,* the servant, brought before them, and eventually extracted from her the information that Bathurst's coat was in the possession of Augustus Schmitz.

They then arrested Augustus, whom they found in one of the low gambling dens he was known to frequent, and as he neither admitted nor denied he had the coat a search was made, and it was eventually found beneath a pile of wood in a cellar. Augustus, being asked how it got there, confessed that he had taken it, but said that he was under

---

* Klitzing, ever jealous of the civil authorities and anxious to find out exactly how they had got their information from Nagel, threatened the girl with a beating, unless she told him. She at once did as she was bid and he then let her go. But the result of her confession was another rupture between Klitzing and the magistrates. (See " Memoirs and Correspondence of Dr. Henry Bathurst.")

the impression it belonged to Herr Meyer, one of
the two Jewish merchants who had put up at the
inn at the same time as Bathurst, and that he
wanted to keep it long enough to get the reward
he fully expected Meyer would offer for it. The
story sounded plausible enough and, had Augustus
borne a good character, it might have been accepted
without question, but, as I have already suggested,
Augustus had a very bad reputation in Perleberg.

He had never settled down to any definite trade
or calling, but divided his time between tramping
about the country and doing odd jobs for his
father ; and, upon being asked how he got the
money he spent on drink, he said he got it in tips,
from acting as interpreter to various of the foreign
officers who from time to time put up at the post-
house (he had, he explained, acquired a certain
smattering of different languages on his trampings),
and by gambling. He volunteered the information
that Mr. Bathurst had two pistols when he came
to the post-house, and was so apprehensive of
being attacked by his enemies that he sent Mrs.
Schmitz into the town to buy more gunpowder.
No one thought of asking Augustus how he came
to know this, or how he spent his time the evening
Benjamin Bathurst disappeared ; neither were
any questions put to Mrs. Schmitz regarding the
matter. Indeed, although grave suspicion would

seem to have attached itself to Mrs. Schmitz and
Augustus, both of whom, it will be remembered,
according to one account, had, in turn, stood by
the horses' heads at the time Benjamin Bathurst
disappeared, and one of whom must therefore have
been the last person known to have seen him alive,
the civil authorities showed no inclination to
subject either of them to anything like a searching
examination. They were arrested, merely on the
charge of stealing the coats, and sentenced to eight
weeks' imprisonment. Klitzing bitterly blamed
the civil authorities for their apathy in the matter,
and it certainly seems as if they were at fault,
though an apparent cause for the subsequent
deadlock in the proceedings and consequent failure
to unravel the mystery of Bathurst's disappearance lies in the behaviour of the civil authorities
in Berlin. They should either have taken up the
case themselves, sending some one to Perleberg
to hold an absolutely impartial inquiry into it, or
else have made it quite clear which of the rival
parties in Perleberg was to have sole charge of the
affair ; but they did nothing definite at all, and the
military and the civil authorities were left to
wrangle and abuse one another to further orders.

Hence, the mystery surrounding the disappearance of Mr. Bathurst, which one feels might and
ought to have been cleared up, is still a mystery,

and the explanation of the disappearance has remained entirely problematic to this day.

Varying theories, based on certain incidents that were said to have occurred from time to time, and reports of which soon got into circulation, were, of course, promulgated. On December 16th two peasant women, inhabitants of Perleberg, went into a wood in the direction of Quitzow to gather fuel, and close to a little path perceived, to their astonishment, lying on the grass a pair of trousers, turned inside out and sodden wet.

The peasant women took them at once to the burgomaster of Perleberg, and they were identified later on as having belonged to Benjamin Bathurst, who, it was believed, was wearing them at the time of his disappearance. On their being examined, two bullet holes were found, but no traces of any blood; and in one of the pockets a half written letter in Bathurst's handwriting to his wife in England. In this letter he expressed grave apprehension concerning a certain Count D'Entraigues, and serious doubts with regard to his getting back to England safely; and, in the case of his death, he implored his wife not to marry again. That was all. Thus, the discovery of the trousers and letter instead of elucidating the mystery only tended to intensify it. Had Bathurst been shot, as the bullet marks suggested, the report of firearms must have been heard, unless, of course, he had been first dragged or decoyed to some remote spot, and both these contingencies would seem to be highly improbable, since the dragging process, no less than the shooting, would have entailed noise, the noise of a scuffle at least, and, according to those present, at the time of his disappearance not the slightest noise of any unusual nature was heard ; and to have decoyed him would have necessitated an artifice of almost superhuman subtlety, in view of the fact that he was on his guard, and therefore not at all likely to be caught napping. Again, if he had been murdered, why were not the trousers hidden or destroyed with the body ? Were they allowed to be found, in order to call attention to the letter in the pocket, and thereby throw suspicion on Count D'Entraigues and the French ? It certainly looked like it and, if such were the case, it is obvious that the perpetrators of the crime were only too well aware of the great haunting fear Bathurst had of Napoleon and his secret agents.

We will allude to this again later. In the meanwhile let us consider the theory, strongly advocated at the time, that the French were actually responsible for Bathurst's disappearance.

In a letter written from Paris by Mr. Thomas Richard Underwood, and dated November 24th, 1816, the writer, who was a prisoner of war in

France in 1809, stated that the French and English he spoke to about Bathurst believed the latter had been abducted by French spies. This view was also shared by the " European Magazine," which, in an article published in 1810, declared Mr. Bathurst had been carried off by French troops stationed at Lentzen.

In Prussia certain people who claimed to be well informed shared this view. They were of the opinion that the French Government had authorized the abduction, and possibly murder, of Benjamin Bathurst for political reasons, in order to obtain possession of certain important dispatches, it was believed, he had on him. In Perleberg itself, it was even asserted in some quarters that French troops had been seen pursuing Bathurst on November 25th as far as Kyritz. However, granting for the sake of argument that the French soldiers who had been seen pursuing him did abduct Bathurst, no one has offered any explanation of the fact that he was abducted (remember he was seen standing at the horses' heads one moment, and the next nowhere to be found) without the slightest noise being made and without any of his assailants being seen.

That the French were at the bottom of the mystery gained much credence in England, and "The Times " for January 23rd, 1810, openly charged Napoleon with being responsible for Bathurst's disappearance. The "Moniteur" of January 29th, 1810, which had previously published a letter * from their correspondent in Berlin, affirming that Bathurst had destroyed himself in a fit of insanity near Perleberg, indignantly repudiated the charge made against Napoleon and, adhering to their Berlin correspondent's statement, maintained that Bathurst had committed suicide. " It is the custom of the British Cabinet," it remarked, " to commit diplomatic commissions to persons whom the whole nation knows are half fools ; " adding a statement to the effect that the accusation of employing bandits, which the English had hurled at the French Government, could be very easily applied to the English themselves.† To those who had formed the theory that Napoleon was responsible for Bathurst's disappearance, this attempt to make out that Bathurst committed suicide, in a fit of insanity, was only a more convincing proof of Napoleon's guilt. Bathurst's letters home showed no signs of insanity, on the contrary they were distinctly coherent and commonplace and, saving for his constant dread of assassination at the hands of French spies, there was no evidence to prove that

---

* *Vide* December 12th, 1809. Several other German and French papers express the same view.

† This was taken to refer to the employment of what were known as the Corsican Rangers in the British Service under Sir Hudson Lowe.

his conduct in Vienna had been anything out of the ordinary. Besides, had Bathurst committed suicide, would not his body have been found ?

The supposition that he had been done away with by the French was, from the very first, entertained by his wife, and no sooner had she received the news of his death than she resolved to go at once to Berlin and Paris, and to make every effort there and elsewhere to clear up the mystery. Having secured a passport to Sweden from Baron Rehausen, she and her brother, Mr. Call, set off to that country, and travelling thence to Pomerania, eventually reached Berlin.

There she interviewed Count St. Priest, the French Ambassador, who, acting on her behalf, obtained a passport * from Napoleon, giving her leave to travel all over the Continent. She received assurances both from St. Priest and the Count St. Marsau, another Minister in the pay of Napoleon, that the French Emperor had had nothing to do with the disappearance of her husband, but was only too anxious to do all that lay in his power to aid her in finding out the true cause of it.

The suavity of St. Marsau, in particular, and the

* According to other accounts, it was through M. Cambacérès she obtained the pass. (See " Memoirs and Correspondence of Dr. Henry Bathurst.")

pains that individual took to try to convince her
of Napoleon's goodwill, only tended to rouse her
suspicions, which were increased when she learned
that he, or Marsau, knew all her movements from
the time she left Harwich to the very moment she
arrived in Berlin. Leaving the latter city Mrs.
Bathurst and her brother proceeded to Perleberg.
Hearing that both Krause and Hilbert had been
suspected of complicity in the disappearance of
Mr. Bathurst, they interviewed them both, and, in
their opinion, both were innocent. It was while
they were engaged in examining these suspects
that a peasant woman named Hacker, who had
been sent to jail for various thefts, made a startling
statement. She declared that when out for a walk
one day in the town of Seeburg, twelve miles from
Hamburg, she met a young shoemaker from Perleberg named Goldberger, whose costume at once
arrested her attention. Whereas, when she had
last seen him, he was poorly clad, he was now wearing new, expensive clothes, while hanging from his
watch chain were several gold seals. The peasant
declared that she was so astonished at the change
in Goldberger's appearance that she stopped and
asked him the meaning of it, whereupon he showed
her a wallet and purse full of gold, and said he had
received them as hush money when the English
stranger about whom so much fuss had been made

was murdered. The story, however, appears to have been discredited by the chief investigators, and it is doubtful if it was ever properly looked into.*

Mrs. Bathurst, who seems to have fully made up her mind that the French alone were responsible for the disappearance of her husband, expressed the opinion that Hacker had invented the story she told, for the sole purpose of obtaining money from her through it. Another story † was current relating to a family named Hacker, but whether the above mentioned Mrs. Hacker belonged to this family or not is by no means clear. The said story was to this effect.

Close to where Captain Klitzing was living in Perleberg was a tavern of ill repute kept by a man of notorious bad character named Hacker. Augustus Schmitz was constantly at this tavern, and certain persons affirmed that on the evening of November 25th, the day Bathurst disappeared, they saw a stranger answering to Bathurst's description leave Klitzing's house and enter the tavern, but they never saw him go out of it. And it was a some-

* It was rumoured subsequently that Goldberger denied the allegations of Mrs. Hacker and offered an explanation regarding his clothes, watch and money, which satisfied the local authorities, but whether this was so is dubious. The author of the article re Mr. Bathurst in " Cornhill " evidently had strong doubts regarding the rumours.

† See " Memoirs and Correspondence of Dr. Henry Bathurst."

what significant fact that three days later the
Hackers left Perleberg and went to Altona, where
they lived in comparative opulence. This story
received a certain amount of confirmation in 1852,*
when Mrs. Kestern, to whom reference has already
been made, told Mrs. Thistlethwayte that she well
recollected Mr. Benjamin Bathurst coming to
Captain Klitzing's house on the evening of
November 25th, 1809. She said that she watched
him both come and go, and noticed that he did not
return by the way he had come, but turned down
the street in which the Hackers' tavern was situated, and this made her wonder whether he was
going to call in at the tavern.

Continuing, she said that, soon after Mr. Bathurst
had left, Augustus Schmitz came to Captain Klitzing and inquired if Mr. Bathurst was there and,
on her pointing out the way he had gone, Schmitz
started off, apparently in pursuit of him. According to this same lady, Augustus died eventually in
a house of conviction and might have confessed
much, had he only been encouraged to do so.
Captain Klitzing always inclined to the belief that
Bathurst had been murdered for his money,
and was of opinion that the Schmitz family
knew more of the affair than they thought fit to
disclose.

* *Vide* " Memoirs and Correspondence of Dr. Henry Bathurst."

Of course, if Bathurst really went to the Hacker's tavern on leaving Captain Klitzing's, the subsequent discovery of his coat in Augustus Schmitz's possession is readily accounted for, but no one came forward to testify to having seen him there, and many, including Krause, Hilbert and the Schmitz family, testified to Bathurst having returned to the post-house that evening, and to his having been seen by them at about nine o'clock standing by the horses' heads.

It must be remembered, however, that most of these witnesses were, in turn, suspected of being in some way implicated in the disappearance of Mr. Bathurst, and it is probable that none of them bore too good a reputation, hence their testimony could not be relied upon to any great extent. Mrs. Bathurst would seem to have placed implicit confidence in it; but her judgment was obviously biased and, firm in her preconceived conviction that the French alone were responsible for her husband's disappearance, she scouted the idea that persons as common and vulgar as Augustus Schmitz and the Hackers had had anything to do with it. Thus, after a very cursory examination of this and various other reports, and discrediting them all, Mrs. Bathurst finally left Perleberg, and having been told by a Mr. Röntgen that a lady in Madgeburg had been heard to say that the English

Ambassador whom every one was looking for was in Magdeburg Fortress she hastened to that city. On arriving there, she interviewed Mr. Röntgen, who declared that directly he had established the identity of the lady who had made the above statement he went to see her, and she told him that what she had said was quite correct. She had danced with the Governor of Magdeburg at a local ball, and in the course of conversation he had remarked, in alluding to the fortress, " They are looking everywhere for the English Ambassador, but I have him safe and sound up there."

This at least was something definite to work on, and Mrs. Bathurst decided to seek an interview with the Governor of Magdeburg without a moment's delay and question him as to the truth of what this lady had said. She had no difficulty in obtaining the interview, and the Governor, with apparent honesty and candour, admitted that he had remarked to a lady, with whom he had danced at a recent ball, that the English Ambassador was at the fortress, but that he had been mistaken. The person whom, at the time he made the remark, he had thought to be Mr. Bathurst, he discovered, later on, to be Louis Fritz, a man who had been employed as a spy on the Continent by Mr. Canning, the English Minister. This man had been seized by a troop of *douaniers* about the time Mr. Bathurst had disappeared, and brought to Magdeburg Fortress, pending examination.

"That may be," Mrs. Bathurst exclaimed, "but you will, I hope, let me see Louis Fritz."

"I'm afraid I cannot do that," the Governor replied. "He is a married man with a wife and family"

"But what if he is? It need not prevent my seeing him," Mrs. Bathurst persisted, "you can have him brought here."

"That is impossible, madam," the Governor responded, "he has gone to Spain."

"Let me see his wife, then," Mrs. Bathurst pleaded.

"She has gone with him," was the immediate answer.

Mrs. Bathurst, however, did not give up without a struggle. For two hours she harangued the Governor, alternately pleading and threatening, but it was of no avail. He maintained without the slightest sign of wavering that the prisoner was Louis Fritz, and that Fritz was now in Spain. Eventually, Mrs. Bathurst had to desist, but she left the fortress unconvinced.

Returning to England in the autumn of 1810, she made inquiries of Mr. Canning, concerning Louis Fritz, the alleged spy; but, as she had anticipated only too well, Mr. Canning informed her that he knew of no such person.

Her suspicions with regard to the Governor of Madgeburg being now confirmed, she was wondering what she should do next, when Mr. Röntgen, who appears to have taken an unusual interest in the case, sent her word that Count D'Entraigues, the man her husband had written about ominously in that apparently half finished last letter of his, found in his trouser's pocket, wanted to see her. Consequently, in spite of her prejudice against him, Mrs. Bathurst immediately invited him to come to her house to see her, and this he did the very next day. Coming to the point at once, he told her that he knew for certain that her husband had been seized on the evening of the 25th of November by a party of *douaniers-montés*, who were scouring the country round Perleberg for English spies, that he had been taken to the fortress of Magdeburg, and that the Governor of the fortress who had written to Fouchet, Minister of Police in Paris, to know what to do with him, had been told by Fouchet to put the mad Englishman out of the way. And this, the Count declared, the Governor had done, the story he had told Mrs. Bathurst with regard to "Louis Fritz" being cleverly invented to fit the occasion. No such person as Louis Fritz, Count D'Entraigues declared, had ever existed.

Shocked but not surprised, Mrs. Bathurst informed Count D'Entraigues that she was prepared to believe what he said about her husband, provided he could give her some kind of proof.

" I can, madam," he exclaimed, " if only you give me time. I will write at once, in cipher, to Paris, and the answer I receive will provide the desired proof."

The interview then terminated.

The Count wrote to Paris as he had promised. Of this Mrs. Bathurst had positive evidence, but in the interim, pending the reply, a dreadful tragedy occurred.

As the Count and his wife came out of their house at Twickenham and were about to step into their carriage to go for a drive, a French footman, who had but recently entered their service, and with whom they were never known to have had any quarrel, came up behind them and stabbed the Countess to the heart. The Count ran into the house for his pistols, and the assassin followed him. Immediately afterwards two pistol shots were heard ; and, when the rest of the household and some passers-by arrived upon the scene, both the Count and his footman were found lying on the floor of one of the rooms dead. Whether they had shot each other, or whether the footman had shot his master and then himself, it was impossible to say. Mrs. Bathurst, having, it seems, ascertained, presumably on pretty reliable grounds, that the

Count played a dual rôle and was actually a spy in the employ both of France and England, formed the opinion that the French Government, furious at his betrayal of the secret of Magdeburg, had bribed the French footman to kill him. For why, she argued, unless this were the case, did the man assassinate two people against whom, as far as was known, he had no personal grudge. Weighing all this over in her mind, together with her experience on the Continent, she was unable to come to any fresh conclusion, and still maintained that her husband had been murdered by Napoleon's agents, solely and wholly for political reasons.

To the outsider, however, it seems incredible that Napoleon himself would have been party to the crime. The war with Austria over, and the peace terms arranged entirely in favour of the French, what possible motive could Napoleon have had for taking Bathurst's life ? Now that the Austrian affair was settled, no great importance would be attached to the dispatches Bathurst may or may not have had on him, and if it were not to secure these dispatches why should Bathurst have been murdered ? Personal animosity ? Hardly likely ! Bathurst was altogether too insignificant an individual to have incurred the hatred of Napoleon. Besides, as far as was known, the two had never met. No, I think the theory that Napoleon was personally responsible for the disappearance of Benjamin Bathurst may be regarded as extremely unfeasible, but, on the other hand, Count D'Entraigues's story of Fouchet being the real culprit seems probable enough.

The *douaniers-montés* may have acted without any specific order from the Emperor, who very likely was quite unaware of what they had done and of Bathurst's subsequent detention and death. It strikes one as quite possible that Fouchet and the Governor of the fortress of Magdeburg did not realize who Bathurst was until after he had been executed, and fearing the consequences, if it should become known that an English Ambassador had been put to death, they agreed to keep the affair a profound secret. Something of this kind seems to me very much more credible than that Napoleon himself should have stooped to assassination.

Lord Bathurst, whether influenced by diplomacy or not, it is hard to say, ruled the French out of it altogether, and maintained that his kinsman had either committed suicide or been murdered, simply for his coat and other valuables. Now the suicide theory, as I have already stated, has very little to recommend it, and those who knew Benjamin Bathurst best ridiculed it ; but that common or garden robbery and murder was the explanation of the disappearance of the English Ambassador does seem to me to be extremely likely. There is also the theory that robbery and murder may have joined hands with political conspiracy.

Close to the post-house at that time, and separated from it only by a street, there lived a local magistrate about whom some strange stories were afloat.* Many people believed him to be a spy in the French Secret Service, and it was said that his two pretty daughters frequently entertained French officers and undesirable foreigners of all kinds at the house, and that " goings on " of every conceivable sort took place in it.

No doubt the Perleberg gossips exaggerated; but, as there is seldom smoke without fire, one may take it for granted that that was sure ground for scandal. The question is how much ? If this local magistrate were really in the pay of the French, and thoroughly unscrupulous, he might well have been in league with either Augustus Schmitz or Goldberger, and Bathurst might have been decoyed to his house that November night and murdered there. His house was not searched, although many thought it would have been advisable, especially after they had heard it said that his widow, on her death-bed, tried to make some kind of confession, but expired in the attempt.

* See " Memoirs and Correspondence of Dr. Henry Bathurst.'

Another house, which was also in close proximity to the post-house, was suspected by many of being in some way associated with the crime. In 1803, the owner, a shoemaker, sold it to a man named Mertens, who at the time Mr. Bathurst disappeared was a servant, either at the " Swan " or post-house, it is not definitely stated which.*

According to one report † there was nothing known against Mertens, who was generally believed to be a respectable, hard-working man, but some surprise was manifested when it leaked out that he had given his two daughters sums of money amounting to £150 and £120 for their marriage portions.

These were large sums for anyone in his position to give, and his friends and neighbours not unnaturally wondered how he had managed to save so much. Still no one, apparently, suspected him at the time of having acquired the money by any but strictly honest means. However, in 1852, some years after his death, the house which had been sold to a man named Kersewelter, and had

---

* Mrs. Thistlethwayte was told in 1852, when she visited Perleberg, that Mertens had been porter at the Crown Hotel. (See " Memoirs and Correspondence of Dr. Henry Bathurst," by Mrs. Thistlethwayte.)

† Mrs. Thistlethwayte was also told Mertens was a man of known bad repute.

got into a very bad state of repair, was pulled down, and under the stone flooring of one of the rooms * was found the skeleton of a man. It was lying at full length, face upwards, and a mark or denture on the top part of the back of the skull suggested the man had been struck a violent blow there with a hatchet or some other heavy instrument. The teeth were very good, but one molar was missing from the lower jaw and, as there were signs that it had been skilfully extracted, it was suggested that the dead man belonged to the upper or wealthy class, since in those days it was only the well-to-do who could afford to go to a skilled dentist.

Hence, it was thought by many of the Perleberg people that the remains must be those of the missing English Ambassador. Indeed, so prevalent was this talk that when Mrs. Thistlethwayte, Mr. Bathurst's sister, arrived in Perleberg, some months later, several of the inhabitants told her, as a definite fact, that the skeleton of Mr. Bathurst had been found, and that there was no longer any doubt but that he had been murdered.

The chief magistrate of the town, who happened to be a medical man, and had the skull of the dead

---

* Whereas Mrs. Thistlethwayte was told it had been found under the flooring of the kitchen, the writer in " Cornhill " declares it was discovered under the stone threshold of the stable.

man in his possession, compared it with a miniature portrait of Mr. Bathurst that Mrs. Thistlethwayte showed him, and after only a few seconds scrutiny remarked, " As a medical man I can attest to you, madame, that the skull I have here "—and he pointed to the skull on a table by his side—" did not belong to the living representative of this portrait, that is to say if the portrait was anything like a good one of him. Examine the skull yourself and tell me what you think."

Mrs. Thistlethwayte did so, and subsequently declared * that she had only to glance at the skull to see that it was not that of her brother, Benjamin. Her brother, it was true, had very fine teeth, she could not say whether he had had one extracted or not, but whereas the skull shown her indicated a very low and prominent forehead with a deep indenture between it and the nose, her brother's forehead was high, and his nose, straight after the Greek pattern, continued in a straight line from it. She was so confident on this score that she did not hesitate to make the following statement in writing to the head of the local police.

" The skull, which was shown to me at Perleberg on Monday, 23rd August, 1852, as having been found near Perleberg in 1852 is certainly not that

* See " Memoirs and Correspondence of Dr. Henry Bathurst," by Mrs. Thistlethwayte.

of my brother Benjamin Bathurst." And she left the town, still clinging to her belief, which was shared by many members of her family, that either Napoleon himself or his Secret Agents were responsible for her brother's disappearance, and that it was therefore futile to look for any real clue to it in Perleberg. It is quite conceivable, however, that both Mrs. Thistlethwayte and the magistrate who had possession of the skull were wrong, and that it did, after all, belong to the missing English Envoy. Mertens being apparently a respectable servant, either at the " White Swan " or post-house, Benjamin Bathurst, momentarily, perhaps, off his guard, might have been decoyed by Mertens into the latter's house that dark November evening, and there murdered ; Augustus Schmitz, or Goldberger, or both, very possibly assisting in the crime.

It must be remembered that Merten's house was situated conveniently near the post-house ; that, after Bathurst's disappearance, Augustus Schmitz had possession of his coat, that Goldberger, hitherto almost a pauper, was possessed of a gold watch and a purse full of money, and Mertens, reputed to be none too well off, was able to give his daughters large marriage dowries.

Another theory promulgated and favoured by some of the Perleberg inhabitants was that Captain

Klitzing behaved treacherously, and himself was responsible for Bathurst's disappearance. According to this theory the story that Bathurst walked round the horses' heads and disappeared was a mere fabrication concocted at Klitzing's instigation, the truth being that Bathurst really had driven away in the carriage that night, but had been waylaid and murdered by the French through the instrumentality of Klitzing and his agents. An elderly lady declared an oath that Klitzing knew all about it, but had sworn he would reveal nothing, while a gentleman, described as a respectable citizen of Perleberg, stated in proof of Klitzing's guilt that, whenever Bathurst's disappearance was mentioned in his presence, he invariably changed the conversation at once.*

It is hardly likely, however, that Klitzing, who as Military Governor of Perleberg held a responsible post, and who afterwards became a member of the Togendbund, would stoop to murder for a mercenary motive, and the only motive conceivable in this case ; and as there appears to be no evidence in support of his guilt, beyond the somewhat paltry statements of two people, an elderly man and woman, I think the theory in question

* See " Memoirs and Correspondence of Dr. Henry Bathurst," under " Translated from the New Pitaval by an Austrian," p. 556, etc.

can be discarded *in toto*. A theory deserving of rather more attention was that held by Mr. George Cotsford Call, brother-in-law of Mr. Benjamin Bathurst.* It was based to a large extent on a story told by the servant of an Agent of the English Government at Königsberg. She stated that late one night, about the time of Mr. Bathurst's disappearance, some one knocked at the front door, and that, on opening it with some hesitation, as her master was away, she saw a man in a travelling cap and cloak, and a sort of roquelaure drawn tightly round him. She said she only got a momentary view of his face, as a strong gust of wind blew out the light she had in her hand almost immediately, but that, nevertheless, the man's features were impressed on her memory, and they tallied exactly with the description subsequently given to her of Mr. Bathurst's features. He asked her if her master were at home, and on learning that he was not, and being asked if he would leave his name and a message, he had replied in some such words as the following :

"Oh, never mind about the name, merely tell him an English gentleman wants to see him tomorrow " (mentioning a certain hour) " at the post-house."

* See " Westminster Review," Vol. CXXXIV., p. 396; and " Memoirs and Correspondence of Dr. Henry Bathurst," p. 179.

He then bade the girl good night and went away.

The following day, at the time specified, the English Agent went to the post-house, but the stranger did not turn up, and as, owing to a terrific storm, several vessels crossing to Sweden, and bound for other destinations, had been lost, it was generally supposed that he must have changed his mind, gone on board one of these ill-fated vessels, and thus perished.

Mr. Call was firmly of the opinion that the stranger was his brother-in-law, Benjamin Bathurst. He believed that, at about nine o'clock, on the evening of November 25th, 1809, Bathurst, full of dread of assassination by the French, had yielded to a sudden impulse and, without telling anyone, had made off alone for Gothenburg, with the intention of travelling thence to England via Stockholm. It was quite natural, he argued, that Bathurst should choose this route, as he had formerly been in the British Embassy in Stockholm and had many friends in that town, besides—and this was more important in his eyes than anything else— there was far less probability of coming in contact with French spies in Sweden than there was in any of the more Southern Continental countries.

The fact of his being lost at sea, Mr. Call argued, would account for his body never being found—if he had been murdered and buried on land, the large

rewards offered by his family and the English
Government would surely have tempted some one
to tell all they knew. But in this, Mr. Call and
others were mistaken, for, again and again, in
murder mysteries has the offering of large rewards
utterly failed to elicit any information.

Moreover, Mr. Call offered no explanation as to
Benjamin Bathurst's overcoat being found in the
possession of Augustus Schmitz, and his trousers,
with bullet holes in them, by the wayside. Mr.
Bathurst may have been in a desperate hurry to
get to Gothenburg, but is it all likely that on a very
cold night in November he would have gone off
without his coat—and in a trouserless state too.

No, I think one must regard Mr. Call's theory,
which, after all, entirely depended on the impress-
sion of a girl, derived, as she herself admitted, from
a momentary glance, as not very feasible.

The theory that Benjamin Bathurst was carried
off by the *douaniers-montés* and murdered at
Magdeburg at the dictate of Fouchet seems more
probable, though it, too, merely depends on the
statement of a single individual, this time a man,
Count D'Entraigues ; and no very great credence,
of course, can be attached to the utterances of a
person who was known to have been in the pay of
two countries, and to have been trying to delude
both of them into the belief that he was acting

solely in their individual interests. Moreover, this theory does not explain how it was that no one in or around Perleberg saw the *douaniers* on the night of the alleged abduction. They could not at nine o'clock in the evening have ridden about the country without being seen or heard by some one, and had they been so seen or heard, the large rewards previously referred to would surely have tempted some one to give evidence. Also, the trousers being found with bullet holes in them, in the wood adjoining Perleberg, does not help the theory, but rather the reverse, since it is extremely unlikely that the *douaniers-montés*, who were a reputable military force and no brigands, would have killed their prisoner and stripped him.

More probable, I think, is Klitzing's theory that Bathurst was murdered by some common or garden thief, such as Augustus Schmitz or Goldberger, in league with some one occupying a house or cottage conveniently situated close by.

In applying for military protection at the post-house, Bathurst, in my opinion, made a most unfortunate move. By the presence at the post-house of a body-guard his fear of political assassination became known; and his murderers took full advantage of it. Knowing that attention would be directed to a quarter from which foul play was suspected, they saw a fair field for themselves, and under cover of it were able to commit the murder with impunity. With regard to the bullet riddled trousers, supposing the above theory were accepted as correct, little mystery would remain. The murderers, at their leisure, had thus riddled them and exposed them to view (with, it will be remembered, part of the letter in Bathurst's handwriting, expressing his dread of assassination by the French, in the pocket) in a secluded part of the wood, in order to further the belief, and thereby render themselves still more secure, that Bathurst, whom, of course, they had been obliged to dispatch without making any noise, had been shot by his abductors for political ends.

CHAPTER IV

THE MYSTERIES OF EISHAUSEN

ONE day, in the year 1803, considerable excitement was aroused in the sleepy little Suabian town of Ingelfingen by a most unusual occurrence, namely, the arrival of strangers. They came in a closed carriage driven by a man in livery, who, it was subsequently discovered, played the dual rôle of coachman and valet, and stopped at one of the most expensive apartment houses in the town. The strangers alighting from the carriage proved to be two in number, a tall, distinguished looking man and a slim, elegant looking woman, whose features were hidden from view by a thick veil and a pair of spectacles.

Both were clad in the height of fashion, and the lady's figure and walk, as she entered the house, gave those who saw her the impression that she was very young. They took a suite of rooms on the first floor, engaged a local woman by the day as maid of all work, and from the very beginning plainly showed they did not wish to have anything to do with their neighbours. The lady never left

the apartment, saving for a drive in the surrounding country, and the only occasion upon which her
features were seen by any of the townspeople was
when the wind blew aside her veil, one morning, as
she was about to get into her carriage. The passers-
by then caught a momentary glimpse of them, and
were immediately struck by the resemblance they
bore to those of the daughter of the unfortunate
Louis XVI. Though apparently a very young face,
it showed signs of great grief and extreme delicacy.
She appeared much disconcerted at being seen, and
stepping into her carriage, in this instance, with
more haste than dignity, was driven rapidly away.
No one ever saw her at any of the windows of her
apartments, but she was occasionally seen in the
garden at the back of the house, albeit invariably
heavily veiled and wearing spectacles. So much
for the lady.

The gentleman, who, presumably, when asked
his name declined to give it, and was subsequently
styled the Count, was not quite so exclusive. He
often conversed with the chemist who lived in the
rooms directly underneath his on the ground floor,
and, evincing a great interest in chemical research
work, he proved to be well up in many of the most
advanced medical and scientific theories of the
day ; and several others with whom he also conversed were impressed by the vast field of his

learning and his apparently intimate knowledge
of many of the topics of the day. Indeed, it seemed
as if he not only took a more than ordinary interest
in European politics, particularly in those of France,
but as if he could not repress a certain eagerness to
ascertain the views held by the people of Ingelfingen regarding the French Government. It was,
in fact, his undisguised prejudice in favour of the
Bourbons, together with his distinguished appearance and that of the lady who accompanied him,
whose relationship to him, by the way, was a
matter of increasing conjecture among the women-
folk of Ingelfingen, that led many to surmise that
he was some French aristocrat, who had been lucky
enough to survive the Great Revolution, but who,
in order to escape its consequences, was still obliged
to live in exile. It was even suggested that the
mysterious stranger was the Duc d'Angoulême,
despite the obvious fact that his age did not in the
least coincide with that nobleman's ; and, in order
to settle the question definitely, attempts were
made to extract information from the coachman,
who apparently valeted his master and was general
factotum and confidential servant besides, but
without success. The coachman-valet persistently
avoided his would-be interrogators and proved to
be quite as much a mystery to the people of Ingelfingen as were his employers ; for his appearance

and manners were not those of an ordinary servant but of a man of superior, if not, indeed, noble birth. He never spoke to the daily woman employed by the Count, excepting to give her instructions from his master, and when not actually with the Count or lady he kept rigidly to his own quarters.

This same woman, who was only too willing to impart all she knew about the strangers, declared that she was never brought into actual contact with "the lady," because she never entered the lady's bedroom while the lady was in it, and if ever the lady happened to come out of it while she (the woman) was on the landing or staircase, she would retreat precipitately to her bedroom and shut herself in. The woman, however, expressed her conviction that the lady was very young, and that the Count himself could not be more than forty. Also, she affirmed that the Count received many letters, all of which bore foreign postmarks; and that whenever he addressed the coachman-valet it was always in a foreign language utterly unknown to her.

Thus, her information, instead of throwing any light on the mystery all Ingelfingen had woven round the strangers, only seemed to intensify it, and the mystery deepened still further, when it was found out one morning that the strangers had gone.

They had apparently made their exit when the good people of the town were still in bed.

Some months later, the "Suabian Mercury" announced the death of a French refugee of considerable distinction, who, it said, had resided for some time in Ingelfingen. Owing therefore to this circumstance, and to the fact that the description given of him tallied exactly with that of the Count, the people of Ingelfingen took it for granted that the defunct refugee and the mysterious stranger who had once resided in their midst were one and the same person, and soon forgot all about him and the veiled and spectacled lady who had accompanied him.

After the lapse of about six years, however, they received a shock. News reached them from Hildburghausen, a neighbouring town, that strangers, the exact counterparts of the Count, the veiled and spectacled lady and the coachman-valet, had suddenly arrived at an inn there called the "Arms of England," and had engaged a suite of rooms. What was the meaning of it ? Was the Count not dead after all, and had the announcement in the "Suabian Mercury" been a fake ? But, if so, why ? What could possibly have prompted such a seemingly motiveless trick ? That is what the inhabitants of the two towns, Ingelfingen and Hildburghausen, found themselves asking one another, and interest in the case soon became widespread. Who were the mysterious two, and where had they hidden during the interval between their abrupt departure from Ingelfingen and their equally abrupt arrival at Hildburghausen ?

None could say. At the " Arms of England," they maintained just the same privacy as they had done at Ingelfingen. The lady never left the inn, saving in the carriage driven by the coachman-valet, and invariably kept in her rooms whenever the woman engaged by the day was anywhere about. Also, rumour again affirmed that the lady was very young, but a fresh rumour got into circulation with regard to the Count, the rumour being that he was a well-known French *émigré* of the name of Vavel de Versay. The local authorities, however, when questioned on the subject, merely shrugged their shoulders.

" He may or may not be the Count Vavel de Versay," they said, " he has not shown us any passport or document to prove his identity, but so long as he pays his bills and behaves like a gentleman, why bother ? We certainly shan't." And they did not.

It was then rumoured in Hildburghausen that Count Vavel de Versay, always accompanied by the veiled and spectacled lady and the sphinx-like coachman-valet, had lived for a while at Frankfort

on the Maine, Mayence and Offenbach, and that he
had gone from each of those places with the same
startling abruptness as he had from Ingelfingen.
Consequently, the people of Hildburghausen were
in hourly expectation that the mysterious two in
like manner would disappear from Hildburghausen.
Nor were they wrong. After remaining at the
" Arms of England " for some months, they left
just as suddenly as they had left their previous
quarters ; but this time, instead of removing to
some far-away town, they merely went to Eishausen, a village about nine miles distant and there
took up their abode in an old mansion on the outskirts of the village, generally known as the château.
It was a large, far from compact building, oak
panelled throughout, and it seemed to abound in
mysterious corridors and staircases. According
to hearsay, in fact, there was something very queer
about the place, and many were the strange stories
told by the villagers, when seated round their cosy
cottage fires in winter time, concerning it. But to
proceed. Former residents at the château, which
was certainly more like a castle than a house, had
kept a retinue of servants, and great therefore was
the astonishment of the simple inhabitants of Eishausen, when it became known that the Count
Vavel de Versay (the Count, it was now apparently
understood, had tacitly admitted his claim to this

title) had only engaged a cook, a man and woman
of the name of Schmidt, and a young girl, all
natives of Hildburghausen, to carry on the work
of his establishment. Also the duties allotted to
the three latter, who were to " live out," would
seem to have been somewhat limited and extraordinary.

The girl was to bring the milk every morning
between four and five o'clock, to hand it through
one of the kitchen windows to the cook, from whom,
through the same window, she was to receive her
orders for the day. These orders were always of
the same nature, namely, to do errands out of
doors, and they were invariably accompanied by
an injunction that she was on no account to
enter the house or to appear in any way inquisitive.
Mrs. Schmidt, albeit her chief job was marketing,
was admitted into the house once a day, at a stated
time, to clean the rooms on the ground floor ; but
no sooner was this cleaning done than she was told
that it was time for her to go ; and never once was
she given a job in any other part of the house.
Besides the cleaning of the ground floor, however,
and the marketing, she had one other duty, namely,
at eleven o'clock every day, to unlock the door
leading into the garden at the rear of the premises,
and to open it for the lady to pass through ; but
so rigidly did the Count enforce his orders that she

should be out of sight when the lady came down-
stairs that, although she regularly performed this
small office for the lady and worked at the château
for over thirty years, she never on any one occasion
actually saw her.

Needless to say, perhaps, since she had even less
opportunity of doing so than Mrs. Schmidt, the
young girl never saw the lady. Neither did
Schmidt, Mrs. Schmidt's husband, who did his
best, single-handed, to keep the grounds in order.

The cook, who lived with the mysterious trio in
the château for over twenty-six tears, only saw the
lady twice, and on both occasions, oddly enough,
owing to the same cause. The Count having been
taken ill in the night awakened the household with
his cries, and the lady, the coachman-valet and the
cook, on hastening to his aid, unavoidably encountered one another. On neither occasion, however, did the cook receive any definite impression
with regard to the lady, her whole attention being
concentrated on the Count.

The extraordinary interest therefore that was
taken in the secrecy surrounding the lady, far from
diminishing, seems only to have increased, as time
went on.

That she was not a prisoner may be gathered
from the fact that she could easily have called for
help, when she took her daily drives in the neigh-

bourhood, often accompanied only by the coachman-valet. Also, when she was sometimes seen perambulating the fields adjoining the château, although on these occasions she was invariably in the company of the Count, she conveyed to those watching her from a distance the very distinct impression that she held the whip hand, and that the Count, willy-nilly, was obliged to do her bidding. It was surmised and believed by many that the Count and the lady were man and wife, but then, again, those who had seen them together thought otherwise.

The mystery, too, deepened as a whole, when it was remembered that the lady's age had apparently remained stationary. Those who saw her on her first arrival at Eishausen, although she was as usual wearing veil and spectacles, were convinced that she could not have been more than seventeen or eighteen at the most. Her figure, her walk, her general appearance, everything about her, in fact, convinced them that she was still in her teens, which certainly seemed very extraordinary, when it was also remembered that the very same opinion with regard to her age had been expressed by the people of Ingelfingen five or six years earlier, and by one Herr Bülow, a resident in Eishausen, at least ten years later.

This Bülow, by the way, appears to have been

something in the nature of a peeping Tom. One day in 1818, chancing to see from the doorway of his house, which commanded a somewhat distant view of the rear premises of the château, some one leaning out of one of the windows, he at once fetched his telescope, and looking through it perceived that the person was a woman, a very young woman, little more than a child he thought, with dark hair and marvellously beautiful features, and wearing a white dress with a dark cloak thrown carelessly round her shoulders. She was breaking up biscuits and throwing bits out of the window to a dog in the garden ; and every now and then, when she clapped her hands and laughed, or called out to the animal, Bülow thought he had never seen a prettier picture. She was full of grace and vivacity ; and yet, underlying all her girlish merriment, he fancied he could detect a spirit of sadness and dejection, which was not to be wondered at, he told himself, considering the fact that she lived in that vast, gloomy old house with no companions of her own age. He concluded that she must be the lady whose identity had been a mystery for so long to every one in Eishausen and Hildburghausen, and yet how was it that she still appeared to be sweet seventeen.

Fifteen years previously those who had seen her at Ingelfingen declared that she was but a girl, and if his telescope was to be relied upon she was but a girl still. What was the explanation of it ?

He stated the case to an old roadmender, who had been at work in the neighbourhood of the château for some time, and, in reply, the road-mender said, " There are two ladies up there in the château, sir. The one is old and ugly, and the other young and pretty. They take it in turns to go out in the carriage, and I have seen them both at different times looking out of it. It frequently passes me while I am at work."

" But how is it," Herr Bülow remarked, " that only one was seen to arrive at Hildburghausen, and to leave, and that the servants at the château de-clare there is only one there, a lady, that no one, saving myself, seems to have seen her without a veil and spectacles."

" I can't explain that, sir. All I can tell you is that I have seen two," the roadmender persisted, " and sometimes they have worn the veil and spectacles, and sometimes not." And he stuck resolutely to his story.

After his talk with the roadmender, Herr Bülow seems to have been more than ever curious regard-ing the inhabitants of the château, and to have been continually trying to pump information about them from the Schmidts, and the young girl. In this, however, he was completely unsuccessful, because neither the Schmidts nor the girl apparently knew more about them than he did himself.

The notorious case of " Casper Hauser " being in progress at this time, Feurbach, who had been told about the mysterious two in the château of Eishausen, conceived the idea that there must be some connecting link between the two cases. Consequently, he brought Casper Hauser to Eishausen and showed him the exterior of the château, in the full expectation that the lad would at once identify the place with the house in which he had lived prior to his coming to Nuremburg.* But in this he was doomed to disappointment, for Casper immediately declared he had never set eyes on the château before. The incident, however, coming to the ears of Bülow, seems to have given him a fresh stimulus, for he thenceforth emulated Paul Pry more than ever, and spent practically all his time hovering round the château, his chief object being to solve the mystery of the lady in the veil and spectacles. On one occasion he trapped the Count out of doors into casually conversing with him ; but, the moment he politely inquired after the health of his good lady, the Count, frowning ominously, bid him a curt good morning. It was soon after Herr Bülow had suffered this set-back

---

* *Vide* " Casper Hauser " in " Remarkable Adventures and Unrevealed Mysteries," Vol. II., by Lascelles Wraxall.

that Schmidt died, and his post at the château was
filled by his son, who, being young and rather unusually " full of himself," was inclined to be a good
deal more communicative than his father. Herr
Bülow, recognizing this, encouraged the young man
to talk, and was at last rewarded in his efforts by
a piece of somewhat startling information. Young
Schmidt, stopping him one day in the road, said
very confidentially :

" I've something to tell you, sir, about the lady
up at the house," and he jerked his head in the
direction of the château.

" Indeed ! " Herr Bülow exclaimed, trying to
hide his excitement, and to appear as usual digni-
fied and indifferent. " What is it, pray ? "

" Only this," young Schmidt whispered with a
a grin, " the old gentleman's jealous of me."

" Jealous—and of you ! " Bülow cried. " Why,
what next ? Explain yourself."

" All right, sir, I will," the youth replied, looking,
however, somewhat crestfallen. " It happened like
this. Yesterday morning, between eleven and
twelve o'clock, as I was walking along the path,
outside the big garden, at the back of the house, I
noticed the wooden door leading into the garden
was open. Now such a thing, sir, I have never
known happen before. Always at that time the
door is locked, because it is then that the lady

promenades about inside. Well, sir, partly through curiosity and partly because I wanted some lettuce to eat with my dinner, I stepped into the garden, and after satisfying myself no one was in sight made at once for the lettuce beds. I had picked a couple—nice big ones too, they made my mouth water—and was about to grab hold of a third, when to my horror, sir, I suddenly heard voices, and before I had time to hide the Count and the lady appeared from behind a cluster of bushes and came straight towards me. They were so engrossed in conversation, that they did not appear to notice me at first, and I was hoping they would pass by without observing me, when the lady suddenly raising her head caught sight of me. To my infinite surprise she smiled, a real smile of delight, and running forward to where I was standing exclaimed, ' My dear Schmidt, I want to speak to you. I ——,' but before she could say another word, the Count was after her like a madman. I have never seen such fury in anyone's face. I can tell you, sir, it made me quake, and I am not easily frightened. Seizing her roughly by the arm, he said something in a jargon I didn't understand, and dragged her away with him to the house. Directly they were gone, I cleared out of the garden, and soon afterwards the Count came to me, and in a voice shaking with rage said ' Schmidt, don't you ever enter that garden again.   If you do, you leave my service at once.'   Of course I promised him I wouldn't, and he went away scowling and muttering."

" And yet they say the lady is not a prisoner, and that the Count is ruled by her," Bülow observed.

" Yes, sir, that's what I've always been told," young Schmidt answered, " and certainly, until now, I've always thought so."

" What was the lady like ? " Bülow asked, not trying to conceal his curiosity any longer.   " Was she wearing spectacles ?   Describe her ? "

" Well, sir," Schmidt responded, " she was young, about my own age I should reckon, certainly no older.   And she was dark, at least darkish, brown hair and eyes."

" What most people would describe as pretty ? " Bülow interrupted.

" I should just think so," Schmidt went on " Pretty isn't the word for it.   And so nice and friendly too.   If it hadn't been for the Count, she ——"

But Bülow cut him short.   He had no desire to encourage too much familiarity on the part of his inferiors.

" There, that will do," he interposed hastily. " She wanted you to go on some errand for her, of course.   Are you sure there is only one lady at the house ? "

"As far as I know there's only one," young Schmidt replied. "If there had been more my mother or father, I'm sure, would have got to hear of it, and they've never spoken of more than one to me."

"And she is always young!" Herr Bülow commented. "Well, well, it's all very queer." And he moved on.

Five years passed, and then a great sensation was caused, in and around Eishausen, by an announcement from the château that the lady was dead and was about to be buried in the garden of a house the Count had bought some years previously in Hildburghausen. The Count declared that the lady—in alluding to her he never called her by any name—had taken a particular fancy to that garden, and that she had expressed an ardent wish to be interred there.

The night of the funeral was one destined to live long in the memory of all who witnessed it. Never had such a funeral taken place at Eishausen before. The hearse left the château at midnight accompanied by the Count, his servants and a large number of villagers, all carrying torches, which cast a lurid glow over the surrounding scenery. Slowly and solemnly, the procession wended its way along the high road to Hildburghausen, arriving at the place of burial shortly before dawn.

Then, by the Count's order, the lid of the coffin was removed, and a figure, clad from head to foot in white, was for some minutes exposed to the view of the more curious members of the crowd, who pressed as near to it as the officiating clergyman and the solemnity of the occasion permitted. After the coffin had been lowered into the grave, and while the crowd were slowly and somewhat reluctantly dispersing, the clergyman who had conducted the ceremony asked the Count for his wife's name, and the date and place of her birth. To the surprise of those standing around, however, the Count replied, " The defunct is not my wife. I have never said that she was, and I must decline to give you any information concerning her." Later on, however, he told the clergyman in confidence that the person buried was " Sophie Botta, spinster, of bourgeois condition, a native of Westphalia, and 58 years of age."

There seems, however, strong reasons for doubting the truth of this statement, and for supposing rather, that the person buried was no person at all, since those who had been nearest to the coffin, when it was opened, expressed their belief that the figure they saw in it was a large wax doll. And this opinion, phantastic as it may seem, received a certain amount of support in a story told by several of the inhabitants of Eishausen, who had seen the

funeral procession set out for Hildburghausen but
had not accompanied it.

They declared that, some time after it had left,
a coach driven by four very powerful looking horses
had dashed through the open gateway up to the
château, and after remaining there for some minutes
had driven away at a furious pace, and that they
had noticed, as it tore past them, that the blinds
were all tightly drawn down. It was an incident,
of course, that naturally led to further disagreement. While some believed that the coach contained the actual corpse of the lady, others maintained that she was not dead at all, and that the
funeral was all a plant on the part of the Count, to
cover the fact that, for some peculiar reason, the
lady had left him. Be this as it may, however,
after her alleged burial at Hildburghausen, the
local authorities visited Eishausen Château for the
purpose of valuing her belongings and making
inquiries concerning her nearest of kin.

And in the apartments the Count informed them
were hers they found 100 new golden coins scattered
about promiscuously and a Catholic book of Hours,
but no documents of any kind. This was certainly
unsatisfactory, and the authorities considered it all
the more so, when, in answer to their statement
that they would have to instigate inquiries elsewhere, the Count laughed and said, " Inquire where

you like, I have taken every precaution. You will discover nothing." However strange as this may seem, after what had transpired, the Count gave the authorities 1470 florins, which he declared to be the exact amount of property the deceased had left, and the authorities eventually agreed to let the matter rest. And officially it did. Later, owing, perhaps, to the misgivings of the general public that were so easily allayed, further inquiries were set on foot, and although very little more, relating either to the Count or the lady, ever came to light, certain details in connection with the case were discovered and are worth recording.

In 1826, while the lady was still living at the château, Hildburghausen, in which town, it will be remembered, the Count had bought a house with a large garden attached, passed under the control of a new municipal council; and this new council tried to bring pressure to bear on the Count to reveal his true identity and that of the lady or ladies of his establishment. But in his dealings with these authorities, also, the Count seems to have come out on top. He refused point-blank to answer any of their questions, declaring that, rather than do so, he would leave the country; and, as he was known to be extremely liberal in his donations to local charities, the council, apparently, not only decided to climb down, but, in order to ensure his

THE DUCHESSE D'ANGOULÊME BELIEVED BY MANY TO BE "THE
MYSTERY LADY" OF EISHAUSEN
(From "Biographie Nouvelle des Contemporains)

continued residence in the neighbourhood, conferred an honorary citizenship of their town on him.

It was also ascertained that one day, when the Count and the lady happened to be in the garden of the house at Hildburghausen, a town councillor, peeping through a crack in the wall, saw the lady without either veil or spectacles, and declared that he was not only struck by her beauty, but by the very extraordinary likeness that she bore to the Bourbon family. And this theory that she was one of the Bourbons in hiding seemed to gain considerably in strength, when, after the Count's death, it was announced that many articles of lady's underwear were found at the château, all marked alike with three fleurs-de-lys. Many people, in fact, then felt convinced that the lady was the Duchesse d'Angoulême, whose head had been saved from the guillotine by the substitution of another in its stead.

But such a supposition does not altogether solve the problem, since not even one of the Bourbons could always remain young ? The roadmender's testimony that there were two ladies at the château, one old and ugly, and the other young and beautiful, would, perhaps, if a single uncorroborated testimony can be accredited, solve the mystery of the lady's age, and it might even suggest, perhaps, that the Count was a Voltairean, a regular *débauché*, and kept a seraglio. But if such were the case, where did he keep his myrmidons and what became of them ? And was he a magician, and had he invested them all with invisibility ? For certainly in the neighbourhood of Eishausen it would have been difficult if not impossible to elude prying eyes, and no one ever knew a stranger drive up to the château or leave it. Besides, who or what did the Count have buried in his garden at Hildburghausen, and who or what, that very same night, was whirled away from Eishausen in the carriage and four with the blinds tightly drawn down ? These were mysteries which no one apparently could solve.

And there were other mysteries at Eishausen too. The coachman-valet being taken seriously ill, the local minister, a Lutheran, was sent for, and on his arrival he was told that a dying man had something he wanted to confess to him ; but the Lutheran minister refused to hear the confession, on the grounds that it was against his creed to do so, and the man therefore died with some sin or secret undisclosed. At the funeral, in reply to the officiating clergyman's questions, the Count said, " The man's name is Philip Sparre. He was between sixty and seventy years of age and came from Switzerland. That is all I know of him." But, if this latter were the case, it was odd that letters addressed to Philip Sparre should have been delivered at the château, periodically, for fully twenty years after his burial, and that not a single one of them should be re-addressed to the postal authorities.

The chief mystery, however, is the Count himself. Who was he? When his death occurred at the château in 1845, this question, always a subject of discussion, was debated more keenly than ever throughout Eishausen and Hildburghausen. Apart from his house property, he only left 15,000 florins in actual money, and nothing to show who he was, or to throw any light on his history, saving the baptismal register (dated 22 September, 1769) of Leonard Cornelius Van der Valck; a passport in the name of Leonard Cornelius Van der Valck, a bundle of letters all signed Ange Barthelemy, *née* Daniels; and one or two documents in the nature of memorandum. The authorities at Hildburghausen, however, concluding that Van der Valck and Vavel de Versay, the name by which the deceased had been known in Hildburghausen, but which no one had ever heard him say was his name, were identical, at once advertised for Leonard Cornelius Van der Valck's nearest of kin, and in due course their advertisement was answered. A Mr. Van der Valck arrived at Hildburghausen with his solicitor from Amsterdam, proved to the satisfaction of the local authorities that he was the nearest of kin to the deceased, and promptly took possession of his house

and money.   Yet, in the eyes of many, the mystery
surrounding the dead man was a mystery still.

It was true that Mr. Van der Valck from Amsterdam had proved that he and his family had been in
constant communication with Mr. Cornelius Van
der Valck * (*alias* the Count) sending him at regular
intervals the dividends on some of his property, but
that was no actual proof that the man who allowed
himself to be styled Vavel de Versay really was
Cornelius Van der Valck.   Not a single one of the
Dutch Van der Valcks, it must be remembered, had
ever seen the dead man, and the fact that the
writing on the letters the Dutch Van der Valcks had
received from Eishausen was similar to that in
certain of the few documents found at the château,
and apparently belonging to the real Cornelius Van
der Valck, was no proof at all that the letters had
been written by him.

Besides, it must be admitted that if the Count
were no Count at all, but a man of distinctly middle-
class origin, such as a man of the name of Van der
Valck would be, his assumption of aristocracy " sat
on him " exceedingly well, since no one ever doubted
his veracity when he alluded to certain members of
the Bourbon family as people whom he had known

* Although it must have been known that letters addressed to
Cornelius Van der Valck were delivered at the château, it apparently
never occurred to the inhabitants of Eishausen to associate the
Count with that individual.

intimately, nor did they even dream that he might be drawing the long bow, when he talked of having been to Vienna for the express purpose of meeting the Emperor Alexander. Hence, his appearance and manners, which were undoubtedly those of an extremely cultured and aristocratic man, negatives the theory that he was Cornelius Van der Valck. But, if he were not Cornelius Van der Valck, who was he ?

In the face of a consensus of opinion as to the place he at one time occupied in the social scale, it would seem almost ludicrous to suggest even that he was, perhaps, merely a clever adventurer, who see-ing favourable circumstances had murdered the real Van der Valck, in order to get his money, and was impersonating him. But should we seriously con-sider this argument, might we not go a step further and suggest that, besides murdering Van der Valck, he had murdered the lady (or ladies) who had lived with him ?

After the alleged burial of " Sophie Botta, spinster, aged 58," in the garden of the house at Hildburghausen, the young and beautiful lady at the château completely disappeared. And the question as to what became of her remains unanswered to this day.

CHAPTER V

PHILIP CHRISTOPHER VON KÖNIGSMARCK

COUNT PHILIP VON KÖNIGSMARCK, son of Count Conrad Christopher von Königsmarck, and grandson of the great Protestant Field-Marshal, Hans Christopher von Königsmarck, was born in 1662. Brought up with his more illustrious elder brother, Count Hans Charles, and his sisters, the Countesses Amalie Wilhelmina and Maria Aurora, at the Agathenburg, near Stade, the stately mansion built by his grandfather, he and his brothers and sisters were frequently invited to the palace of Duke George William of Brunswick-Lüneburg in the neighbouring town of Celle.

It was therefore at a very early age that he first became acquainted with the Duke of Brunswick-Lüneburg's daughter, Sophia Dorothea, who was destined to play such an important rôle in his subsequent fate. The two were children and play-mates together, and it is extremely probable that a match between them was planned at that period by Count Philip's mother and the Duchess of

Brunswick-Lüneburg, who were great friends. The
young Count, being related to several sovereign
princely houses, and the Princess's mother being,
though a member of the French nobility, not of
royal blood, the match would not have been so
unequal as it might, at first sight, have appeared.
Anyhow, we may confidently surmise that the two
mothers favoured it, and the Count and the little
Princess, who was several years younger, were
allowed to be constantly together, so that they
naturally became greatly attached to one another
Before Count Philip had passed out of his teens,
however, he was sent with his brother on a succession of visits to foreign Courts to improve his education, and while he was thus engaged, the Princess
Sophia Dorothea, then only sixteen years of age,
was persuaded, one might almost say coerced, into
marrying her cousin, George Louis, Crown Prince
of Hanover, and afterwards George I of England.

Seven years later, Count Philip von Königsmarck,
now a proud, handsome, chivalrous cavalier,
returned to Germany and presented himself at the
Hanoverian Court. It may be taken for granted,
perhaps, that the emotions of the Princess on seeing
him again were of a somewhat conflicting nature.
Pleasure at the thought of renewing social intercourse with her old playmate was, in all probability,
marred by the knowledge that he could never be

anything more to her now than a friend.   It was no
secret that her marriage was a very unhappy one.
Her husband, a coarse brute—there is little question
on that point—seldom treated her with any cour-
tesy, let alone affection, and openly insulted her by
making love in public to a lady of the Court.   When
comparing him with the gallant and chivalrous
Count Philip von Königsmarck, and thinking,
perhaps, how different her lot would have been had
she married the latter, the Princess Sophia must
indeed have felt sad, and it is possible that she made
Count Philip the confidant of her sufferings.   Very
likely, too, she derived consolation for the ill-
treatment she was so certainly enduring at the
hands of her husband in the young Count's society.
Anyhow, it is alleged they were often together,
though there is no evidence to show that they ever
behaved in any other than a strictly proper manner,
or that the Count paid the Princess any more
attention than the respect and courtly gallantry
that were characteristic of those days demanded.

There were persons who believed that certain
letters forming a correspondence between the two
and proving a guilty intercourse had been found in
Sweden, but the unbiased mind can only regard
such documents as forgeries, since it is more than
improbable that the letters of both Count Philip and
the Princess should have fallen into the hands of the

same person. Also, it is inconceivable that either
the Count or the Princess would willingly have
parted with their letters, no matter what they contained, and had they been procurable the Hanoverian Government itself would have been first in
the field; in which case they could have been
relegated to the National Archives and kept there
under lock and key.

However, to proceed with this story, Count
Philip von Königsmarck, being, as I have already
said, extremely handsome, had the misfortune to
attract the attention of Countess von Platen, the
beautiful and powerful mistress of the Elector
Ernest Augustus, Princess Sophia's father-in-law.
Inflamed with an uncontrollable passion for the
young Count, this woman resorted to every device
imaginable to secure his affection, and when she
failed, failed utterly, owing, she imagined, to his
love for the Princess, her love, if love it can be
called, turned to the most virulent and violent hate.
Hence, it became her one desire to ruin the young
Count and the Princess, and with that object in
view she immediately set to work to poison the
mind of the Elector Ernest against them both. It
was at this stage in the affairs of Count Philip von
Königsmarck that he was called away from Hanover
by the death of his grand-uncle, Field-Marshal Otho
von Königsmarck, who fell a victim to what, for

want of a more technical name, was called the Plague. He died on September 15, 1688, and his body was taken to the family vault at Stade, Count Philip accompanying it. About this time, too, Count Philip's brother, the notorious Hans Charles, and also his uncle, Count Otto Wilhelm, died, and as he inherited their money, as well as that of his grand-uncle, he suddenly became one of the richest men in Europe. He had several palatial country residences, and at his town house, in Hanover, he is said to have had twenty-nine indoor servants, a prodigious staff for those days, and to have kept over fifty horses and mules.

The Elector Ernest had frequently tried to induce him to enter the Hanoverian Army, and in 1689 he did so, obtaining a commission as Colonel of Dragoons.

The following year, he saw service under Prince Charles of Brunswick-Lüneburg against the Turks, in 1691 and 1692 he was serving under William III of England in Flanders, and in 1693 he was commanding an army against the Danes, who were threatening to invade Prussia.

During these campaigns, it must be noted that, whenever a temporary cessation of hostilities occurred, he returned to Hanover, and that the Princess Sophia welcomed him openly, displaying every token of regard and friendship, but never any

warmer feeling. On the other hand, the sight of
the young Count, flushed with victory in the field
and more handsome than ever, seems to have caused
a revulsion of feeling in the breast of the Countess
von Platen, who, once again, became desperately
enamoured of him.

As before, she resorted to every artifice that
she thought likely to induce him to yield to her
advances, which seem to have been of the most
passionate and ungovernable nature, and when, as
before, she failed ignominiously, her sentiments
towards him finally underwent a complete change,
and she became imbued with only one desire,
namely, revenge. The Princess Sophia, with an
almost incomprehensible lack of ordinary tact,
which was indeed remarkable in one who was
credited with rather more than an ordinary share
of feminine caution and common sense, showed the
Countess very plainly that she knew of her hopeless
infatuation for the Count, and her somewhat
unaccountable and foolish assumption of the rôle
of successful rival simply goaded the Countess to
desperate measures. In her fiercely rekindled
hatred of the handsome soldier, who, unmoved by
her passionate appeals, would have none of her
love, and the pretty Princess, who feeling secure in
her exalted position at the Palace, openly flouted
her, she set to work to arouse the jealousy of the

Crown Prince by spreading the most infamous calumnies about his wife, and using every other means in her power to persuade him to believe that the relationship between the Princess Sophia and Count Philip was of an immoral nature. Even to a casual observer, perhaps, it was obvious that she meant mischief, and Field-Marshal von Podewils, one of Count Philip's truest friends, warned him seriously against her and advised him to leave Hanover without a moment's delay. But Count Philip turned a deaf ear. Dashing and reckless in the field, he defied any sort of danger, and he laughingly told Podewils that having faced the Turks, who were generally deemed the most savage fighters in Europe, he certainly did not fear a woman, however powerful she might think herself. Hence, it was not until he found it impossible to see the Princess alone, owing to the interference of Court officials and servants, who, instructed by the Crown Prince, at the instigation of the Countess von Platen, were evidently spying on them, and the attitude of the Elector and Crown Prince towards him became absolutely insufferable, that he resolved to leave Hanover. He realized, of course, that promotion in the Hanoverian service would henceforth be barred to him, but, what was more important to him, he now felt convinced that his presence at the Court would bring trouble to the one being

he loved.   He therefore sent in his resignation as an
officer in the Hanoverian army, and immediately
afterwards entered the service of Saxony as a
general.   After remaining some days in Dresden,
paying his respects to his new patron, the Elector
of Saxony, he returned to Hanover, heedless of the
warnings of his friends, determined to see the
Princess Sophia Dorothea once more, and to explain
to her that his affection for her was in no degree
diminished, but that he must for her own sake bid
her a final farewell.   Arriving in Hanover he put
up at the Hotel de Strelitz in the New Market, and
on Sunday evening, July 1, 1694, he was seen to
enter the Electoral Palace.

After that no one outside the Electoral Palace
ever saw him again.   Four days later, that is to
say on July 5, Hildebrand, the Count's secretary,
becoming greatly alarmed at the continued absence
of his employer and at certain rumours that were
afloat in the town, to the effect that he had been
arrested for a criminal liaison with the Princess and
confined in a dungeon, reported the matter to the
Elector of Saxony, the Countess Marie Aurora von
Königsmarck, and various others of the Count's
relatives and friends, and this news aroused a storm
of indignation.

The Elector Frederick Augustus at once dis-
patched Colonel Bauer, as Saxon Envoy extra-

ordinary, to the Court of Hanover, demanding the instant release of his general; whilst, at the same time, the Countess Marie Aurora von Königsmarck and her sister sent a messenger demanding the immediate release of their brother; but neither envoy nor messenger achieved the object of their mission, and the replies made to them were couched in such subtly evasive language that, with regard to the Count's whereabouts, they learned absolutely nothing. However, the Count's relatives believed that he was alive, and his heirs, the Königsmarcks of Kötzlin and Roddahn, in order to settle the question which affected them so materially, sent one of their number, Lieutenant Frederick William von Königsmarck, to Hanover, with instructions to prosecute the most vigorous inquiries.

The Lieutenant, on arriving at Hanover, went at once to the Palace, but he was not only refused admission, he was warned by the officer whom he interrogated that he would be shot off hand if he ever dared show his face there again. He deduced, however, from the officer's manner, that Count Philip von Königsmarck was still alive, and he returned home under that impression. More efforts were then made to obtain Count Philip's release, his cousins joining forces with Countess Marie Aurora, her sister, and the Elector of Saxony, but without avail.

The Elector of Hanover remained inexorable ; moreover, he was silent as the sphinx, and not a word regarding the whereabouts or fate of the young man could be got out of him. The Count's heirs, naturally, were in despair. Owing to the absence of any proof of his death they could not inherit his estates ; besides that, none of the title-deeds to his property could be found. Köller, their agent, conjecting that the will and other legal documents relating to the Count's property were in Hanover, went there, and was told by Privy Secretary Bacmeister, whom he interviewed, that the papers he wanted were in the Archives of the Palace, and that he would secure them for him.

Very significantly, however, Bacmeister died soon after the interview, and although his successor, Privy Secretary Reiche, assured Köller that he would look into the affair and see that the papers were forthcoming as soon as the King absented himself from the Palace, this promise also was unfulfilled, and consequently the case remained *in statu quo*. From time to time fresh inquiries were made, and as late as the middle of last century the Königsmarck family again petitioned the Court of Hanover to restore to them the missing man's papers and property, but they did not succeed ; and, as before, no definite information with regard to his fate could be obtained.

Of the various accounts of Philip von König-
marck's life, up to the time of his disappearance,
that briefly outlined in the foregoing pages is, I
believe, generally deemed to be the most authentic.
In its main features, at least, it is demonstrably
true, and there is every reason to suppose that it is
also true in detail. As to what happened to the
unfortunate man after he was seen to enter the
Electoral Palace on July 1st, 1694, one can only
surmise, and perhaps form some theory from the
many rumours, et cetera, concerning it that were
circulated at the time, both in Hanover and elsewhere. A manuscript, purporting to be a true
solution of the mystery, was discovered by Carl von
Weber in the State Archives of Dresden.   Written
in somewhat faulty French, and bearing the signature of Count Maurice de Saxe, one of Count Philip
Christopher von Königsmarck's nephews, it sets
forth the story of Count Philip's life and disappearance, up to a certain point, strictly in accordance with well-established facts, albeit, these facts
are accompanied by a wealth of detail, which is
certainly marvellous ; but commencing with Countess von Platen's infatuation for Count Philip, and
her determination for revenge, when her advances
are rejected, there is a distinct departure from the
story in its generally accepted form. Count
Maurice de Saxe in this document states that when

the Countess von Platen failed in her first efforts to poison the mind of the Elector Ernest Augustus, who is here described as a prince of mild and gentle character, against Count Philip and the Princess, it was the Elector Ernest Augustus himself, and not the Elector of Saxony, who advised Count Philip to get a discharge from the Hanoverian service and enter that of Saxony.

" I know all, Philip," the Elector (according to this document) said to him one day. " Here is a letter for Prince Frederick Augustus ; go to him. When you are in Hungary, ask for your discharge from our service ; the Prince is attached to you, your brother-in-law serves under him, and you will get on there.   Farewell, and remember the friendship which I show you."

Count Maurice de Saxe then goes on to state that at that time, Prince Frederick Augustus, who was brother of the Elector of Saxony, commanded the Imperial Army in Hungary.   This, however, is one of the many misstatements in the manuscript, as Prince Frederick Augustus did not take over the command of the Imperial Army till after Count Philip von Königsmarck had disappeared.   Continuing, the writer asserts that when Count Philip—the campaign in which he fought under Prince Frederick Augustus over—asked for a few days leave to go to Hanover, Prince Frederick, knowing the danger that threatened the Count should his presence in Hanover be discovered by the implacable Countess von Platen, at first refused to let him go, and only very reluctantly, on being persistently pressed, at last granted him leave.

Also, the real reason for Count Philip's return to Hanover, Count Maurice de Saxe assured us, was his burning desire to repossess himself of a love token, a ribbon, which, in his hurried departure from Hanover, he had inadvertently left behind. Shortly before Count Philip resigned his commission in the Hanoverian Army, according to Count Maurice de Saxe, he had taken part in a tilting tournament and won the first prize. It was a bouquet tied round with a ribbon, and the Princess Sophia Dorothea had presented it to him. He had fastened the ribbon to the colours of his company, and, as already stated, the object of his return to Hanover and visit to the Palace (where we presume the colours were kept) was to reclaim it.

To go on with the story, as Count Maurice de Saxe tells it, Philip, on arriving at the Palace, interviewed Count von Platen who had succeeded him in his command, and was a relative of the Countess von Platen, and demanded the ribbon. Count von Platen declared he had given it to Countess von Platen, whereupon Count Philip

von Königsmarck asked him to go immediately to
the Countess and request her to restore it at
once.

" Tell her," he said, " if she refuses, to beware of
me, for not even the Elector himself shall protect
her against my vengeance."

Count von Platen delivered the message and the
Countess was delighted.   The chance she had long
waited for had at last come, Count Philip was in her
hands.   Pretending that she had mislaid the ribbon
and would return it to Count Philip directly she
had found it, she at once made preparations for
his murder.   First of all she prevailed upon the
Elector, by dint of coaxes and threats, threats to
leave him unless he did exactly what she wanted,
to give his assent to her designs, keeping the affair,
of course, a profound secret.   She then secretly
negotiated with two Italian desperadoes who had
been employed by her before, in all probability for
a similar purpose, and, in conjunction with the
Elector, issued orders to two *chasseurs* and the
Court furrier.   But while the Elector instructed the
two *chasseurs* and the Court furrier to secrete themselves in a room on the ground floor, close to the
staircase leading to the apartments of the Princess,
and when Königsmarck appeared on the scene, to
seize and carry him alive, and without doing him
any injury, into the laboratory, and to keep him

there a close prisoner, the Countess, unknown to the Elector, told the two Italians to kill him.

The Elector then asked the Crown Prince to spend the night in the country and to take certain of the Royal Household with him, naming those officials whom he and the Countess feared might get to know too much, and on whose silence they did not feel they could depend, and those servants whose duties would necessitate them being in the way. Whether the Crown Prince had any inkling of what was in the air, or not, he raised no objections, but at once fell in with his father's proposition. The next step was to entice Count Philip to the Palace. In order to accomplish this the Countess resolved to make a tool of Fräulein von Knesebeck, the Princess's great friend and confidante.

Consequently, knowing that she could only get hold of Fräulein von Knesebeck, who was naturally not very friendly disposed towards her, by the employment of strategy, the Countess sent a message to Fräulein von Knesebeck purporting to be from Fräulein Dillon (presumably a friend of Fräulein von Knesebeck) asking to see her at once on a matter of urgency, and naming a meeting-place. Falling into the trap Fräulein von Knesebeck set off, but on the way was stopped by the Elector, who commanded her to go immediately to the Countess von Platen.

Full of apprehension, Fräulein von Knesebeck obeyed, and was told by the Countess to sit down at once and write the following note to Count Philip von Königsmarck :

MONSIEUR LE COMTE :

Ma Princesse désire de vous voir ; elle ne peut vous escrire, s'estant bruslée la main, et m'a ordonné de vous faire scavoir que vous pouvez vous rendre chez elle par le petit escalier comme autre fois ; elle me paroist inquiette de votre silence, à Dieu, tirez bientost * de doutte la plus amyable Princesse du monde.

Not daring to disobey, as the Countess † threatened her with torture and death if she did, she wrote as requested, and put her signature to the epistle.   It was then given to one of the Countess's male followers, who, disguising himself, in accordance with her commands, conveyed it to Count Philip.

Overjoyed at the prospect of seeing the Princess,

* Note the misspelling of words.

† Count Maurice de Saxe furthermore states that the Countess, fearing that Fräulein von Knesebeck might betray the plot, at once had her conveyed to Scharzfels Castle and immured in a dungeon, intending no doubt to have her murdered later on. Fortunately, however, a man who was employed repairing the roof of the castle, caught sight of the unhappy prisoner, and being struck by her beauty, and also being of a chivalrous disposition, effected her escape.

and regardless of his own safety, Count Philip immediately repaired to the palace, and arriving there before the conspirators expected him passed safely into the Princess's apartment. Upon learning the cause of his visit and seeing the note, the Princess, guessing the truth, told Count Philip that he was betrayed by the Countess von Platen, who meant to do him bodily harm, and that he must fly at once. Count Philip, then, more for the Princess's sake than his own, endeavoured to leave the Palace. In the hall, on the ground floor, the five hirelings surrounded him. The furrier said in a low voice :

" Do not defend yourself ; we mean you no harm."

But Count Philip took no notice of him. He thrust out right and left, and in the desperate struggle that ensued he killed the two *chasseurs* and one of the Italians, and, in all probability he would have escaped had not the furrier, seeing that the battle was going against his companions, resorted to strategy.

Picking up the cloak which the Count had cast aside, he slipped back, as if badly wounded. The Count, then believing the furrier to be *hors de combat*, came out of the corner from whence he had made so successful a stand, and was about to dispatch, as he thought, his one surviving assailant, when the cloak, held in readiness all the time, was flung over his head ; and it was while he was trying to disengage himself that the Italian thrust him through the body, so that he fell senseless to the ground. At this moment the Princess, whose attention had been directed to the sounds of the scuffle by the barking of her little dog, appeared on the scene.

Perceiving that her worst fears had been realized, and that the body the two men were in the act of picking up was that of her beloved Count, with a heartrending cry, followed by a despairing moan, she fainted. The furrier and Italian between them carried her back to her apartment, and then hurriedly conveyed the body of the Count to a subterranean vault. Leaving him there, they hastened back to the scene of the fight, in order to remove all evidence of it, and to bury the three slain men in the nearest convenient spot. The furrier then informed the Elector of what had happened, and sought to exonerate himself from all blame for the death of Königsmarck.* He declared that the surviving Italian had repeatedly stabbed the Count, and that it was in vain that he had expostulated with him, and tried to prevent him, since the Italian was only acting in accordance with the

* The writer of this asserts that Königsmarck was not really dead, but that the furrier believed him to be so.

instructions given him by the Countess von Platen.

The Elector made no comment, he was apparently too deeply affected to speak.

Shortly after the tragedy, the Princess sent for the Elector and Crown Prince, and when they entered her apartment, she exclaimed :

" I have only two words to say to you. I will not humiliate myself by persuading you that I am innocent. I am guilty ; but only in so far that, in cowardly obedience, I broke my faith to Count Königsmarck. I loved Königsmarck before the duty was forced upon me of obeying you. I recognize with terror the mistake of allowing him admission to my presence, and the remainder of my life shall be devoted to repentance and recollection.

" I am the cause of his death and it is left to me to avenge him. So you may prepare for all the horrors which revenge can suggest."

Much alarmed, the Elector (according to the author of this document, a poor weak creature) implored the Princess to calm herself. He declared it was not his fault if any harm had befallen Count Philip von Königsmarck, as he had given explicit orders that he should not be harmed. It was entirely due to an accident, he said, and begged the Princess to dismiss the Count from her life and to devote herself entirely, in the future, to her husband.

The Princess laughed scornfully. " That will do, sire," she ejaculated. " There is no happiness in this world for me. If I am alive now, it is only because I am anxious to avenge Philip von Königsmarck. No one shall deter me from that."

The Elector did not wait to hear more, but taking the Crown Prince by the arm hurriedly left the room with him.

Leaving them conferring together as to the best course to pursue with regard to the Count, whom the Elector's surgeon reported to be alive, but in a somewhat critical condition, we must now return to the Italian desperado who had stabbed him. Upon quitting the Palace after the fray, and returning to his quarters in the town, which he happened to be sharing that night with two strangers, he went to bed, but had not lain down long, before he awakened his fellow lodgers and implored them to summon the landlord at once, as he was dying. On the landlord's arrival the Italian begged him to send for a priest, and was terribly upset when told that there was not a Roman Catholic priest in Hanover. Declaring that he had been poisoned by the Countess von Platen,* he begged God to forgive him and his dead comrade, whom he was about to join,

* According to Count Maurice de Saxe, the Countess von Platen had ordered her waiting woman to give the Italians poisoned refreshments immediately before they lay in ambush for Count Philip ; and apparently this had been done.

for their sins ; and after giving utterance to this
pious hope he died. The two strangers, Count
Maurice goes on to assert, left Hanover the next
day, but not before mentioning the incident of the
night to certain people in the town, who spread it
broadcast, and who, putting two and two together
—for the disappearance of the two German *chasseurs* had already been remarked upon—not
unnaturally came to the conclusion that the words
of the dying Italian were associated, in some way,
with Count Philip von Königsmarck's disappearance.

Continuing, Count Maurice de Saxe states that
all this talk coming to the ears of the Countess von
Platen she grew alarmed ; and, acting on the
principle that dead men tell no tales, determined
that Count Philip von Königsmarck should die ;
but with the diabolical cunning that was characteristic of her she resolved that the Elector alone
should be suspected of his murder. Hence, she so
contrived that everything looked black against him,
and she so worked upon his feelings and imagination, that, in the end, he really began to believe he
was responsible for all the mischief she had done.
Several members of the Privy Council * were, more
or less, under her thumb and afraid of her, conse-

* The rest of the Privy Council were smuggled out of the way,
while the Princess Sophia Dorothea was sent under a heavy armed
escort to Ahlden Castle.

quently she took them into her confidence ; and, when, at her suggestion, the Elector appealed to them as to what had better be done with the imprisoned Count, they unanimously agreed he must be poisoned, arguing, as Countess von Platen had told them to do, that, since the Saxon Ambassador had demanded his liberation and the Elector of Saxony had appealed to the Court at Vienna, it would never do to keep the Count any longer in the Palace.

Therefore, since he could neither be kept in the Palace nor liberated with any degree of safety, surrender to the Elector of Saxony, it was argued, would be tantamount to an admission of cowardice, besides which, the Count, freed, would doubtless bring forward accusations against the Elector, which he, the Elector, could not face, the only alternative was to put him out of the way. It would merely be announced, of course, that the Count had died, and then, when it once became known to his friends that he was dead, no further stir would be made in the matter. This was the decision these Privy Councillors arrived at, and the Countess von Platen, while thus cunningly shelving the authorization of the murder of Königsmarck on the Privy Council, still allowed the public to believe that the Elector himself was responsible for whatever had happened to Count Philip.

To continue, in accordance with the document of Count Maurice de Saxe. Whilst the Countess von Platen was thus plotting to murder Count Philip at the Palace at Hanover, Count von Lewenhaupt,[*] Count Philip's brother-in-law, determined to solve the mystery of his disappearance, applied to the King of Poland for leave to go to Hanover and investigate.

The King not only gave him permission, but furnished him with credentials. Realizing that Count Philip might have to be rescued by force, Lewenhaupt decided to take a band of trustworthy men with him, and, in addition to some of his own servants, he secured the services of several officers in the Saxon Army and those of Ziegler, Count Philip's *chasseur*. Ziegler proved invaluable.

On the arrival of the party in Hanover he set to work to make love to the wife of the furrier who had attacked Count Philip, and so won her over with his flattery and attractions, that she confided in him all she knew of the affair, telling him at the same time where Count Philip was. Ziegler, then, biding his opportunity, stole a key to Count Philip's apartment, and hastened with it to Count Lewenhaupt, whereupon Lewenhaupt at once decided to go to the Palace and carry off the prisoner without any further delay. Fortune aided

* Also spelled " Lewenhauft."

his enterprise, in as much as the Elector and his
Court were in the country and the Palace was
consequently very nearly deserted. He chose for
the venture Sunday morning, February 15, 1695,
and an hour when most of the people in the town
would be going to early service.

On reaching the palace gates he instructed certain
of his followers to simulate a quarrel among themselves, so as to draw off the attention of any Court
official that might happen to be present, while he
and Ziegler made for the quarters where the
prisoner was confined.   Fortune still favoured him.
No one stopped them, and they reached the laboratory in which Ziegler had been informed Count
Philip was confined without mishap.   When, however, they burst in—the key did not fit the lock of
the door after all—the room was empty.

There was evidence that the bed had been slept
in quite recently, and scribbed on the whitewashed
wall with charcoal, in a handwriting which Lewenhaupt instantly identified as that of his cousin, were
these words :

" Philippe de Königsmarck a rempli sa destinée
dans ce lieu le 14 February, de l'année 1695."

Lewenhaupt, then realizing that he had come too
late, silently left the room, and, accompanied by
Ziegler, made his way back to his followers.   Later
on in the morning, he met his wife coming out of

church ; and, learning from her that Superintendent Bilderbeck,* the minister of the church, had said something in his sermon that suggested he knew a good deal concerning the fate of Count Philip, Lewenhaupt at once hastened off to interview him.

" You need not tell me why you have come to see me," the Superintendent exclaimed, on Lewenhaupt being ushered into his presence. " I can guess, and I shall be glad to tell you all I know. I have no fear of the Elector, for I have long been suffering from a slow fever, and the shock I have just sustained has, I can feel, precipitated my end."

He then informed Lewenhaupt that he was commanded the previous day by the Elector to give the last consolations of the Church to Count Philip von Königsmarck, who was about to be poisoned at supper that night by order of the Court, and he was forbidden to disclose the fact till after the Count had eaten. The Superintendent said he declined to go at first, but on being told that if he did not no other minister would be called in, and Count Philip

* Count Maurice de Saxe states in this document that the Superintendent chose as his text these words : " A certain man went down from Jerusalem to Jericho and fell among thieves," and in his concluding remarks made use of these words : " I have on the past night comforted a perturbed soul; I trust I may not survive him, for our city is stained with the blood of the innocent, and the palace of the Prince is a murderer's den."

would be left to die without holy ministration, he
very reluctantly assented.   Continuing, he said he
went to the laboratory that evening at seven
o'clock and was received with joy by Count Philip,
who laughingly said :

" I am not afraid that you have come to prepare
me for death, for I do not think my enemies would
wish to do me any further harm."

They then sat down to supper, the Count still
smiling and gay.   The Superintendent, on being
invited to partake of the food and wine, politely
declined, excusing himself on the grounds that it
was not his habit to eat or drink on such occasions
He sat down at the table, however, and, in a state
of mind defying description, watched the Count
take up his spoon and dip it in the soup.   After a
few mouthfuls the Count paused and throwing down
the spoon, looked fixedly at the Superintendent and
said :

" I see now why you have come to me : I am not
angry with you ; you could not help it.   But what
do you say to such men ! "

He then got up, and while the Superintendent was
making preparations for him to take the Holy
Sacrament, wrote on the wall with the charred end
of a stick.   Two hours later he died.

This was the minister's story as narrated by
Count Maurice de Saxe, who subsequently states

that the minister hlmself died very shortly afterwards.*

Returning to Saxony, Count Lewenhaupt reported all that had occurred to the Elector Frederick Augustus ; but, while the Elector bitterly deplored the cruel murder of one whom he greatly esteemed and liked, he declared himself powerless to do anything in the matter, and consequently no further action was taken. Count Maurice de Saxe adds that the Hartoges,† merchants at Hamburg, with whom Count Philip had left many valuables, declined to part with them, until Count Philip's will or written authority was produced. And, as his heirs were not able to do this, the Hartoges retained the property.

With this material statement, one of the few, perhaps, in the foregoing narrative that is capable of verification, Count Maurice de Saxe concludes his document. His story of Count Philip von Königsmarck and his mysterious disappearance is probably based on what his mother, the Countess Marie Aurora, sister of Count Philip von Königs-

* According to documentary evidence, generally accepted as sound, Superintendent Bilderbeck did not die till 1706. (See footnote to " Remarkable Adventures and Unrevealed Mysteries," Vol. II., p. 180, by Lascelles Wraxall.)

† In the work " La Saxe galante " the name of the Hamburg firm which refused to give up Count Philip's valuables is given as " Kastrop Brothers."

marck and mistress of the Elector Frederick
Augustus of Saxony, told him, and possibly, too,
on some first-hand information supplied to him by
Count Lewenhaupt.

It is, however, so erroneous in detail, as, for
instance, in its description of the Elector Ernest
Augustus, who, far from being timid and weak, was
rough and brutal, that great discredit has been
thrown on it, as a whole.

At the same time, although condemning Count
Maurice de Saxe's narrative on the whole as somewhat wild and improbable, the majority of writers
on the subject are of the opinion that there is no
small amount of truth in it. They do not doubt,
for instance, that Count Philip was murdered by
the Countess von Platen's order. They believe,
however, that the murder took place on the evening
of July 1, 1694, directly after his interview with the
Princess Sophia Dorothea, and apparently deeming
the affair of the two Italian assassins a myth, and
basing their theory on the alleged confessions of
three halberdiers, namely Buschmann and the two
Lüdus, who, likewise, stated that they had been
hired to assassinate Count Philip, they maintain that
the Princess was entirely ignorant of the plot to kill
her lover that night, and accordingly Count Philip
left her presence without the least suspicion that he
was about to be murdered. Strolling leisurely

along, and finding the staircase at the end of the corridor leading from the Princess's quarters closed, fearing nothing, he made for the grand staircase, and had come to the vestibule near the palace chapel, when the halberdiers, in ambush, suddenly sprang out and attacked him.   In the struggle that ensued, and which was carried on in the dark, one of the halberdiers * was killed, but in the end his colleagues triumphed, and the Count fell mortally wounded.   Again, according to this theory, it was the Countess von Platen, and not the Princess, who then appeared upon the scene, and she, candle in hand, mocked the man with whom she had once been so deeply infatuated, and who now lay dying and helpless at her feet.   Bending down she flashed the light of her candle in his face, and so held it that he could see the smile of exultation on her lips. With regard to what followed there seems to be considerable disagreement, notwithstanding the fact that all the evidence collected was said to be derived from the same source, namely, the aforesaid confessions ; and while some writers assert that Count Philip cursed the Countess von Platen, in consequence of which she subsequently lost her sight and ended her days in misery, others express their belief that he simply repeated the declaration

---

* We conclude from the account that four halberdiers were hired to assassinate Count Philip.

THE STRANGE CASE OF COUNT PHILIP CHRISTOPHER VON KÖNIGSMARCK
(*From "Remarkable Adventures and Unrevealed Mysteries" by Lascelles Wraxall*)

he had formerly made to her, namely, that his friendship with the Princess was entirely innocent, and that no immoral relationship whatever existed between them.

However, every writer on the subject would seem to be agreed, that, in all probability, Count Philip was unceremoniously interrupted in his speech by the halberdiers, who, upon receiving a signal from the Countess, gave their victim the *coup de grâce*.

Also, it seems to have been unanimously agreed that, later on, his body was covered with lime and let down into a sewer under one of the rooms, the sewer being then bricked up and, as far as is known, never again disturbed.

Thus the theories concerning Philip von Königsmarck's disappearance advanced by the majority of writers, although varying in detail, in the main undoubtedly agree ; but, since they all hinge on the alleged confessions of certain hired assassins, and, as far as I can see, there is no positive proof that such confessions ever took place, not one of them, in my opinion, can be logically accounted either very sound or very convincing.

However, setting aside all theories, no matter whether based on authentic sources of information or otherwise, we may surmise much from the Countess von Platen's known antagonism to Count

Philip ; and it is highly probable he was actually murdered through her command.

At the same time we cannot say positively that this was the case. All we can say for certain is* that he was seen to enter the Royal Palace at Hanover on the evening of July 1, 1694, and that from that time onward, as far as his family and the public were concerned, he was never seen again.

* This statement is made in accordance with that of Sir Lascelles Wraxall.

CHAPTER VI

WHAT BECAME OF MARTIN GUERRE

SOMETIME, during the sixteenth century, there lived in the little town of Artigues, in the district of Rieux, a young couple named Guerre,* about whom very queer stories were told. The reason was this.

Bertrande Rols, when little more than 13 years of age, was married to her playmate, Martin Guerre, a youth of about 16 ; but, despite the fact that they were both strong and healthy, Bertrande possessing, in addititon to a sound constitution, considerable physical attraction, they had no children.

Hence, the good citizens of Artigues, who like the majority of people at that time were very super-stitious, came to the conclusion that the Guerres were bewitched ; and consequently extraordinary rumours soon got into circulation concerning them. It was said, for instance, that they had gathered flowers in a certain woodland glade reputed to be fairy haunted, and that, as a result, they had come

* See " All the Year Round," June 29th, 1867, and " Celebrated Crimes," by Alexandre Dumas.

under a spell; and, again, that they had offended an old itinerant mendicant believed to possess the evil eye, and that he, in revenge, had cursed them.

Their friends and relatives, believing either one or other of these stories, and anxious to deliver the alleged sufferers from the charm or curse, as the case might be, recommended all sorts of supposed antidotes, such as consecrated cakes, the branch of an elder tree, a horseshoe (nailed over the entrance of their abode), and the red flowers of the hypericon or St. John's wort (to be worn round their necks),* while the priests of the district composed special prayers for their benefit, and nearly drowned them in holy water. However, it was all of no avail; the enchantment continued: no children would come.

Now among the many admirers of Bertrande Guerre were several young men, who, being envious of Martin, combined with Bertrande's friends and relatives in trying to persuade Bertrande to divorce him and marry some one else, attributing her being childless to him, and declaring him to be a

---

* Bassardus Visontius (ant Philos) commends to one troubled with heart-melancholy " Hypericon or St. John's Wort " gathered on a Friday in the hour of Jupiter, " When it comes to his effectual operation (that is about the full moon in July) ; so gathered, and borne or hung about the neck, it mightily helps this affection and drives away all phantastical spirits." (Burton's " Anatomy of Melancholy," Part II., sec. 5.)

thoroughly worthless and abandoned character, capable of almost any wickedness. But Bertrande, who was devotedly attached to her husband, indignantly repudiated all these charges, and refused to be separated from him.

Then an event happened, which for the time being, at all events, led to the total discomfiture of Martin's accusers. Bertrande gave birth to a child, a boy, who was subsequently christened Sanxi* ; and this, of course, rendered any attempt at divorce extremely difficult, if not impossible. However, not long after the birth of this child, a robbery took place one night on the farm belonging to Martin's father (who, though of Biscayan origin, lived in Artigues), and owing to the discovery of certain tell-tale clues, suspicion at once fell upon Martin ; and, whether he could have exonerated himself or not, no one could say, for while his wife and father, who believed him to be innocent, were waiting for him to take that step he suddenly vanished.

He left his cottage one summer morning and set off down the road, in the direction of his father's farm, and, after that, all trace of him was lost. His enemies, naturally, spread the report that he had absconded, remarking that if any sure proof of his guilt had been needed, he himself had now furnished it. Fearing arrest and the severe punishment

* Bertrande was now just 20 years old.

meted out to thieves, they said (in those days no matter how small the theft hanging was the penalty) he had simply fled.

" You are well rid of him," they told Madame Guerre. " If he hadn't robbed his father, you may depend upon it he would have robbed some one else."

But again they were nonplussed ; Bertrande stolidly refused to be set against her husband. Moreover, she declared, in public, her absolute belief in his innocence, and was ceaseless in her efforts to trace his whereabouts. In this she was helped by Martin's father, who, although somewhat dubious now as to his son's innocence (the circumstances, it must be remembered, appeared to be dead against him), was still fond of him, and only too willing to welcome him back to Artigues.

However, despite the exhaustive inquiries made by these two, no tidings of the missing man could be obtained. He had not been seen in any of the neighbouring villages, nor apparently had he been encountered by anyone in any of the roads or lanes round and about Artigues.

The years passed by. Martin's father died, and to prove that he bore Martin no ill will he left the bulk of his property to him. In the absence of any positive proof of Martin's death, the legal view of the matter was that he was still alive, a fact Martin's father, of course, would be well aware of when he drew up the will.

In Artigues, however, the opinion that Martin Guerre was dead prevailed, and great therefore was every one's astonishment, when, at the expiration of eight years from the time of his disappearance, the news was suddenly spread that he had returned. What actually happened was this.

One morning, a sunburned, weather-beaten man called at the house where Madame Guerre was living in solitary retirement, and asked to see her. Now the moment Madame Guerre caught sight of the stranger, perceiving at once that his features and stature were identical with those of her lost husband, with a wild cry of delight she threw herself into his arms. Later, the Guerres' friends and neighbours, becoming acquainted with the news, came crowding to the house, and as soon as they saw the stranger they also unanimously expressed the opinion that it really was Martin come back, and straightway greeted him with the utmost cordiality.

The stranger, whom I will now call Martin, then chatted away with them, gossiping about old times, various escapades in which he had participated as a boy, and numerous adventures that had befallen him in more recent years, until finally, when they left him and returned to their respective houses, there was not one among them who was not fully convinced that he was and could be none other than Martin Guerre.

And it was the same with Martin Guerre's four sisters. They had no sooner set eyes on the stranger than they hailed him as their missing brother, while their uncle, Peter Guerre, following suit, acknowledged him to be his nephew, and subsequently made him his heir. So far, then, all was well. Martin Guerre had come back to life, and since, naturally perhaps, bygones were allowed to remain bygones, he was soon comfortably ensconced in the home he had left so abruptly, and under such a cloud.

And no one could have been happier than his faithful Bertrande, who, in course of time, presented him with two more children. One of them, it is true, died in its infancy, but this apparently was a mere detail, apart from which everything seemed to be going on quite swimmingly in the Guerre household. Nothing, in fact, of an unpleasant nature seemed in the least degree likely to happen, when one day a startling report concerning Martin was suddenly launched forth and spread throughout the village. It originated thus.

A soldier, arriving in the village from Rochefort, upon being told the story of Martin's disappearance and return, electrified his informers by declaring that the man whom they had welcomed, open armed, as the lost Martin Guerre was an impostor, and that the real Martin Guerre, whom he knew intimately, was still alive, although he had lost a leg in the recent war in Flanders.

The story was variously received. While some were inclined to believe it, others did not, arguing that, if it were true, the one-legged man would assuredly have come forward long ago and claimed his pretty wife and not inconsiderable property.

Now, it was while the citizens of Artigues were thus engaged in a somewhat heated controversy that the harmony in the Guerre household was threatened with a serious rupture.

Although Peter Guerre had handed over to his nephew the property he had inherited from his father, and of which he had been appointed trustee, he had not rendered an account of his trusteeship, and this omission gave rise to an incessant wrangling, which soon led to a violent quarrel. Martin brought an action against his uncle, and his uncle, losing his temper one day, knocked him down with an iron bar and would have killed him, had not the devoted Bertrande opportunely interfered and prevented him. Henceforth, however, Peter Guerre became Martin's inveterate enemy, and, with the intensity of feeling which was characteristic of him,

gave himself up entirely to thoughts of revenge.
Nor did he have to wait long for an opportunity to
gratify such thoughts.

Martin, who seems either to have become
suddenly aggressive or to have developed the unfortunate idiosyncrasy of arousing other people's
animosity, quarrelled with a man named Jean
d'Escarboeuf, who, somehow, managed to get him
put into prison. Here, then, was the opportunity
Peter was looking for. Taking advantage of
Martin's ignominy and absence, he did his level best
to persuade Bertrande to desert her husband,
declaring him—although he had up to that time
unhesitatingly accepted him as his nephew—to be
an impostor, and even going so far as to threaten
to turn them out of their house if she refused.
Bertrande, however, did refuse. She said the story
told by the soldier from Rochefort was untrue,
merely another device on the part of Martin's old
enemies, and that she was positively certain the
man she had welcomed back as her husband was
her husband.

" If it isn't Martin," she said, " then it is the devil
in his skin."

This sentiment found an echo in the minds of
many, including one Jean Loze, a highly influential
person living near Artigues, who, upon Peter's
applying to him for a loan to commence proceedings

against Martin, indignantly refused to advance him
a sou, at the same time remarking :

" If I part with any money, it will only be to
defend Martin Guerre against those who are once
again trying to deprive him of his good name."

The day after Peter Guerre's application had
been thus summarily dismissed—it was said that he
went out from the presence of Jean Loze raging—
another sensation was caused in Artigues. Peter
Guerre, accompanied by his four sons-in-law, all
armed to the teeth, went to Martin's house, while he
was at breakfast, and taking him by surprise,
before he could lay his hand on any weapon with
which to defend himself, marched him off between
them to Rieux, where he was once again lodged in
the jail which he had only quitted a few hours
previously. Intensely surprised though they were
upon hearing of this outrage, the inhabitants of
Artigues were still more astonished when they
learned that it had been approved of by Bertrande
herself, and even perpetrated at her request. There
seems, indeed, to be little doubt that such was the
case, but it is extremely probable that Peter Guerre
and his sons-in-law had " got at " her, and that she
would not have acted as she did, had they not
resorted to forcible persuasion, or what is termed
in other words undue influence. There is, however,
some uncertainty with regard to what were her real

feelings and belief at this juncture. Some are of
the opinion that she had long ago discovered that
the man she was living with was not her husband,
but that she had resolved to say nothing about it,
since she had grown really fond of him, a state of
affairs that would account for her not having
yielded to the previous persuasion and threats of
Peter Guerre ; whereas others maintain that she
still believed the arrested man to be her real
husband and, having full confidence in his ability
to prove himself such, she considered it advisable
that he should have an opportunity of doing so in
public. At any rate, as a sure indication, we may
take it, that she still had some regard for him, about
three weeks after the commencement of his incar-
ceration, she sent him clothes, clean linen and
money.

The trial before the Court of Justice took place
at Rieux. He was put down on the indictment
sheet as Arnold Tilh, commonly called Pansette, a
native of Sagias,* and charged with having assumed
the name, rank and person of Martin Guerre,
claimed his wife, appropriated and spent her property, and contaminated her marriage. His chief
accusers were Peter Guerre and the latter's sons-
in-law.

* Arnold Tilh had mysteriously disappeared about the same time
as Martin Guerre.

The accused defended himself, and the story he told was apparently pronounced with so much candour and simplicity that, if he really were the impostor he afterwards declared himself to be, one can only say he should be classified among the very cleverest and most unscrupulous of criminals. He said that having seriously offended his father (although he was innocent of the robbery) he thought it best for financial reasons and his wife's sake to leave Artigues, and consequently he went off, without making known his intentions to a soul. Wandering about from place to place—he mentioned them by name and the various people he had come in contact with in each—he eventually enlisted, and served in the French army for eight years. Tiring at length of that, he deserted, and after being a soldier in the Spanish army for a short time, finding he could return to France without fear of punishment, he came back to Artigues, and being instantly recognized by his wife, his four sisters and all his relations and friends, he naturally resumed his old life. He described in detail the instant recognition of him by his wife and sisters, and the welcome they gave him, throwing themselves into his arms, and then said :

" If Bertrande, after thus receiving me back and living with me perfectly happily for three years, is now one of my accusers, it can only be because she has been intimidated and forced to turn against me by my enemies, of whom my uncle is the most bitter. I once had the misfortune to quarrel with him, and ever since then he has sought every opportunity to do me harm. I beg of you to have my wife released from his power and placed under the protection of some reliable and disinterested person."

The Court granted this appeal and deferred giving a verdict till inquiries concerning the truth of certain of his statements had been made, and more witnesses called. The trial was therefore adjourned for a while. The result of the inquiries having tended to corroborate the statements of the accused, regarding the towns he had visited and the people he had encountered, the trial was resumed, and the accused subjected to a rigorous cross-examination. He neither wavered nor contradicted himself, but spoke easily and naturally about his parents and wife, commenting on the dresses worn by some of those present at his marriage, and recalling an amusing incident that happened the night preceding that event, namely, a serenade given him by a number of young men in the village, all of whom he mentioned by name.

His accusers, however, noticing with satisfaction that he had not made any allusion at all to the rumours that had, at one time, been current in

Artigues, with regard to the bewitchment of Martin
Guerre and his wife, commented upon this point to
the judges, who at once examined him on it, but his
replies to all the questions put to him were perfectly
satisfactory, and tallied in every detail with a statement in writing, relative to the same subject, made
by Bertrande Guerre.

A hundred and fifty witnesses were now called
to say whether they identified the accused as Martin
Guerre or Arnold Tilh.   About sixty of them could
not decide one way or the other.   Forty drew attention to certain marks on the accused, namely, a scar
on the forehead, a misshapen nail on the forefinger
of his right hand, several warts on various of the
other fingers of the same hand, and a conspicuous
mole over one eye, declaring that Martin Guerre,
whom they remembered as a youth, had all these
marks, and therefore they were convinced that the
man they now saw before them in the person of the
accused actually was Martin Guerre ; whilst, on the
other hand, fifty witnesses pronounced the accused
to be Arnold Tilh of Sagias, whom they had known
as a boy, and who, they thought, might quite
possibly have possessed marks on his person similar
to those said to have been seen on the person of
Martin Guerre.

As a further test, Sanxi, the acknowledged son of
Martin Guerre, was brought into Court.   The

majority of those present decided that he bore no resemblance whatsoever to the accused ; but, on the other hand, they observed that Martin Guerre's four sisters, who had preceded Sanxi in the witness box, bore a very close resemblance to the accused.

Thus the pros and cons in the case seemed to be about equal, and considerable excitement ensued, when the judges, after conferring together for some time, returned to pronounce their verdict. It was to the effect that the accused, being found guilty of all the charges against him, was sentenced to be executed and quartered.

He made an appeal to a higher tribunal, and another trial was consequently arranged before the High Court of Justice, at Toulouse. In due course it took place.

One of the first witnesses called was Bertrande Guerre. Her past life, the fact that for eight years she had remained wholly loyal to her absent husband, resolutely refusing to divorce him or to marry again, had created a very strong impression in her favour, and this impression was enhanced by her extreme beauty, simple air and very modest bearing. It seemed impossible that she could descend to falsehood, or that she would have lived with a man, unless she had been thoroughly convinced he was her lawful husband. Yet, on being confronted by the accused and asked by him in his usual calm, steady voice to tell the Court whether he was or was not the real Martin Guerre, she dropped her eyes, looked confused and declined to give any definite reply. Fortunately for the accused, the judges were of the opinion that this hesitation on Bertrande's part was due to intimidation on the part of Peter Guerre and his sons-in-law. She was afraid to speak the truth because of them.

Thirty of the people who had figured as witnesses in the previous trial were re-examined, and, as before, they could not agree. While some of them declared the accused was Martin Guerre, others were equally positive he was Tilh. Those who remembered both Martin Guerre and Arnold Tilh as youths agreed that the likeness between Martin Guerre and Arnold Tilh had been remarkable, but that there were certain differences. Arnold Tilh, for instance, was more robust looking and upright than Martin Guerre. I have already referred to certain marks the boy Martin Guerre was declared to have possessed ; some of the witnesses who had already affirmed that Arnold Tilh had several, if not all, of those marks, now differed as to the position of some of them, some declaring, for instance, that the scar had been over the right eye, and some over the left. Indeed, no two witnesses agreed *in toto*. And with regard to other testimony it was just as conflicting. An innkeeper of Rieux in the witness box swore that the accused had once told him in confidence that he was, in reality, Arnold Tilh ; and two other witnesses said that, on a certain occasion, seeing the accused out of doors, in company with some of Martin Guerre's relatives, they were about to greet him as their old friend Arnold Tilh, when he signalled to them to be silent, and shortly afterwards one of them received a present from him with a message to the effect that silence was golden.* Also, an uncle of Arnold Tilh, on seeing the accused in Court in chains, at once identified him as his nephew, and burst into tears, which involuntary demonstration on the part of a witness made a great impression on the judges, who regarded it as very telling evidence for the prosecution.

Yet, as against all this and more testimony of a condemning nature, certain witnesses, including the brothers of Martin Guerre, were emphatic in their belief that the accused was the person he purported to be, urging in support of their contention the character of Arnold Tilh. Was it possible, they argued, that such an incorrigibly lazy, mendacious and disreputable individual as Arnold Tilh admittedly had been could have lived for three years in

---

* In addition to this rather damning testimony, it was known that the youthful Martin Guerre had been a good swordsman and could speak Basque, his father's native tongue, whereas the accused had been proved to be a poor swordsman and to be utterly ignorant of Basque.

MADAM GUERRE AND THE MAN WITH THE WOODEN LEG
(From " Crimes Célèbres par M M Alese Dumas, Vol. VII., p. 2)

perfect harmony with a woman of such an upright and estimable a character as Bertrande ? This was a poser. The judges were perplexed ; they did not know what to decide, and it is highly probable they would have given a verdict in favour of the accused, had not the prosecution, at this psychological moment, created a big sensation in Court by producing a new witness in the person of the man with the wooden leg, already referred to, who styled himself the real Martin Guerre.

The accused, on being confronted with this new witness, did not appear in any way startled or disconcerted. On the contrary, he maintained the same calm demeanour which had characterized him throughout. He declared the man with the wooden leg was simply an impostor, bribed to appear against him by Peter Guerre, and that it was all part of a conspiracy to deprive him of his lawful wife and the property he lawfully inherited.

In giving his testimony, the man with the wooden leg, while vehemently denying that he had been bribed, and protesting he was the real Martin Guerre, appeared very flustered, and his evidence struck many of those present as forced and unconvincing.

The next step, however, on the part of the prosecution, and one which had probably been well rehearsed beforehand, was to confront the man with the wooden leg with the Guerres. This proved fatal to the accused. Directly the eldest of Martin Guerre's sisters saw the new witness, she threw herself into his arms, calling him her dear lost brother. Her three sisters followed suit. Then, amid the most tense silence, Bertrande was called. The moment she entered the Court and saw the man with the wooden leg, she became greatly agitated, and bursting into tears fell on her knees before him, crying out that he was her real husband and imploring his forgiveness.

That, in the opinion of the judges, settled the matter. They at once pronounced the accused to be guilty of all the charges brought against him, and sentenced him to be executed. Four days later, that is to say on the 16th of September, 1560, the sentence was carried into effect.

The condemned man, bareheaded, clad only in his shirt, holding in one hand a burning taper, and with a rope round his neck, was, first of all, made to kneel before the door of the Church of Rieux and ask pardon of God, the King, the local authorities, the presumed real Martin Guerre, in other words the man with the wooden leg, and Bertrande. Then, with a cruelty characteristic of those times, he was taken to a scaffold, which had been erected just outside Martin Guerre's house, and in the presence of Bertrande and all the Guerre family, he was slowly strangled, his body being subsequently burned.

If Bertrande did feel any pity for him, she certainly did not manifest any, but seems to have remained perfectly indifferent to his sufferings. That he was an impostor should not, perhaps, be doubted, since it is said that he made a full and spontaneous confession of his guilt without any coercion whatever.

But, at the same time, it seems to me quite conceivable that this unfortunate man really may have been Martin Guerre, and that he made a false confession with regard to his identity, anticipating torture if he did not.

The question as to whether the man with the wooden leg was the real Martin Guerre may, I think, safely be answered in the negative. It must be remembered that the soldier from Rochefort had publicly declared, most probably at the instigation of Peter Guerre, that the real Martin Guerre, having lost a leg in the wars, was wearing a wooden one. What an inducement then for an adventurer, chancing to have lost a leg, to pretend to be Martin Guerre, the owner of no inconsiderable property and a pretty wife! Learning, too, of Peter Guerre's fanatical hatred of the man who had for three years passed as Martin Guerre and was now accused of being Arnold Tilh, he would, of course, bank considerably on Peter Guerre's support, reckoning that with such an influential ally the risk of exposure would not be very great.

Or, again, and what, I think, is more likely, Peter Guerre may have engineered the whole thing and have bribed the man with the wooden leg to play the rôle of Martin Guerre.

As I have already stated, the man with the wooden leg appeared very confused in Court ; his replies to questions put to him were evasive and shifty, and he gave not a few of those present in Court the impression that he was not genuine and merely acting a part he found extremely difficult to maintain. Were he the real Martin Guerre, many argued, he would surely have made known his presence in Rieux or Artigues before his appearance at the trial, and the fact of his not having done so suggested he was purposely kept out of the way, lest he should be asked too many questions.

The fact that Bertrande and Martin Guerre's sisters proclaimed the man with the wooden leg to be the genuine Martin Guerre the moment they set eyes on him proved nothing, since they had all been just as ready with their recognition in the case of " Arnold Tilh," so that, if they had been so easily deceived on one occasion, why should they not be on another ?

But apart from the fact that their identification was thus proved to be futile, it is more probable than not that, in the case of the man with the wooden leg, they had all acted under the coercion of the vindictive Peter Guerre.

However, if neither the man with the wooden leg nor the man who had been executed was the real Martin Guerre, what had become of him ? He was last seen, it will be remembered, that summer morning, some seven or eight years after his marriage, walking along the road leading from his home, through lonely lanes and fields, in the direction of his father's house. He was well known to have had several inveterate enemies, youths who bitterly resented his prosperity and coveted both his wife and fortune. What more likely, then, than that these envious youths had banded together and murdered him, burying his body in one of the many unfrequented spots all around Artigues ?

I can find no definite statement that this explanation of his disappearance was seriously considered at the time, but so obvious is it that there was both motive and opportunity for murder, that were it not for Bertrande's having been so sure, to begin with, and apparently up to the commencement of his trial, that the man who claimed to be her husband, and with whom she subsequently lived for three years, was her husband, I should say that, without doubt, Martin Guerre was murdered. It is the inconsequent and unsatisfactory behaviour of Bertrande herself that, in my opinion, makes any certain solution to the mystery of her husband's disappearance impossible.

CHAPTER VII

THE NUN OF GIBRALTAR

ASSOCIATED with the fine old mansion, which—now in all probability demolished— was occupied at the beginning of last century by the Governor of Gibraltar, is the strangest and, perhaps, saddest of all the sad and strange stories that Gibraltar boasts. An equally ancient edifice standing near the aforesaid mansion, and used by the latter's occupant for housing military stores, is also, though in a lesser degree, associated with this story, the action of which took place many years previously, when the one building was a convent, and the other, according to Major Hort,* a monastery, and when, it so happened, that the Holy Inquisition was at its height.

It was at this period, then, of Spanish History that one stormy night in autumn, when the wind was blowing furiously, and the rain descending in sheets, that a party of horsemen came dashing over the rough and uneven track that led to the convent,

* *Vide* " The Rock," by Major Hort. Published 1839.

and drew up sharply at its entrance.   One of their
number, dismounting immediately, approached the
door and knocked loudly on it with the hilt of his
sword.

The noise of the elements, however, presumably
prevented his knock from being heard by those
within, a circumstance which drew forth the most
terrible imprecations from one of the still mounted
party, and it was not until the knocks and the oaths
had been repeated over and over again, with increasing vigour every time, that there was any
response.   The door was then opened by an ancient
female janitor, who drew back in alarm at the sight
of so many men.

" It's all right, mother," the horseman who had
sworn so volubly exclaimed, " I am not here to do
you any harm.   I have come to see the Abbess.
Conduct me to her at once."

" I cannot do that," the old woman croaked,
" she has retired for the night, and must not be
disturbed.   Were it not for this dreadful weather,
I should have gone to bed, too, but we are keeping
open in case travellers should call who cannot find
shelter elsewhere."

" Look here, old woman," the horseman exclaimed, taking a gold ring with a large seal attached
to it from one of his fingers, " give this to the Abbess
and tell her that the owner of it demands instant

admission. Delay, and the consequences will be the reverse of pleasant for you and for every one else within these walls."

He spoke so sternly that the old woman, for once in a way cowed, took the ring from him and, as she ambled off with it across the tessellated floor of a spacious but gloomy interior, a flash of forked lightning, which was followed immediately by a terrific peal of thunder, pierced its diamond paned windows, illuminating the armorial bearings on its walls and throwing into relief certain marble effigies and other objects of a similar sepulchral nature. Indeed, the very atmosphere of the place, and not only its complete isolation and utter stillness, seemed closely associated with death. The apparent leader of the party, the rider who had given his ring to the old woman, now threw aside his cloak, and revealed a young girl seated in front of him. Dismounting, he helped her to alight. He then seized her by the arm, and led or rather dragged her with him into the convent. They were both very striking in appearance. He, tall and graceful, with handsome, regular features and dark, deep-set eyes. According to the fashion of the times he wore a large Spanish hat with a single feather drooping over one shoulder, with a doublet hose ; and by his side hung a rapier and poniard, ready for instant use. The girl, like so many

Spanish women of pure descent, was fair. She had
large liquid grey eyes, so dark that they might have
been mistaken for black, a slightly *retroussé* nose,
a lovely mouth, all the more attractive for the teeth,
which were of a pearly white and absolutely even,
and was, indeed, even in that age when Spain was
renowned for the extreme good looks of its women,
noticeably beautiful.

" Hurberto," she cried, as the young man pushed
her forward, " for the love of Heaven do not leave
me in such an awful place as this. If thou dost, I
shall die."

" So much the better," Hurberto replied savagely,
" seeing that thou hast disgraced one of the noblest
houses in Spain. When I think of thee on the
terrace of our beloved castle, as I found thee last
night, being courted by the scion of a House that has
ever acted basely towards our family, by all the
Powers Above "—and here the young man stamped
on the ground in his fury—" I could slay thee and
him a dozen times over."

" But I knew not of this feud," Alitea de Lucerna,
for that was the name of the girl, pleaded, " I swear
before Heaven I knew it not, Hurberto, and I vow
I will never see or have anything to do with Silvano
again. Ah, dearest brother, have pity on me.
You used to love me when we were children.
Love me again," and bursting into tears she knelt

at his feet and caught both of his hands in her own.

Hurberto thrust her from him without ceremony.

"Have done with thy whimpering," he said sternly. "I do not believe thee when thou sayest that thou knewest not of the deadly feud between thy lover's family and ours. Has not all Spain heard of it ? And as for this Silvano of thine, if ever I alight on him, and I shall leave no stone unturned in my search, the fires of the Holy Inquisition shall scorch his bones ; and that not until he has been first made to suffer torments, such as the brains of the officers of the Grand Inquisition alone can invent. Come, make an end of thy cringing and get up ! "

Hurberto spurned her with his feet as he spoke ; but still she did not move. In a state of frenzy almost bordering on madness she implored him to retract and allow her to depart. However, when he again spurned her and mocked at her tears, she suddenly sprang up and stood before him, angry and defiant.

"Very well, Hurberto," she said, "I will no longer plead with one who has ceased to be a brother and become a cruel master. But know this, that all the love and affection I once had for thee and for our parents is now turned to hate. Get thee gone quickly, Hurberto, for I detest the very sight of thee. We shall meet again, once, but only once, and something tells me that that meeting will be as fatal to thee as to me."

She turned her back on him as she spoke and refused either to look at him or say another word. And thus brother and sister parted.

Months passed, autumn merged into winter ; winter, in its turn, gave way to spring, and spring once more to summer.

Gibraltar, though still wholly Spanish—that is to say, free as yet from any foreign control—was even then a seaport of some size and international fame. Hence, ships of all nations might be seen lying tranquilly on the smooth water of its harbour, while its narrow, winding streets teemed with cosmopolitan life. Swarthy dagos, for example, in wide brimmed hats, gleaming earrings, and weapons of all sorts in their gaudily fringed waistbands, rubbed shoulders with sturdy, sunburned English sailors, and dapper, disputatious, little Frenchmen ; and as a result, perhaps, quarrels very frequently occurred. An English sailor in a fit of drunken levity would jostle a Spaniard or insult his sweetheart, whereupon a knife would instantly flash in the air, and blood flow, and in nine cases out of ten the drunken reveller would be killed, and his lifeless body left on the ground, for the flies to settle on, and the half-

famished street dogs to sniff at with a horrible
longing in their eyes. Unhappily, such sights
attracted no attention from the authorities in those
days, so long as the victim was only some ordinary
seaman or foreigner of no account, and consequently,
since no one cared what happened to it, the body
of such a one would usually lie where it fell, till it
was devoured by ravenous curs or became so insani-
tary that some passer-by, in self-defence, would give
some one a trifle to cart it off, for impromptu burial
in the harbour.   Thus, in all probability, more than
one fracas of this description was in progress, when
one evening, in response to the chiming of the bells
of the ancient monastery adjoining the convent
heretofore mentioned, a long stream of gaily clad
men and women threaded their way through the
picturesque but exceedingly smelly streets of the
town, in order to be present at some special
ceremony in the Monastery Chapel.   It was easily
seen, upon entering, that the service about to be
held was one of unusual interest, and also an occasion for rejoicing.   Long chains of bright coloured
flowers were wreathed round the two rows of pillars
supporting the lofty ceiling of the edifice, and
similar chains festooning the pulpit and certain of
the seats gave the interior of the chapel, as a whole,
an appearance that was almost fairylike and unreal,
which was enhanced, perhaps, by the soft light

issuing from several silver candelabra suspended by long chains from a transverse beam extending across the ceiling from east to west. The air was full of the most delightful perfume—indeed, nothing that could in any way appeal to the senses was wanting—and as the subdued strains of sacred music suddenly arose a procession headed by the Venerable Superior of the Order walked slowly and solemnly up the central aisle, and the service began. It proceeded much as usual at first; but, when it had reached a certain stage, apparently much curiosity was awakened, on the part of the worshippers, by the sudden emergence from amongst them of a singularly prepossessing young man wearing the dark habit of a religious Order, who making his way to the altar stood in front of it, and took the vows which were to cut him off for ever from the outside world. He was evidently a stranger in the neighbourhood, and many of the younger and more romantically inclined of those present, who saw him then for the first and, perhaps, last time, wondered whether it was zeal for religion only that had induced him to such a step, or if he had been impelled to it through some unfortunate love affair.

Again, time passed. One evening, exactly twelve months after the above incident, the young man, now no longer a mere novice but a full fledged, ascetic friar, entered the penitential box in a remote corner of the chapel precincts, to hear confessions. Person after person came and went, and none awoke any particular interest in the friar, until, finally, a woman stepped into the box and, in silvery tones, inquired if there was any hope for one who having sworn to give up the world still clung to memories of it. The friar started. There was something about the voice he seemed to recognize, something that re-called memorable moments in the not so very long ago past. Forcing himself to be calm he said there was hope for every one and bade her unburden her soul.

" I will, father " she replied, and continuing, said that she still constantly thought of some one in the outside world, still loved him.

The Father, then, unable to restrain himself any longer, exclaimed, in a voice trembling with agitation :

" His name, tell me, I beseech thee ? "

" Silvano," the woman answered almost hysteri-cally. " Thou, thou knowest him ? "

" In very truth I do," the Father responded joyfully, pure joy, for the moment, obliterating every other consideration, " for I am he ! I have found thee at last, Alitea ! "

And thus it was that the two lovers, who had been

so cruelly torn asunder, found themselves now separated by the merest pretence at a partition. In low tones they discussed all that had happened since they last met ; how Silvano, finding out, at length, that Alitea had been forcibly taken to the convent at Gibraltar and intimidated by her brother into taking the vows, had entered the monastery, adjoining the convent, so as to be near her. They spoke of the hardships they had endured and of their utter repugnance to a life for which neither of them was in the least degree suited, and vowing that they would stand by each other, come what would, they determined to do their level best to find some means of escape. Exactly how they succeeded in getting out of convent and monastery respectively we are not told,* but the moment they did get out, they stole unobserved, as they thought, into the town, bought two suits of male attire from the Jewish owner of a second-hand clothes shop, and then, disguised as ordinary citizens, they went on to the quay and inquired of the seamen there if they knew of any vessel that was about to sail for England. Apparently, it was no easy matter to obtain information on this score, and it was only after much bribery that they at last discovered the name and whereabouts of the captain of an English merchantman. This man they interviewed, and he

* Major Hort in his account does not explain.

promised, though not without a bribe, to book them as passengers on his ship, which, however, much to their dismay, was not to sail for two days. They begged, of course, to be allowed to go on board at once, but to this neither entreaties nor bribes would induce the captain to consent. Two days hence, he declared, at noon, they would find a boat waiting at the quayside to convey them to the ship, and with this arrangement they had to be satisfied. The two days having passed uneventfully, Silvano and Alitea stood on the quay on the day and at the hour specified, awaiting the boat that was to convey them to the ship. It was nowhere in sight, and Alitea looked sad and despondent.

" Do not lose heart, my beloved," Silvano whispered, " the boat is sure to come. The English captain is evidently fond of money, and for that reason only will keep his word."

" I wish I were as hopeful as thou art, Silvano," Alitea answered with a sigh, " but I have a horrible presentiment of some impending evil. Last night I dreamed we were both dead, and when I looked into the mirror this morning methought it suddenly turned black."

" It was thy imagination, dear one," Silvano replied with a laugh. " See, here is the boat with three good rowing men in it."

Sure enough, as he spoke, a boat suddenly shot round the head of the quay, and was seen to be slowly approaching the spot where they stood. Instead, however, of drawing right up to the steps leading down to the water side, it remained several feet away, and when Silvano asked the men to come nearer they shook their heads and pointing to some rocks showing under the water, close beside the steps, called out :

" We can come no further, master. Thou and thy lady must jump from the steps ! "

" But, it's impossible," Alitea cried, wringing her hands. " Alack, alack, I knew something would happen to prevent our escape."   And then, addressing the boatmen, " For the love of Heaven, draw a little nearer, so that we may jump with some chance of alighting in safety."

But the men only grinned at one another, and again shook their heads.

" It's no use asking them. I'll jump first," Silvano said, " and when I'm on board, thou must jump too, and I'll catch thee. See, a number of people are coming this way from the town, there is no time to lose ! "

He ran down the steps as he spoke and, measuring the distance between himself and the boat, took a sudden leap.

He alighted upon one of the seats, and had the

men caught hold of him all would have been well, but this, for no apparent reason, they did not do, and, consequently, owing to the tipping of the boat he lost his balance, and fell headlong into the water. Without even a pretence at trying to rescue him the men in the boat rowed away, and Silvano being unable to swim sank out of sight. Speechless with horror Alitea was about to hurl herself into the water after her beloved, when two men in the much dreaded garb of the Inquisition, who, it seemed, had suddenly appeared from nowhere, crept up behind her, and throwing a large black cloak over her head held her imprisoned in it. She struggled desperately, but could not free herself, and such was the terror which the Inquisition inspired that none of the spectators, and a large crowd comprising people of all nationalities had assembled, dared venture to her assistance. Consequently, she was overpowered, and as she eventually sank fainting into the arms of her brutal captors, who commenced dragging her in the direction of the adjacent convent, one of them, who was recognized by the bystanders as the cruel and tyrannical young Count, Hurberto de Lucerna, said mockingly, " Thy words, Alitea, have come true. We have met once again, and for the last time." The crowd watched the Inquisitors drag the hapless girl away, and after the trio had reached the bend in the narrow, winding

street leading to the gates Alitea disappeared for
ever from the world. She was never seen again
outside the convent ; and as, on that same night,
the trembling crowd saw lights at an unusually late
hour passing along the corridors and in the cloisters
and garden of the convent, the while the bell tolled
dismally, it was inwardly wondered whether, after
that night, anyone ever saw her again inside the
convent. However, although almost certain of the
sinister significance of what they saw and heard,
none dared speak their thoughts aloud, and none,
of course, dared ask any questions of the convent
officials.

Consequently, as no allusion was ever made to
this tragic affair by the nuns or friars and nothing
ever divulged by them regarding Alitea de Lucerna,
after her capture by the Inquisitors and forced
return to the convent, her exact fate must for ever
remain a matter of surmise, and her untimely death,
logically at least, an open question. I repeat
nothing was proved, but about two hundred years
later, that is to say in the early summer of 1838,
some workmen, when repairing the pavement in the
banqueting hall of the Governor of Gibraltar's house,
which was formerly the chapel of the aforesaid
convent, came across the skeleton of a woman. It
was lying on its back two or three feet below the
surface, and close beside it was a small iron crucifix,

such as the Spanish nuns in olden times used to wear. There was no clue whatever as to the identity of the remains, but those who knew the story of Alitea de Lucerna wondered if the skeleton were hers.

CHAPTER VIII

JEAN PETIT, "LORD OF THE BLOODY HAND"

ABOUT the year 1363, when a veritable reign of terror was paralysing France, the whole country being overrun by numerous bodies of discharged soldiers, who plundered and killed everywhere they went, an army of ruffians, under the leadership of a man of monstrous size and the most ferocious mien called Jean Petit, suddenly appeared one day on the outskirts of the town of Mirepoix and took up a position there in a most aggressive and menacing manner.

The citizens of Mirepoix realizing their inability to cope with such a force, and having heard that Jean took fearful vengeance on all who dared oppose him, unanimously decided to offer no real but only a pretended resistance. Consequently, Jean had an easy " walk over " ; and, entering the town with a great clattering of arms and waving of banners, he contented himself with hanging a score or so of the more affluent of the people and purloining their property, and let the humbler of the citizens alone.

Instead of passing on to other fields of conquest, however, the beauty of the town appealing to him, he decided to take up his abode in it, and he was strolling through its narrow winding streets one day, looking for a house that was likely to suit him as a residence and headquarters, when he was nearly ridden down by a party of richly clad people, on gaily caparisoned horses. As their steeds jostled against him he swore roundly, and a young girl, whose attire surpassed in splendour that of any of her companions, disapproving of such language, especially from one whom she took to be a private soldier, drew her whip smartly across his face. With a yell of rage and pain, Jean's huge hand at once sought his sword, and he was on the verge of taking a mighty slash at his assailant, whose horse came to an abrupt halt, when he suddenly checked himself. Her great beauty completely overcame him, and although such a ruffian was, undoubtedly, incapable of actually falling in love certain it is that he became so wildly and madly infatuated with her that he resolved to make her his wife, at all costs.

" *Mon Dieu !* " he exclaimed, wiping the blood from his face with a fold of his coarse jerkin, " but that slender hand of thine can lay it on heavily. What is thy name, lady, and whence hailest thou ? "

" What business is it of thine, fellow ? " the

young girl said scornfully. " Come, move aside, or
I will call to my followers to hew thee down."

Jean laughed.

" Prettily spoken," he replied, " for the most
comely wench it has ever been my lot to see.
Hark ye, lady, Jean Petit has taken a fancy to thee,
and what Jean Petit sets his heart on, Jean Petit
always gets. Dost understand ? " and he stretched
out his hands to lay hold of the bridle of her horse.
The lady, however, was too quick for him. Cutting
him again with her whip, so smartly across the face
that he sprang back with a loud cry of pain, she
succeeded at the same time in urging on her horse,
and in a few seconds had rejoined the rest of the
party, who were about to turn back in search of her.

To return to Jean. Far from being cured of his
infatuation by the sharp chastisement he had
undergone, he now became more than ever anxious
to gain possession of the charming, though vixenish,
author of all the trouble.

Consequently, he inquired of certain persons he
met, and ascertaining that the object of his admiration was Marie de Monségui, daughter of one of the
richest noblemen in the province, he proceeded at
the head of his desperadoes to this nobleman's
castle, and peremptorily demanded the hand of
his daughter in marriage. The Baron de Monségui,
whose rage and indignation knew no bounds,

haughtily refused to give her up, whereupon Jean promptly attacked the castle, and having worsted the defenders, carried off Marie by force. We are told she fought desperately with her captor and, not content with scratching his face, even bit him in her fury ; but her struggles were of no avail, they only made Jean laugh the louder, and he brought her home with him to Mirepoix. There, in his domain, he set about trying to tame her.

Now, as may be supposed, Marie had many admirers, but she cared for none of them, saving a young neighbour of her father's called Count Albert.* Overwhelmed with horror and consternation, when he heard of his lady love's abduction by the much dreaded robber chieftain, Count Albert at once tried to get people to join him in an attempt to rescue her. So great was the terror with which Jean inspired the whole countryside, however, that no one dared do anything against him, and so Count Albert, on her behalf, ventured forth alone. His one hope of success lay in this. Now that Jean had got all he wanted in the way of money and power— he styled himself and was, in very deed, Lord of Mirepoix—it pleased him to pose as a lover of equity and wise judge, a Solomon in fact, and accordingly he instituted what he termed a Court of Justice, placing himself at the head of it, and ordained that

* His name in full is not given in my authority.

it should sit daily in Mirepoix, and pronounce judgment in all kinds of criminal and civil cases.   The
following story may be cited as an example of the
justice meted out by him.

A man was brought before him charged with
stealing grapes.   It is true that the fellow was
proved to be guilty, but his punishment surely out-
weighed his offence, since he was condemned to be
tied to a post in a public thoroughfare, with a
placard by his side bearing these words, " This man
is a thief.   The law of retribution demands that
every passer-by, man, woman and child, should
pluck a hair from his beard.   Let no one omit to
do so."

Signed : " Jean Petit, lord of Mirepoix."

The wretched thief of course was soon both bald
and beardless.   This, as well as many other stories
of a similar nature about Jean, had come to the ears
of Count Albert, but having a clear conscience and
a good cause he resolved to play a bold card and
appeal to Jean's much vaunted love of justice, no
matter what happened to himself in consequence.

Accordingly, he went one day to the great hall
where Jean was presiding as judge, and after several
cases had been heard and settled asked if he might
be allowed to speak.

" Why certainly," Jean Petit said, " who art
thou, young man, and what is thy grievance ? "

"I am Count Albert," Albert replied boldly, "and I am here, because I have heard it said that Jean Petit, lord of Mirepoix, metes out justice with an impartial hand and expounds the doctrine that every man should restore what he hath unlawfully taken. Am I not right?"

"Why, yes," Jean Petit replied slowly, "I have heard of thee, Count Albert, and understand the drift of thy speech. Thou meanest that I should hand over to thee the daughter of Baron de Mon-ségui. But, why should I, seeing that the lady is my wife."

"It is not true," Count Albert exclaimed hotly, "or, if it is, then she was forced into wedlock by thy brutal threats."

"Thou poor fool," Jean laughed, "thou thinkest that my wife loves thee and is here now against her will. Well, I will send for her, so that she can disillusion thee." Beckoning to a page, he bid him go at once to the Comtesse Marie and say that the lord of Mirepoix had need of her immediate presence in the Court of Justice.

After the lapse of a few minutes, Marie de Mon-ségui appeared, and Count Albert perceived that she was pale as death and trembling, so that she could scarcely stand.

"Tell me, Marie," he exclaimed, kneeling before her and raising one of her hands deferentially to his lips, " is it true that thou art married to this robber chieftain of thine own free will, and art living with him happily ? "

Marie made no reply, her lips moved as if she were going to speak, but the words did not come. However, her looks gave Count Albert his answer, they needed no words to interpret them.

" I knew it was a lie," he shouted joyfully, and taking off one of his gloves he threw it on the floor in front of Jean. " My hand is yours, Marie," he said gallantly, " as well as my heart. Let him who dares dispute it pick up my glove."

He hoped of course that Jean Petit would respond to his challenge by picking up the glove, and that a duel with him would naturally follow, but to his intense surprise and disappointment Marie, leaning forward, picked up the glove herself. Feeling sure, however, that she did so only to save him from risking his life on her behalf, he refrained from uttering the words of vexation that involuntarily rose to his lips.

Jean Petit laughed, long and mockingly. " Ha ha, my fair bantam cock," he said, " all that crowing, which thou hast, no doubt, rehearsed in the privacy of thy home, promises to come to naught. But let this console thee, *Thou wilt hear sometime from Jean Petit.* And, now, get thee gone."

He waved his hand in the direction of the door as he spoke, and Count Albert, perceiving that it would be useless to remain, walked sadly, but haughtily, out of the building.

Days passed, and he received no challenge from Jean Petit. Then, one evening, as he was strolling sadly through the forest of Bélène near Mirepoix, trying to formulate some fresh scheme to rescue Marie de Monségui, he suddenly perceived the tall figure of a man in highly polished armour advancing in the moonlight towards him.

For a moment or so his heart stood still, for the forest bore the reputation of being haunted, and he thought the figure was a ghost.

He was speedily disillusioned, however, for when the man was a few paces from him he threw back his vizor and displayed the sinister features of Jean Petit.

" Well, my fine bantam," he said savagely, " thou see'st we have met at last. I have kept my word, and I now intend making thee keep thine."

" What meanest thou ? " Count Albert cried, laying his hand on his sword.

" Didst thou not say thy hand belonged to the Comtesse Marie—my wife ? " Jean related menacingly.

" To Marie de Monségui," Count Albert replied haughtily, " and my heart too."

" Well, call her by what name thou wilt," Jean said with a coarse laugh, " she shall have thy hand.

As to thy heart, that will do for the crows!" And, so saying, he drew his sword and slashed furiously at Count Albert, who, parrying the blow, attacked him, in turn.

The fight, of course, was too unequal to last long. Jean Petit was encased in armour from head to foot, whereas Count Albert wore no armour of any kind, and although Count Albert, as an expert swordsman, was Jean's equal, the latter had the advantage in reach, being nearly seven feet in height. After a very short time therefore Jean broke through the Count's guard, and stretched him on the ground, with a terrible cut on the head. Then bending over him, as he lay there bleeding and helpless, he severed his right hand, and struck him with it in the face.

"Thy hand says good-bye to thee, Count Albert," he said. "I now take it to give to the Comtesse Marie, my Marie, who shall sleep with it under her pillow. Fare thee well." And thus leaving his victim to bleed to death, Jean Petit strolled leisurely away.

Arriving at his home in Mirepoix, before dawn, he entered the apartment wherein Marie was sleeping, and shaking her roughly by the shoulder, exclaimed, "See, what I have brought thee." He then flung the severed hand on her pillow and left the room, laughing. Marie, who was very ill at the time, received so severe a shock that she died soon afterwards. Her death had a marked effect on Jean. He evinced a sudden antipathy to Mirepoix, and informed his followers that he intended quitting the place and seeking a habitation elsewhere.

The day of his departure arriving, the main portion of his old army assembled outside the town, while the remainder, carrying lighted torches, ran through the streets, setting fire to houses and cottages in all directions. As a result, half Mirepoix was destroyed. Jean Petit, mounted on his favourite charger, watched the conflagration for some time, and then, bidding his troops be ready to march southwards in an hour or so, rode away, alone, in the direction of the Forest of Bélène. He was seen by certain citizens of Mirepoix, whom he passed on his way to the forest, and after that it cannot be said for certain that anyone ever saw him again.

As he did not return when he was expected, some of his old followers went to look for him, and, according to their statement, the whole forest was searched thoroughly, but not a trace of him could be found. Hence, to this day, his fate remains a mystery. An extraordinary story * relating to him

* " Legends and Traditionary Stories." Anonymous. Published 1843.

eventually got into circulation, the origin of which, seemingly, was as follows.

Several years after the events just narrated had taken place, Philip de Levis, the scion of an ancient and much honoured family in Mirepoix, returning to his old home, after an absence spent in fighting in the service of some foreign potentate, was elected lord of the town by a council of citizens, and, in order to justify his election, immediately set to work to make good the damage done by Jean. He personally supervised the rebuilding of the town, and while he was thus engaged never once took a holiday ; but directly the work was finished, and the town had once again attained its former air of prosperity, he decided to take a little recreation.

Now, above all things he loved hunting, and against the warning of the good citizens of Mirepoix, who firmly believed that the Forest of Bélène harboured demons, he went hunting one day in it. Luck, however, was against him. Mile after mile he rode, but of game there was no sign. At last, weary and disappointed, he was about to return, when an old man, on horseback, with a long white beard suddenly emerged from a thicket and confronted him.

" Well, my good fellow, what can I do for thee ? " Philip inquired good-naturedly.

To his surprise the man made no reply, but,

signalling to Philip to follow him, leisurely turned his horse round and rode off down a side track into a wide avenue of magnificent elms. Philip was much impressed by this fairylike vista, but what interested him much more than the avenue itself was the sight of a long procession of knights and ladies, squires and dames, moving along it, in absolute silence, neither looking to the right nor to the left, but walking noiselessly and steadily forward, with their eyes fixed straight in front of them.

The old man fell in with the rear of the procession, and Philip again obeying his signal did the same. Thus they rode on, till they came to a part of the forest that seemed quite new to Philip, although he was under the impression that, as a youth, he had explored the whole of it. Here the avenue became less and less regular, and, whether it was actually owing to the gloom or not, the trees that were now more varied seemed to be much darker too, and to be assuming strangely fantastic shapes, that might have proved alarming to anyone possessed of a more nervous and timid temperament than Philip. In between the trees, the spaces were covered with unsightly hillocks, long and narrow, and unpleasantly suggestive of graves ; and this suggestion was considerably enhanced by the sepulchral stillness, and a damp, mouldy smell. The sun, by this time low in the horizon, was rapidly fading from sight, and with its disappearance weird shadows, that seemed to lack material counterparts, appeared on all sides. A little way on, and the scenery became wilder and more barren ; strangely fashioned boulders took the place of trees, and here and there, between them, glimmered the surface of deep, silent pools of water. Then, in the distance, right ahead of the procession, that all this while had been steadily advancing, there loomed the black outlines of a massive, turreted building, surrounded by a moat. Crossing the drawbridge, that slowly descended, creaking and groaning on its rusty hinges, the procession passed through a gateway and under an arch into a vast stone-paved courtyard. A squire, handsomely attired, now approached Philip, to help him dismount, but the old man, speaking for the first time, warned Philip on no account to accept anything from anybody, or to utter a syllable, if addressed.

Dismounting therefore without help, and, tethering his horse to a pillar in the yard, Philip followed the old man through a long vestibule full of soldiers and pages, engaged in all kinds of occupation. While some were throwing dice and playing all manner of games, mostly of a gambling nature, others were burnishing weapons, and others hastening to and fro, as if with messages. Apparently, however, everyone spoke in the lowest tones possible, and consequently the whole place seemed full of whispering, a whispering that had a strange, ghostly effect. Passing through suites of rooms, some full of gaily dressed people, also whispering, and others empty, and awful in their intense silence and gloom, they eventually came to a huge hall, in the centre of which was a table, laid for a meal. All around the table, with folded arms and sardonic smiles on their evil faces, stood men, clad from head to foot in tightly fitting red, red caps, red tunics and red hose, while seated at one end of it was a gigantic man, also in red, with very forbidding features, but a sad and weary expression. At a sign from him, and a gesture of approval from the old man, his conductor, Philip sat down, and almost immediately a ruby-clad page entered the hall with a large silver dish and, setting it down in front of the tall man in red, removed the cover. To Philip's intense horror, a bloodstained hand, with out-stretched fingers, was all the dish contained. It was speedily removed and another dish brought in its stead, but the same thing happened. Directly the cover was taken off, a bloody severed hand lay revealed to view, and so it was with dish after dish, on each one of them, a bloody hand and nothing more. Finally, when the last dish had been removed, a richly clad page brought round wine, and was about to fill Philip's glass, when the latter, remembering the old man's warning not to take anything offered him, waved him aside.

The big man in red, who had hitherto maintained silence, now commenced speaking. He asked Philip a number of questions—where he came from, if he had ever been to Mirepoix, whether he had heard any news lately concerning that town, and a host of other things, and he spoke so earnestly, and with such an appealing look in his eyes, that Philip was more than once on the verge of answering. However, he checked himself in time, and was apparently so obdurate that his questioner at length exclaimed, with his eyes fixed on Philip more appealingly than ever :

" *Mon Dieu*, I can't think why it is that no one ever speaks to me, ever replies to my questions, when they must know that it would please me mightily to learn what is going on in the world."

At the conclusion of this speech Philip's conductor, who was standing close beside him, motioned to him to rise. They then left the hall together. On their way back, along the same route as they had come, they saw on walls, ceilings, tapestry and furniture the imprints of a bloody hand, but no human being. Instead of rooms, corridors and vestibules being filled with gaily dressed crowds, all were now empty, and the only sounds that broke the universal deathlike hush were

Philip's footsteps; they seemed to echo and re-echo at every step he took, whereas the old man's feet made no noise at all.

When they had at length quitted the castle and were once again mounted, the old man explained what they had seen. He told Philip that, during the burning of Mirepoix, Jean Petit, it was quite true, had gone off, alone, into the Forest of Bélène, but that he had been subsequently joined there by his followers, who knew all the time where he was, and who, under his command, had attacked and brutally butchered a party of pilgrims, though not before one of their number, a relative of the unfortunate Count Albert, had pronounced a terrible curse on them.

It was to the effect that for the many crimes they had committed they should meet with violent deaths, and, their punishment not ending there, they were to remain earthbound in the forest, tied to the spot where their last cruel deeds had been perpetrated. And Jean Petit, as their leader, who had previously murdered the highly gifted and beloved Count Albert, was to undergo an additional punishment. He was to be for ever haunted by bloody hands. They were to be served to him at meals and to appear before him wherever he looked and went; and this curse was to continue, till some scion of a noble Mirepoix family, taking compassion

on him, should erect a church in Mirepoix to his
memory.

That was the sum and substance of the pilgrim's
curse, and no sooner had he spoken it than he fell
back dead. The following day Jean Petit and his
men were suddenly attacked by a large army of
wandering pillagers like themselves, and entirely
destroyed; their spirits chained to this earth, to
the great phantom castle Philip had just seen, had,
ever since the curse was pronounced, haunted the
forest.

" It lies in your power, Count Philip," the old
man added, " to free them from their doom.
Should you conclude from all I have said and what
you yourself have witnessed that they have suffered
enough, then go back to Mirepoix, and there build
a church."

Philip, who, upon looking round, perceived that
they had now come to a part of the forest that he
knew well, was about to make some reply to the old
man, when, to his utter astonishment, he found
himself alone. His companion had utterly and
quite inexplicably vanished.

Convinced that he had but just encountered the
Unknown, Count Philip rode thoughtfully back to
Mirepoix, and on the morrow consulted the Town
Council with regard to selecting a site for
a new church, to be built at his expense and

dedicated to the memory of the unhappy man, Jean Petit.

The site being duly found, the building was begun in 1370 and finished in 1402. At a later date, a wonderful spire was added, and, adjoining the church, a magnificent episcopal palace was erected.* Such is the tradition relating to the disappearance of Jean Petit, generally known as " Lord of the Bloody Hand." Though most of it is too fanciful to be regarded as fact, there is, very probably, a substratum of truth underlying it.

It may have been that Jean Petit, tired of town life, had gone off into the Forest of Bélène with certain of his followers, and having seized a castle, or built one there, for himself, lived in it till he was subsequently killed in some foraging affray.

Some such happening as this might, of course, explain the tradition relating to the existence of a phantom castle, but the suggestion on my part is simply an unsubstantiated theory. All that is known for an actual fact regarding the disappearance of Jean Petit I have already stated, and I repeat, that while the town of Mirepoix was burning he was seen to enter the Forest of Bélène; after that the annals of Mirepoix assert, he simply vanished, and what became of him none knew.

* The entire building is still in existence.

CHAPTER IX

THE PRISONER OF WEICHSELMUNDE

ONE summer morning in the year 1811 a big, well built, and tolerably well-dressed man, who, to judge from his round, red face and smiling eyes, seemed the very soul of jollity and good humour, came strolling into the market place of Danzig, to see the soldiers (belonging to one of the crack regiments of the Imperial Army) mount guard for the first time since their arrival in the town.

A number of citizens, of both sexes, some richly clad, others wearing workaday clothes, and others, rags and tatters, were already assembled to watch the ceremony, and as our jolly looking friend advanced a tall, lanky individual, with sleek, black hair and cadaverous cheeks, stepped out of the crowd and shook him warmly by the hand.

" Why, Fritz, friend," he ejaculated, " you look wonderfully well for a man of your years. I wish I carried half as much weight as you do. The doctor told me again last night that I am in a decline and cannot live long, But—*Donnerwetter !*

What ails you, man ? What are you staring at ? "

" Your ring," Fritz rejoined, pointing to a gold ring that Karl was wearing, inset with a large carbuncle that shone a brilliant red in the sunlight, " where did you get it ? "

" From a French officer," Karl responded. " I gave him five crowns for it only last week. It's a beauty, isn't it ? "

" It's mine," Fritz exclaimed excitedly, " I should know it anywhere. It was stolen from my house some months ago."

" I can't believe it," Karl stammered, his naturally long face suddenly becoming much longer, " the officer who sold it to me assured me it was his. You must be mistaken."

" Oh, but I'm not," Fritz said emphatically, " it was my father's, and his father's before him, and so on back and back, for quite 200 years. It's an heirloom, and we kept it in a glass case on a table in our parlour. Know it again, why I'd stake everything I have in the world that it's mine." In the heat of the argument they unconsciously raised their voices, thus attracting the attention of those standing near, and a French officer, seeing a crowd about to gather round the two, approached them and asked what it was all about. Fritz and Karl then calmed down, and would have walked away, had not an old woman, who had been listening to every word of the conversation, touched the officer on the shoulder, and in a croaking voice exclaimed :

" It's about a ring, monsieur ! The fat gentleman declares that the ring the thin gentleman is wearing on his little finger is his, and the thin gentleman declares that he bought it only a week ago for five crowns from an officer belonging to your Army."

" Is that so, monsieur ? " the French officer ejaculated, glaring fiercely at Karl from under his shako, " you dare to assert that an officer of the Imperial Army sold you a ring ? "

" It is as true as I live, monsieur," Karl faltered, his white face a degree or two whiter. " An officer wearing a uniform exactly similar to yours sold me this ring," and he pointed to the gleaming carbuncle, " for five crowns."

The officer looked at the ring intently for some seconds, and then, turning to Fritz, remarked :

" And you assert this same ring is yours ? "

" I call God as a witness that it is mine," Fritz replied in tones of great solemnity, " and I can give you a sure proof."

" That can come later, my friend," the officer observed. Then addressing himself again to Karl, he said, " Can you describe the officer who sold you the ring ? "

" Why, certainly," Karl responded, and in a very

quavering voice he at once began a very elaborate and detailed description.

He had not got far, however, before Fritz, who had been listening with rapt attention and eyes that grew wider and wider every moment, broke out with a loud :

" *Mein Gott!* Captain Alswanger ! "

The officer started. " It certainly sounds like Captain Alswanger," he muttered. Then aloud to Fritz, " Do you persist in your statement ? "

" Why, yes, monsieur," Fritz stuttered, " the ring is mine all right, but if it means getting the Captain into trouble—well, there, I will drop the matter."

The officer cast a hasty glance around, and to his chagrin perceived among the crowd several French soldiers of various ranks.

" It's too late," he said in a low voice, " the matter cannot rest here now." He then beckoned to a corporal and told him to search about for a field officer and Captain Alswanger, and bring them both to the spot at once.

There was now an interval of some minutes, during which the crowd swelled to a very large extent, and then a field officer, accompanied by Captain Alswanger, a tall and good looking man of about thirty-five years of age, joined the trio.

" What's all this fuss about ? " he asked angrily. " Why are we sent for ? "

The officer who had been talking to Fritz and Karl saluted, and then proceeded with an account of what had happened.

" Before we go any further," the field officer said, turning to Fritz, " kindly explain to me the circumstances under which this ring, which you say is yours, was stolen ? "

" I do not want to press the case, monsieur," Fritz stammered. " Indeed, I would rather my friend Karl kept the ring and no more was said about it."

" Impossible," the field officer remarked, " it has been suggested by you that an officer of the Imperial Army is a common thief, that is enough. The matter cannot end here. State all you know."

Seeing there was no loophole of escape Fritz very reluctantly began a stammering account of what had taken place. He said that for some months Captain Alswanger had lodged in his house, and that all the time he was with him he had behaved in the most exemplary fashion, always keeping regular hours and behaving in every way as an officer and gentleman. After Captain Alswanger left, however, he missed a ring which he valued very much and always kept in a glass case that stood on a table in his parlour. The ring in question was the ring he now saw on the hand of his friend Karl.

" And you declare it was sold you by Captain

Alswanger ? " the field officer observed addressing Karl.

Karl nodded. " Yes, monsieur," he stuttered, " for five crowns."

" Is that true ? " the field officer said, looking at Alswanger.

" Yes," Alswanger replied, " but I did not steal it. It was given me by my sister who is married and lives in Paris."

" Well, what have you to say to that ? " the field officer ejaculated, turning again to Fritz.

" The ring is mine," Fritz exclaimed. " I can prove it." Then addressing Captain Alswanger, " Do you know its secret ? "

The Captain shook his head. " It hasn't one," he laughed.

" Hasn't it ? " Fritz said excitedly. " If my friend Karl will let me have it for a moment, I will soon show you that what I have said is correct." He then took the ring Karl handed to him, and, drawing the field officer aside, pressed one of the small knobs surrounding the stone in the ring with his pocket knife, whereupon the stone at once flew up on a hinge, and revealed to view a small hollow cavity.

" There's the secret," Fritz exclaimed triumphantly. " In olden times—the ring I know dates back to the sixteenth century—a deadly poison was kept in that hole, to be used whenever the wearer thought it necessary.   Have I proved my case, and my ownership ? ”

“ I think so,” the field officer said thoughtfully, then, tapping Alswanger on the arm, he bid him and the officer who had first appeared on the scene accompany him to the general in command.   Now, it so happened that the military governor of the town, General Rapp, was about to review certain of the French regiments belonging to the garrison, and on being informed by the general that Captain Alswanger was under arrest, charged with theft, he was greatly upset.

“ *Peste*,” he ejaculated, “ and Captain Alswanger of all people !   The most popular officer in the garrison.   It’s most annoying, just at a time, too, when it’s of the utmost importance that the Imperial soldiers should be thought well of by the Danzig populace.   Keep an eye on him, general, and let a Court of Inquiry be held to-morrow.”

The general saluted the governor, who was in complete authority in the town, and retired.

The following day the Court of Inquiry, consisting of a number of French officers, assembled in the town hall, and Captain Alswanger appeared before them, to answer the charge made against him.

The Auditor-General, an old friend of his, presided, and addressed him as follows :

" Captain Alswanger, you are accused of stealing a ring, what have you to say in answer to so shameful a charge ? "

" It is true, Your Excellency," Alswanger replied calmly. " I stole the ring and was stupid enough to sell it in this town."

" What ! " the general exclaimed in horror, while a murmur of amazement ran through the Court. " You plead guilty ! Do you realize the enormity of the offence ? An officer of the Imperial Army to stoop so low as to steal a paltry ring ! You must be mad or drunk ! "

" I am neither, Your Excellency," Alswanger said in a firm voice. " I needed money, and yielding to the temptation of the moment I took the ring. There is nothing more to be said."

" Incredible ! " the general ejaculated, " are you aware of the consequences of what you say, Captain Alswanger ? "

" Most certainly, Your Excellency," Alswanger responded, " I know the law of the Imperial Army exacts that I shall be deprived of my commission, expelled from the Army and not allowed to enter France again."

" And, in spite of all that, you persist in pleading guilty ? "

" I do. Justice demands it," Alswanger replied.

The Auditor-General sighed. He had done all

that he could do to save his friend, and failed.   The law would now have to take its course.

A report of the proceedings was consequently drawn up, and after being signed by the general, officers of the Court of Inquiry, and prisoner, was delivered to Governor-General Rapp.   The governor seemed greatly distressed, he had, as a matter of fact, been present during the Court proceedings and witnessed the whole affair.

"Gentlemen," he said to the Auditor-General and officers accompanying him, " We have lost through his own confession a man whom we all respected, and even loved.   A true friend and brave officer. It will be the hardest thing we have ever been called upon to do to condemn him, but our duty to France forbids us to flinch.   A court martial will assemble to-morrow under General O,* and I trust the sad business will be ended as speedily as possible."

There is no occasion for a detailed account of the legal proceedings.   The court martial had, of necessity, to find Alswanger guilty, and their verdict was summed up in these words :

" As Captain Alswanger has declared himself guilty by signing the *procès-verbal* of the preliminary inquiry he must be punished as a common thief. He will accordingly be cashiered as infamous in front of his company, removed from the Officers'

---

* The name in full is omitted by Sir Lascelles Wraxall.

Corps as morally dead, confined in a fortress for a year, and then sent back as a private soldier to the company he has hitherto commanded. We recommend him, however, to the mercy of the Emperor, on account of his previous good conduct and services."

On hearing the verdict, Governor-General Rapp remarked it was a severe sentence; but, as the crime had been of the meanest description, the honour of the Army demanded a fitting punishment.

Alswanger was then sent for, and, on appearing under escort, was asked if he appealed against the sentence.

"No," he answered firmly. "I will undergo it." But it was noticed his hand trembled, as he signed the separate protocol.

He was then removed to prison and told that his degradation was to take place shortly, in public.

The open-air spot selected by the court-martial for their ceremony was the Langenmarket, and a vast concourse of people, consisting largely of fashionably dressed women, collected there to witness the unhappy spectacle. The townsfolk who had houses overlooking the Langenmarket charged exorbitant prices for their windows, and even sold seats on their housetops. When the Governor-General Rapp and staff arrived, Alswanger was conducted to a reserved space in front of him, and the process of degradation commenced.

First of all, the decorations the condemned man had gained by his valour on the field were removed from his tunic, then his sword was broken, his epaulettes and facings torn off, and a common forage cap placed on his head, whilst his handsome shako together with his epaulettes and facings were cast contemptuously at his feet. All this he bore in silence and apparently unmoved, until he was about to be led away in chains, when he begged to be allowed to speak, as he had an important communication to make. His request was readily granted ; and the gist of his statement was as follows :

He was not Captain Alswanger at all, but the son of a Strasburg tradesman named Diderici. For seven years, very much against his will, for he had always longed to lead an outdoor life, he served as an apprentice to a shoemaker ; and, when freed from his apprenticeship, he immediately joined a troupe if travelling actors. Weary, at last, of forced companionship that was often uncongenial, he set off alone, earning just sufficient with his guitar to provide him with food and lodging. After undergoing many adventures he arrived one day at Aguila, and was drinking lemonade in a café, when some young French officers, one of whom bore an extraordinary likeness to himself, sauntered in and catching sight of him burst out laughing.

" Why, Alswanger," they cried, holding their sides with merriment, and addressing one of their number, " you never told us you had a twin brother ! Why, you and this fellow with the guitar are as like as two peas."

" Mother of Moses, you're right," Alswanger replied, " I can see the likeness myself. By Jove, I've an idea. It will tickle everyone to death and muddle the whole regiment. Look here, you fellow," he went on, addressing Diderici, " you look a bit down on your luck. Would you like a job, quite a soft one ? "

" I should, indeed," Diderici responded, albeit rather dubiously, for he thought Captain Alswanger was making fun of him. " What is it ? "

" Why, I am looking for a valet," Alswanger answered, " to take with me, whilst I am going about with the regiment, and you will just do."

He named a salary, and Diderici, to whom in his hard-up condition it seemed truly munificent, closed with the offer at once.

The relationship between Alswanger and Diderici soon proved to be that of friends rather than master and servant. Alswanger, who, as I have already said, was fond of practical joking, just to hoax the officers and men of the battalion, often used to change clothes with Diderici—the likeness between himself and Diderici being then so extraordinary that one or other of his fellow officers would invariably fall into the trap, and suddenly find themselves talking, perhaps confidentially, to his valet, instead of himself. On these occasions, of course, Diderici's ready wit and experience as an actor enabled him to carry on the deception, and once, so good an actor was he, that dressed in his master's clothes, and posing as Captain Alswanger, he entertained a number of officers and their lady friends to dinner, his real identity never being even suspected by anyone.

In this fashion, time passed quite smoothly and pleasantly for Diderici. Then there was a change. One autumn evening, Captain Alswanger was taken ill. He came home looking very pale and complained of a violent headache and giddiness. Diderici put him to bed and left him. In the morning, when he went into his room with his usual early cup of chocolate, he found him dead. It was then, as he stood by the body of his dead master and double, that the idea of impersonating him permanently flashed through his mind. What he had done for a joke, he might easily do for gain. Captain Alswanger had a liberal allowance from his father, a rich banker in Rome, why should he not make a bold bid for it ? The thought was no sooner con-

ceived in his fertile brain than he resolved to put
it into execution.

Taking off his clothes he put on Alswanger's
uniform, and carrying the latter's body into his
own room, he put it into his bed. He then made
certain other alterations, and, when all was complete, rushed out of his quarters in an assumed state
of panic and summoned the regimental doctor.

" It's my valet," he said, as soon as the latter
arrived. " He's either in a fit or dead."

" Humph ! " the doctor exclaimed, bending over
the supposed Diderici and examining him, " he's
dead, that's what's the matter with him. You look
none too well yourself, *Captain*."

" No," Diderici exclaimed, helping himself to a
glass of brandy. " I've not been any too grand
lately, and the shock of this fellow's death—I was
quite attached to him—has entirely unnerved me."

" What you want is a rest," the doctor replied,
" a month's sick leave. I'll advise the C.O. to that
effect, if you like."

" I wish you would," Diderici said, " for I really
feel I need it."

" There's no doubt on that score," the doctor
responded, and then, once again, turned to the
corpse.

Two other doctors, both civilians, were subsequently called in, and a certificate to the effect that

Diderici, valet to Captain Alswanger, had died of apoplexy was signed by all three. The real Diderici now obtained a week's sick leave, and employed it reading through the dead man's correspondence and imitating his handwriting. He also set to work improving his Italian—he could already speak that language tolerably well—and in his assumed name of Alswanger sent the burgomaster of Strasburg, his native town, intimation of the death of Diderici, his valet.

In short, he acted with such cleverness that no one, so far, suspected him. But, to ensure success in the future, he had a more difficult part set to play. He was desperately short of money, and needed an advance on the allowance, which he knew was not yet due, or a loan. But how was he to get it ? Should he write to Captain Alswanger's father or apply to him in person. After turning the matter over in his mind, he resolved to visit the Alswangers, arguing that he would, in any case, have to face them sooner or later. Consequently, pretending that he was suffering from a complete breakdown and needed a change of scene, he obtained a month's sick leave, and at once set out to Rome. His visit was, on the whole, a success. Captain Alswanger's pretty sister, Prudence, evidently believed him to be her brother, for she received him with every demonstration of affection, while Mr. Alswanger, making no comment at all upon his personal appearance, also appeared to be very pleased to see him. It was only Mrs. Alswanger of whom he was afraid, since he constantly caught her regarding him with an expression of the greatest perplexity on her face.

It was, indeed, fear of detection on her part that made him cut his visit short. Pretending that he had to see some friends to whom he had been introduced by his commanding officer he left the Alswangers several days earlier than he had intended and, to his intense relief, Mr. Alswanger, on the morning of his departure, presented him with a substantial cheque.

The pleasure this gift gave him, however, was somewhat marred by Mrs. Alswanger's parting words. Heaving a sigh of relief, she ejaculated, " Go, in Heaven's name," and this speech increased his apprehensions to such an extent that for days after he lived in constant dread of exposure. Yet none came. Soon after this, he was ordered to the Front and at Jena he won his first decorations.

This gained him considerable popularity in his regiment, and everything went smoothly till Mr. Alswanger died. The remittances, which he had received regularly from Rome, then ceased, and he was once again haunted with the evergrowing dread of exposure.

This concluded his confession, and the effect it had on Governor-General Rapp was amazing; every one present commented on it.

His previous inclination to sympathize with the prisoner had suddenly vanished, and he appeared to be imbued with a hatred so violent that it seemed almost an obsession.

"Infamous impostor!" he cried, as soon as Diderici had finished speaking. "Wretch! It's my belief you poisoned Captain Alswanger. The sentence I regarded as too severe on you is not nearly severe enough. You ought—but, bah! Why waste words," and turning to the soldiers who had hold of Diderici, he said, "Away with him!"

And thus ended the first step in the Diderici drama. A report of the case was, in due course, sent to the Emperor Napoleon, who it was believed would reprieve Diderici, on account of his gallant conduct at Jena and other battles. Greatly, however, to every one's surprise Napoleon declared the sentence passed on Diderici to be altogether too lenient.

For his admitted impersonation of Captain Alswanger he ordered him to be branded, in public, as a common felon, to be then sent to the fortress of Weichselmunde, and at the first favourable opportunity to be transferred thence, as a prisoner for life, to the galleys at Brest. The severity of this command appalled every one but Governor-General Rapp, who expressed himself perfectly satisfied.

"The scoundrel," he was heard to remark, "has got no more than his deserts." Under his directions the branding of Diderici took place in the Langenmarket of Danzig, and, as on the occasion of the prisoner's previous degradation, a vast crowd, comprising members of both sexes, assembled there. Diderici bore his punishment without flinching and was removed in irons to Weichselmunde. His treatment there was rigorous and brutal in the extreme. Herded with criminals of all kinds, he was employed every day, from dawn to dusk, at the hardest of hard labour, receiving little food and plenty of blows and lashes, if he ever dared pause in his work or complain.

In 1813, two years after Diderici had been sentenced, the fortress passed into the hands of its original owners, the Prussians. An envoy from the French Government, accompanied by several mounted officers of the Imperial Army, arrived one morning at Weichselmunde and informed the governor that his services were no longer needed there, and that all the French military prisoners, no matter what their offences, were to be released at once, adding that it was particularly stated in his orders that he himself should effect the setting free of the prisoners.

The governor, expressing his readiness to comply with these orders, at once called to the head jailer, and telling him that the prisoners were to be released set off with him to the cells, accompanied by the envoy and the latter's escort. Beginning with cell No. 1 they visited all in turn, releasing their inmates, till they came to cell No. 80, and this, the jailer, who led the party, was about to pass by. The envoy, however, called him back.

" We must not omit Diderici," he said, looking at the list of prisoners he held in his hand. " I recollect his case well. Open the door ; I should like to see him."

The jailer looked at the governor ; but, failing to catch his eye, advanced to the door and turning the key in the lock threw it open. No one was there.

" Hullo, how's this ? " the envoy exclaimed, putting his monocle to his eye and staring at the governor in blank astonishment. " Where's the prisoner ? "

" No one knows, Your Excellency," the governor stammered. " A very extraordinary thing happened, and I should, perhaps, have told you about it before. One day, when the prisoners were out in the grounds taking exercise, No. 80 suddenly disappeared."

" Disappeared ! " the envoy echoed. " But surely the prisoners were in chains ? "

"Why, yes, Your Excellency," the governor replied. "As I have just said, it was an extraordinary thing to happen, and all we can think of to account for it is that the prisoner may have jumped into the Vistula, which flows past the fortress, and been drowned."

"But some one, surely, would have seen him," the envoy said, "or heard a splash; and, besides, his body would have been found. No, I think the drowning theory very weak. Have you nothing better to suggest?"

The governor evidently had not, for he said nothing; and what became of Dederici has remained to this day an unanswered question. While some believed that he was drowned in attempting to escape, others believed that he was murdered either by order of General Rapp, who, as has been shown, evinced a sudden and most violent antipathy to him, or at the instigation of Mrs. Alswanger, who bitterly resented his impersonation of her son, and, in all probability, shared General Rapp's belief that Diderici had poisoned him.

At any rate the matter was never cleared up, and for years afterwards No. 80 was called "the mystery cell."

CHAPTER X

A NORTHAMPTON DISAPPEARANCE*

ONE morning in the winter of 1864 Richard Warren, a labourer of Ringstead, Northamptonshire, was cleaning out a dyke or ditch in a lane leading from the village of Denford to that of Keystone, when his spade hit against something hard. At first he thought it was a stone, and he was about to toss it casually aside, when something in its appearance striking him as peculiar he examined it more closely, and was surprised to find it was a human skull. The instant he made this discovery he dropped his spade, and set off to find his employer, who was in a field near by.

" See 'ere, master," he cried in a great state of excitement, pointing to the skull which he held in one hand, " see what I've bin and found in yon ditch," and he jerked his thumb in the direction of the spot where he had been working. " I'm thinking as 'ow this mebbe the 'ead of Lydia Atley, who yer may recollect disappeared mysteriously close on thirteen and a 'alf years ago."

* " News of the World " and other papers, March, 1864.

" Let me have a look at it," his employer said, coolly taking the skull and examining it curiously. " What makes you think it is a woman's skull ? It might, surely, be a man's."

" Women's 'eads are smaller than men's, master," Warren replied, " and this 'ere is a small 'ead. You may depend on it, it is Lydia Atley's."

The employer shrugged his shoulders.

" It is possible, of course," he said, " but weren't there any bones with it ? "

" I didn't wait to see, master," Warren answered, " I was too hexcited at finding this 'ere."

His employer smiled. " Show me the spot, Warren," he observed, " and we'll dig around and see if we can unearth anything else."

Warren did as he was bid, and, after digging a very short while, came upon an entire skeleton, that is to say entire all but the head. It was lying at a depth of only a few inches, breast downwards, with its neck towards the hedge and its feet to the road. There was no sign of any clothing, nothing but the mere bones. The two men at once informed the local police, who, in their turn summoned the local doctor.

The latter pronounced the remains to be those of a female of medium height and between twelve and twenty years of age. There were no signs that any violence had been committed, and nothing in any way peculiar about the skeleton, saving that a double tooth on the left side of the jaw was missing. The discovery of the remains, close to the spot where Lydia Atley was said to have been seen on the evening of her mysterious disappearance thirteen and a half years before, striking the police as singular, they resumed the inquiries they had dropped, with the result that William Weekly Ball, a well-to-do butcher of Ramsay, Northumberland, was arrested and tried on the charge of murder.

I have no wish to enumerate all the details of the case, set forth at the trial, for one thing I have not enough space, and for another they are far too sordid, but in order to have a correct understanding of the principal features in it, I will give a brief outline of the history of Lydia Atley, up to the time of her disappearance, in strict accordance with the evidence elicited at the trial.

Undoubtedly the belle of the little village of Ringstead in the year 1849, Lydia Atley, then barely out of her teens, had all the vivacity and charm of healthy girlhood, coupled with a grace of figure and piquancy of feature that made her quite extraordinarily attractive. Had she been born in rather better circumstances, and belonged even to the middle class, she would doubtless have made a good match, and have wedded, perhaps, some well-to-do farmer, but being only of the labouring class, she had nothing to look forward to, wedded or single, but a life of toil. Now most of her companions, being plainer than herself, and perhaps more sensible, were quite resigned to their lot, but with Lydia it was different. The attention she had received from the village swains, not a few of whom imagined themselves to be head over ears in love with her, had made her very vain and, being naturally rather " giddy," she speedily developed into what is vulgarly termed a regular little minx. At least that was the title awarded her by the elderly and more respectable members of Ringstead society, and whenever they saw Lydia pass by their cottages, decked out, as they put it, in all her trumpery finery, to catch the men, they invariably said to one another, " Just look at that minx, dressed up to the knocker again, you may depend upon it she'll come to no good."

At first, Lydia, sometimes overhearing and sometimes being told of these remarks, " took them to heart," but, by and by, as she grew accustomed to them, she no longer winced and turned red ; whereupon she was dubbed a bold hussy and no good at all. And, yet, all the harm she had done so far was to wear gaudy ribbons in her hair, and to discard the elastic-sided boots custom demanded of her class, for very cheap and rather high-heeled shoes. The wearing of the latter was apparently an unpardonable crime. Well, things were at this stage when Lydia, unfortunately for herself, happened to attract the attention of Mr. William Weekly Ball, a young Ringstead tradesman, who, by reason of the fact that he lived in a house, not a cottage, and was doing well in business, was much looked up to and envied by the villagers. Ball, who was married, was very proud of his " position " and respectability, but being by nature a gay Lothario, a fact he had tried to keep from his wife and the elect of Ringstead, he could never resist having a little *affaire*, when the opportunity offered, provided there was little likelihood of his being found out. Therefore, as Lydia Atley was admittedly the prettiest girl in Ringstead, the idea of having a flirtation with her struck him as extremely nice, if only it could be indulged in with safety.

Deciding at last to take the plunge and the risks, he commenced his campaign of conquest by making eyes at Lydia, having first made sure that no one was looking, and nodding pleasantly to her whenever they passed one another in the road. As he had shrewdly foreseen, Lydia's vanity was the source of her undoing. Delighted at being noticed by some one whom she regarded as " quite a swell," she returned his oglings with compound interest, and when he turned round to look at her after he had passed he saw her smiling at him coquettishly and waving her hand.

That was the beginning of it, how it ended no one to this day knows. It was fairly conclusively proved that they used to meet almost every evening, when he was supposed to be away from home on business, in one or other of the lonely spots near Ringstead, and she was not infrequently seen by the village constable stealing her way home after one of those meetings, sometimes late at night, and sometimes in the early hours of the morning. Now the village constable, like most men, with a little leisure, was a bit of a gossip (I would here remark that, with regard to gossip, I cannot agree that women are the greatest sinners) over a glass of ale, and sometimes, without that incentive, his tongue would wag, simply for the love of wagging, and he would say things that in his cooler and more reflective moments nothing would have persuaded him to utter.

It was then, that owing to his fondness for imparting sensational news, the constable disclosed the secret of Weekly Ball and spoke about seeing him with Lydia Atley in the dead of night. Now nothing travels faster than scandal, and it was not long before the whole village got talking. " To think of 'er carrying on with Ball and 'e a married man. She ought to be ashamed of 'erself, and 'e, too, as far as that goes. Pity some one doesn't tell 'is wife."

These were the remarks made, and, in due course, some well-meaning individual repeated them to Ball.

" If I was you, Weekly," he added, tapping Ball on the arm by way of emphasis, " I'd drop Atley. If you leave her alone, she'll soon take up with some one else."

" It's not a case of my leaving her alone," Ball laughed bitterly, " it's she that won't leave me alone. Why, she's always after me morning, noon and night."

" Humph," his friend ejaculated somewhat dubiously, " well take care, Weekly. These kind of friendships often end badly."

Ball made no reply, he had very good reasons to fear what his friend hinted at might prove true. Indeed, he had so far committed himself with Lydia Atley that it was no easy thing to shake her off. Again and again, he cursed himself with having been such a fool, he might truly have added, and knave, but that didn't help matters. What was done, was done, there was no getting away from that, the question that confronted him now was what was going to follow.

Should he flatly deny that the child she was about to have was his and send her to the right about, or, by offering her money, try to effect some kind of compromise. By adopting the latter course he might avoid an actual row with Lydia, and for a time, at least, prevent his wife getting to hear of his " indiscretion." It was a problem, and he lay awake at nights wracking his brain to know what to do for the best, the best, that is to say, as far as he was concerned. Several weeks passed, and the conundrum still remained unsolved. He had, however, taken to seeing less of Lydia, putting off appointments with her, or breaking them altogether, and when they did meet he was perceptibly cooler to her. That was the state of affairs at the commencement of the third week of July, 1850.

Early in the afternoon of the 22nd day of that month Lydia Atley, looking very flushed and excited, called at the cottage of Mrs. Groom, one of her few really intimate friends in the village, and complained bitterly of the manner in which Weekly Ball was treating her.

" Now that 'e's robbed me of my good name," she began angrily, " 'e thinks 'e can throw me aside like a bundle of dirty rags, but 'e little knows who 'e's dealing with. I've made an appointment with 'im this evening, and if 'e dares break it—but 'e daren't, not after the scolding I gave 'im yesterday in the street."

" 'E's a wretch to treat you as 'e's doing," Mrs.

Groom said sympathetically. " I never did like 'im. With all them airs 'e gives 'imself, 'e's only in trade, same as one of my 'usband's relatives ! If 'is wife got to 'ear of 'is b'aviour to you, 'e'd sing small."

" And she will," Lydia Atley cried, clenching her hands in her fury, " I'm going to tell 'im she will, unless 'e pays me 'andsomely for keeping quiet. It's money I want now, not 'im, the beast, and it's money I mean to 'ave."

Mrs. Groom nodded approvingly.

" I only 'opes you gets it, Lydia," she said, " and plenty of it, 'e can afford it. But take care ; remember, 'e's a man, while you're only a woman."

" Pooh ! " Lydia Atley exclaimed scornfully. " Do you think I'm afraid of the likes of Weekly Ball ? Not me, Mary Groom ! 'E's got to give me a tidy sum of money, or there'll be a row I can tell you," and with the gleam of battle in her eyes Lydia Atley strode off to her house.

That was the last Mary Groom ever saw of her.

The clouds that had been hanging low in the sky all the afternoon gradually cleared away, and the evening proved to be wonderfully fine, a glorious silvery moon amidst myriads of scintillating stars, and scarcely a breath of wind stirring. An ideal summer evening, so Joseph Groom, husband of the aforesaid Mrs. Groom thought, as he wandered through the village on his way to the inn, pausing every now and again to look up at the sky and revel in the delicious odour of the roses and honeysuckle. It was during one of these halts, when he was standing close to the entrance to Weekly Ball's orchard, that he heard voices engaged in a seeming altercation. Wondering what it was all about he looked around for the speakers, but could not see them, as they were hidden from him by some boarding. Straining his ears to catch what they were saying he presently heard one of them, whose voice he now recognised as Lydia Atley's, exclaim very wearily, " I did not intend coming in here with you to-night, Weekly Ball, for I've got the feeling you intend killing me. Isn't it so ? " Anxious to hear what the reply would be and who made it, Groom listened very eagerly, but he couldn't catch the slightest sound. There was, instead, a most emphatic silence that lasted till Lydia Atley spoke again. " The Lord have mercy on me, if I am to die in my present state of sin," she said, but in tones that seemed to have grown very much feebler.

After this there was again silence, and Groom coming to the conclusion that it was, perhaps, nothing more than an ordinary lovers' quarrel, in which he had best not interfere, went on his way. That was at about a quarter to ten.

A few minutes before Groom had paused at this

particular spot, another villager called John Hill, also attracted by the beauty of the evening, was taking a stroll through neighbouring fields.   Hearing voices and footsteps in the lane running alongside the fields, and filled with a sudden curiosity to see who the speakers were, Hill went up to the hedge that intervened between him and the lane and peered through.   Not altogether to his surprise the speakers proved to be Lydia Atley and Weekly Ball.   The whole lane being bathed in moonlight he saw them very distinctly, especially Lydia Atley, who looked white and haggard.   They appeared to be on anything but affectionate terms, to put it in his own blunt language, " they were not 'anging to one another's arms, as lovers are wont to do, there was nothing in the way of canoodling."   They were merely walking along, at a distance of a foot or so apart, and, as they passed close to where Hill was standing, he heard Lydia say in very angry tones, " I won't, Weekly Ball, I won't do or say nothing of the kind.   It's yours, yours I tell you, and no one else's."   He couldn't hear what Weekly Ball said in reply, for he spoke in very low tones and seemed cowed.

They went on down the lane, and Hill, keeping a short distance behind them, on the other side of the hedge, followed them with his eyes till they got close to the wooden door leading into Ball's orchard.

He then lost sight of them amid the gloom and shadows of the thick foliage. Hearing, however, a noise like the clicking of a latch he concluded they had entered the orchard, and accordingly wended his way homewards.

Lydia Atley was never seen again. On her failing to return to her home that night, the local police were notified the following morning, and all Ringstead soon awoke to the fact that she was missing. Suspicion at once falling on Ball, his orchard was searched, as, indeed, were the neighbouring fields and spinneys, but not a trace of Lydia Atley could be found. She had vanished, *in toto*, without leaving the slightest clue as to her whereabouts or fate. An anonymous letter was received by a local magistrate stating she had been seen, since her reported disappearance, by the writer in Gold Street, Northampton, but this letter was not regarded as a valuable clue, although it might easily have proved to be, but, instead, was merely regarded as a hoax.

However, Weekly Ball was, in fact, generally suspected of being the cause of Lydia Atley's disappearance, and it was thought he knew a great deal more than he chose to disclose; at the same time nothing could be actually proved against him, because no body was found. The Government offered a reward of £200 to anyone giving any information concerning her whereabouts or fate, but it

remained unclaimed, and the affair was soon relegated to the category of unsolved mysteries. Rather
more than thirteen years passed, and then came the
discovery of the skeleton of the woman in the ditch
by Richard Warren.

Taking into consideration the following facts,
namely, that a certain tooth in the left side of the
jaw of the skull of this skeleton was missing, and a
labourer called Henry Dix, declared he had drawn
a corresponding tooth for Lydia Atley about a fortnight before her disappearance ; that John Hill
had seen Lydia Atley and Weekly Ball together, on
the night of the 22nd July, and that they had
presumably entered Ball's orchard ; that Joseph
Groom, shortly afterwards, on the same night, heard
two people talking in Ball's orchard, and that one
of them was Lydia Atley ; that the remains of the
woman with the missing tooth was found near this
orchard ; and that the writer of the anonymous
letter received by the magistrate now came forward
and stated he had been asked to write the letter by
Ball, who, at that time, was a friend of his ; taking,
I repeat, all these things into consideration, the
police could not help coming to the conclusion that
the skeleton was actually that of Lydia Atley.
Consequently they arrested Weekly Ball ; and he
was brought before the Thrapston magistrates
charged with the murder of Lydia Atley. He

pleaded not guilty. In his defence it was urged that, although it was quite true he had met Lydia Atley on the night of the 22nd of July, and that she had accompanied him to the door of his orchard, he had parted with her there, and had never set eyes on her since. He gave her money, on the understanding that she was going to leave Ringstead at once, and he believed she had done so. Though the police claimed the skeleton found in the ditch was that of Lydia Atley, the defence maintained no proof that such was actually the case had been produced. On the contrary, there was evidence to show the remains discovered were not hers at all.

In the first place, had the remains discovered been those of Lydia Atley, evidences of her condition of expectant motherhood would have been found too,* but they were not ; and, secondly, there were strong reasons for supposing the remains found to have been those of some one else. When the police had been digging up the ground in and around the ditch, hoping to find some article that would establish the identity of the skeleton in dispute, they unearthed the skeletons of a man and two other women. Now it was a well-known fact that the spot had been, for years, used as a camping ground by gipsies, and it was urged the finding of the remains suggested that the gipsies had also used it as a burial ground.

* Medical testimony had affirmed this.

There was far more reason, the defence argued, for supposing the skeleton under discussion to be that of a gipsy than there was for supposing it to be that of Lydia Atley. The missing tooth was apparently the only mark of identification to which the prosecution could point, but since hundreds of people had lost a tooth from the left side of their jaw could the missing tooth, it was asked, be regarded as an identification mark at all. With all these points raised by the defence the magistrates agreed, and the case against Weekly Ball being regarded as incomplete and insufficient, he was discharged. No one else was arrested, and the fate of Lydia Atley remains to this day problematic.

Had she, as Weekly Ball suggested, left Ringstead and gone to swell the number of unfortunate beings like herself in London or some other big city, and ended her life, perhaps by her own hand, or died of some loathsome disease ; or was the skeleton found really hers, and had Weekly Ball, knowing the spot to be frequented by gipsies, very cunningly buried it there, anticipating that, should it ever be unearthed, it could not be distinguished from and could be mistaken for the remains of some Romany. I think most people will incline to the latter theory.

CHAPTER XI

THE CRIPPLE OF MOGSDEN

IN the eighties of last century, at Mogsden,* a
village in the Midlands, there lived a family
named Harper : a Mr. and Mrs. Harper and their
son, John. A cripple from his birth, John's case
had been regarded as quite hopeless till just before
his nineteenth birthday, when he suddenly showed
signs of getting better, and, to every one's surprise,
was not only able to leave his bed but to hobble
about the house and garden. Congratulations were
showered upon him, for he had always borne his
sufferings patiently, and being of a generous,
sympathetic nature, though somewhat super-sensi-
tive, he was beloved by all who came in contact
with him. Parents, servants, friends, to whom he
had never said an unkind word, and who, it is
equally certain, had never said an unkind word to
him, were all equally delighted.

Up to the time of his getting better, his one hobby

* Owing to the desire on the part of the people who told me this
story for absolute secrecy, I have given fictitious names to all
persons and places in it. The truth of the case has, however, been
vouched for.

had been reading, his favourite authors being Harri-
son Ainsworth and James Grant, whose works are
chiefly of a romantic nature ; but, after he had
partially recovered the use of his limbs, he took, in
fine weather, to gardening and tending to the
poultry, and when he was not thus occupied he
would sit on the lawn in the front of the house, a
spot from which he could command a long vista,
both ways, of the high road to Birmingham, and
watch the passers-by. Sometimes a brake full of
holiday makers would attract his attention, sometimes a party of children blackberrying, and sometimes a pretty face, for John was an extraordinary
mixture, a strange blending of the materialist and
the idealist, the doer and the dreamer. At one
moment, intensely practical, not to say commercial,
he would be calculating how much he ought to get
for his chickens and eggs, and the next, a simple
romanticist, he would be lost in admiration of some
pretty girl who happened to be passing, and for the
next half hour, perhaps, would sit wondering who
she was, where she lived, and how she spent her
time.

So diverse, indeed, were his tastes and so complex
his nature, that his parents, had they been compelled
to launch him on the world to earn his living, might
have found it difficult to map out a course for him.
As they were well off, however, there was no need

for him to earn money, and he seemed perfectly content to amuse himself in whatever way he fancied.

Thus his days were passing, apparently, pleasantly enough, when he received a letter one morning from some friends in Quintox, a village about 20 miles distant by rail from Mogsden, inviting him to spend the day with them.

In John's eyes it was an event of the greatest importance, and, naturally, he was no little excited. After being looked upon as a hopeless invalid all his life, never going anywhere or seeing anyone, saving when they came to his house or happened to pass by, to be asked by his friends to spend the day with them, just as they would ask a normal boy, why, it was absolutely heavenly, and, quite overcome with joy, he showed the letter to his parents, saying how delighted he was, and that he should write off at once to accept the invitation.

His parents did not know what to do ; he had evidently set his mind upon going, and they dreaded disappointing him.   With the aid of a crutch, it was true, he could hobble about the grounds, but he had never walked further than the pillar box, which was within sight of the house, at a stretch, and, to get to Quintox, he would have to walk to the railway station, a distance of at least a quarter of a mile, there being no other means of getting there.

Reading perplexity in his parents' faces, and fearing they intended to dissuade him from going, John exclaimed :

" You needn't look so worried, mother. I shall be perfectly all right. If I am strong enough to be out of doors all day gardening and looking after the poultry, surely I am capable of walking to the station and travelling by train only twenty miles. If I should want help getting into the carriage, which I'm sure I shan't, the porter would lend me a hand this end, and the Browns are going to meet me the other end, so what harm can come to me ? There's no change."

" No," John's father replied hesitatingly, " there's no change, it's a straight run."

" Of course it is, and you can't think of anything to prevent me going, now, can you ? " John said coaxingly. " Besides, it's not until next week, and I shall practise walking every day between now and then, so as to be in good form."

After this John's parents thought it best to drop the subject for the present. John was naturally obstinate, and having once made up his mind to do anything, it was difficult to deter him ; and in this instance, so far, it seemed quite impossible.

He at once began hobbling up and down the road outside the house, and gradually going further and further, he was at last able to walk as far as the railway station, which was about a quarter of a mile in a direct line from the house, with apparent ease. This pleased him immeasurably, and he certainly seemed in very good condition ; but, to his parents' dismay, he insisted upon going to Quintox alone.

" It takes away all my pleasure, if I have to have some one with me," he explained. " I am nineteen, and I can't bear to be thought not capable of looking after myself ; you can come to the station to meet me, when I return."

" We will certainly do that," Mrs. Harper rejoined, " but we should be much happier if you would only be sensible and let us accompany you."

But John remained obdurate.

" No, mother," he said firmly, " it's you who are not sensible, because there really is no occasion for anyone to come with me, and I want to go alone, so that everyone can see that I'm no longer a poor stick and tied to your apron strings."

His parents still persisted, but, seeing, at last, that there was no chance even of a compromise, they eventually gave in.

Well, the eventful morning arrived. It was an ideal summer day, the sky serenely blue with not the vestige of a cloud, and the whole country-side aglow with golden sunlight. The entire household, including John's old nurse, who had known him from babyhood, and the cook, housemaid, between-maid and bootboy, covertly watched him depart, and Mr. Harper walked with him as far as the station. There he left him. He saw him hobble up to the window of the ticket office and ask for a ticket and then, as he knew that John was positively aching to be " on his own," and consequently would prefer that he did not wait till the train came in, he turned his back on the station and walked homewards.

To Mr. and Mrs. Harper the day passed very slowly. They had refrained from asking John to send them a wire on his arrival, in deference to his strongly expressed desire that no fuss should be made, and it had not occurred to them before that they might have asked the Browns, in strict confidence, to send them a wire, unknown to John, to apprise them of his safe arrival. Hence they spent the day in a fever of anxiety, lest the fatigue and excitement of the journey had proved too much for him and had led to a collapse. Those were the days before telephones, or, at any rate, before telephones came into general use, and although it did occur to them that they might wire to the Browns they thought it best not to do so, since John would probably know if they did, and would consider that they were taking an unfair advantage of him. They therefore, instead of running the risk of upsetting him, bore the suspense as best they could, and at half-past five set off to the station, in plenty of time to meet the train he was to return by.

Never had they awaited anyone's arrival so anxiously, and never had they felt such trepidation, as when they at last saw the signal fall and the train suddenly round the curve, known locally as " the elbow." With almost breathless excitement they watched it getting nearer and nearer, and when eventually it slowed down as it approached the platform and, after what seemed to them an eternity, stopped, they began systematically peering into one carriage after another in search of John. He was nowhere to be found. Thinking that he must be in the train, and that, having fainted, perhaps, he had been unable to attract their attention, they spoke to the station master, who of course knew them well, and asked him to delay the train, while they looked again. The station master acquiesced, and every compartment was examined ; but it was of no avail ; in none of them was John to be found.

" Don't worry, ma'am," the station master remarked to Mrs. Harper, in a kindly endeavour to relieve her anxiety, " no doubt Mr. John will come by the seven o'clock. He doesn't go out visiting, you know, every day, and he's making the most of of the occasion."

Thinking that there might be some **truth in** this remark, the Harpers resolved to wait at **the station** for the seven o'clock, which was the next train due at Mogsden from Quintox. Needless to say the time went slowly enough, and when they again watched the signal fall, and the train from Quintox round "the elbow," their excitement had reached a limit.

This time the station master joined in the search without being asked, but neither he nor anyone else —for porters and passengers assisted in the search— could find John, for the very simple reason that John was not in the train.

The Harpers were now almost out of their minds. They anticipated the worst; and the station master, anxious to allay their fears, said he would wire at once to the station master at Quintox and ask him to send some one to Mr. Brown's, to find out why young Mr. Harper hadn't returned.

Again, there was an interval of seemingly endless waiting, and when the reply did come it proved a veritable thunderbolt. John was not at the Browns', and he hadn't been there.

" We expected him by the first train in the morning," they wired, " but he didn't come. What has happened ? "

" Good God, what can have happened ! " Mr. Harper ejaculated. " What can we do ? "

" Very possibly he forgot to get out of the train

at Quintox and was taken on to Birmingham," the station master remarked.

"But he's not at all forgetful, and it was to Quintox that he was so bent on going," Mr. Harper replied. "Besides, even if he had gone on to Birmingham by mistake, surely he would have taken the first train he could catch back, and have arrived at the Browns' later on in the day."

To this there was no answer; Mrs. Harper was, in fact, too overcome to speak, and a general silence ensued.

Though no one had actually seen John get into the train at Mogsden that morning, it was regarded as pretty certain that he had done so. The booking clerk could testify to having given him a ticket, presumably for that train, but he could not say for certain whether it was for Quintox. Owing to his having issued quite an unusual number of tickets that day, both for Quintox, where a fair was being held, and other places, he had been extremely busy and could not possibly remember whether young Mr. Harper had asked for and been given a ticket for Quintox or elsewhere.

In a state bordering on utter distraction Mr. Harper took the train to Quintox, and arriving there questioned the station officials; but none of them could give him any definite information. The porter who took the tickets from the passengers, as they left the platform, said he thought a lame gentleman was among those who had arrived by the train in question, but he couldn't be sure. More people than usual seemed to have come by that train, and, as they passed out of the station all together, he had not noticed anyone in particular. Baffled again, Mr. Harper hastened to the Browns', who had arranged to go to the station to meet John, and learned from them that owing to an unavoidable delay, they unfortunately did not get to the station till five minutes after the train John was to come by had left.

There was then, they said, no one on the platform, saving a porter and an old woman, and concluding that something had prevented John coming—if he had come, they argued, he would surely either have started off to walk to their house, in which case they would have met him on the road, or have waited for them at the station—they returned home.

They were almost as upset as Mr. Harper himself, and remarking that possibly John had gone to the fair, as they had often heard him express a great desire to see one, they suggested searching the fair for him. Mr. Harper then, accompanied by Mr. Brown and his eldest son, a youth of about John's age, immediately set off in the direction of the fair. Arriving there they made a thorough search of all the booths and the grand stand, making inquiries wherever and whenever possible, but all without avail. No one had seen a young man answering in the very slightest to the description of John. At last, wearied and dispirited, they left the place, and were wending their way to the station, when some children came running after them.

" Are you looking for a lame old gentleman ? " they asked.

" Not a lame *old* gentleman," Mr. Harper replied impatiently, " a lame young gentleman."

" Well, we don't know what age he really was," one of the children, a girl, said, " but he seemed old compared with us. He stopped us outside the station this morning, as we were going home from school, and inquired the way to some house."

" Was it The Lindens ? " Mr. Brown asked eagerly—The Lindens being the name of his house.

But none of the children could remember. One of them thought the name might have been The Lindens, but the others disagreed. It was a name more like The Buttery they thought. Anyhow, they could say nothing more definite on that point.

He went on, they said, and took the lane leading to the canal. Asked to describe him, they could not agree again. Whereas some of them startled Mr. Harper by declaring that the lame gentleman wore a straw hat and kind of grey flannel suit (John had, actually, worn clothes answering to this description) the others were equally positive that he was wearing a brown bowler and suit of much the same colour. Also, while one girl thought he was very fair, with just the suspicion of a moustache (this description, too, fitted John), another declared he was dark and quite clean shaven ; while the rest were absolutely sure he had white hair and side whiskers, just like old Johnson, the village under-taker. However, contradictory and confused as all these statements were, there was sufficient unifor-mity in them to suggest that possibly the stranger, so variously described, and John were one and the same person, and concurring in this opinion Mr. Harper and the Browns bent their way in the direction of the canal.

The sun having now sunk completely out of sight, in lieu of the brilliant blending of crimson and gold in the western sky there was merely a faint glow, against which the rest of the heavens showed dark and lowering.

Silence too—utter silence that seemed to be in absolute harmony with the shadows from the tall, motionless trees that skirted the lane on either side and with the general gloom—hung around them as they walked. And the further they advanced the more accentuated this gloom became.

The trees thickened into a wood and the scene was soon rendered all the more drear and forbidding by the appearance, in the distance ahead of them, of a long strip of water, which in some places, namely, where the glow from the horizon fell on it, was glimmering, and in others black as ink.

The three men trudged steadily on, keenly alert and on the look out ; but, as if afraid to break the awful stillness by giving voice to their dismal thoughts, they seldom spoke. As they approached the water, the scene grew even more lonely and depressing. Here and there, trees had fallen down, and their rotten trunks, overgrown with moss and rank vegetation, assumed in the uncertain light strange and fantastic shapes that were positively alarming ; and, nearer still to the water's edge, reeds and bulrushes, growing in profusion, rustled dismally, as the cool, night breeze swept over them.

Facing the pedestrians, as they now approached what appeared to be a fork or branch of the canal, was an obviously disused lock, the stone walls of which were mouldering and overgrown with weeds ; and close to it stood a derelict wooden hut. Indeed, dreariness and desolation were here depicted in no uncertain form, and a chilly, almost visible dampness in the air put, so to speak, a further touch to the picture.

" This is a ghastly place," Mr. Harper exclaimed, shivering, as he bent down and peered into the stagnant, weed-covered water. " One might imagine anything happening here. I hope——" But his speech was cut short by a loud, wailing cry from the neighbouring trees.

" A night bird of some kind," the younger Brown observed with a somewhat forced laugh. " They make rather a nasty noise."

"Are you sure it was a bird ? " Mr. Harper queried nervously. " It couldn't have been—John ? "

" No," Mr. Brown senior remarked, " that was a bird right enough. Come, cheer up, Harper. Those children were probably wrong ; the man who asked them the way, perhaps, wasn't lame at all, and therefore couldn't have been John, and when you get home you will find him waiting there for you."

" I wish I could think so," Mr. Harper said gloomily, " but I can't ; I feel dreadfully depressed. Something tells me that John did come to this horrible place this morning, and I believe that he is here, somewhere, now. Indeed, I am sure of it. Let's examine the hut."

They did so, but there was no sign of John, and as night was now fast coming on, and they had no lanterns, it was decided that it would be useless to proceed further. The Browns therefore returned home, and Mr. Harper took the last train back to Mogsden.

Hoping against hope that John would be at home when he got there, Mr. Harper simply flew from the station to his house. His wife and their old and valued servants were on the doorstep waiting for him, but there was no John. Nothing whatever had been heard of him.

Not much sleep did either of the Harpers have that night, and early in the morning, long before the arrival of the post, Mr. Harper was making inquiries at the police and railway stations. At neither of those places, however, had any news been received of the missing youth.

That day and the two following days search was made all along the line from Mogsden to Birmingham, ditches, lanes and woods were scoured, and the old, disused branch of the canal, which Mr. Harper and the Browns had visited, was dragged, but the result was nil. Not a trace of John could be found, and from that day to this his fate has remained a conundrum.

The police inclined to the theory that John's disappearance was voluntary. He was generally thought, they said, to be not quite normal, people who have been cripples from their infancy, they argued, seldom are, and it was not improbable that he had taken himself off of his own free will, in accordance with some sudden whim or fancy. Such cases were very far from uncommon. Indeed, they happened almost daily.

Mr. and Mrs. Harper, however, took a very

different view. They scouted the idea of John purposely hiding from them. He was as devoted to them, they declared, as they were to him, and they were quite sure that he would never knowingly cause them the slightest pain or grief. Besides, if he were still alive, some one must know where he was, for he could not pass unnoticed, on account of his infirmity, and surely that some one having seen the description of him in the papers and at the various police stations, would have come forward with some sort of information concerning him, if not for common humanity's sake, for the sake of the reward the giving of such information would secure.

No, in the Harper's opinion, an opinion that was shared by many, John had been murdered, murdered on the morning of his disappearance, in that lonely spot by the canal. It was a spot, they declared, much frequented by gipsies and tramps, especially in the summer, and some evilly disposed vagrant, lurking there, seeing that John was a cripple, and therefore unable to offer much resistance, had killed him, merely for his clothes and the money he had on him. Had he cried for help, it was more than probable that no one would have heard him, since few visited the spot, saving undesirables, and in that locality it was easy enough to hide a body where no one was at all likely to find it. It was true the police had searched the district, but it was not possible that they had looked everywhere, and dragged waters still have a knack of retaining their secrets.

Oddly enough, the idea of suicide in connection with John does not seem to have occurred to anyone. And yet, considering John's complex character, his extreme sensitiveness, allied to a love of the material and physical, and in no less a degree to a love of dreaming and romance, what was more likely than that he had committed suicide ? Just as jarring elements in a physical body often lead to rupture and catastrophe, so do jarring elements in the spiritual body. By their constant friction they create a mental discord and chaos that the outsider little dreams of, and from which the sufferer sees only one channel of escape—suicide.

In the course of my life I have known quite a number of people who have committed suicide, and in most of them I have noticed a singular complexity of character. In some, for instance, there has been a combination of the devout churchman and man about town, in others, a combination of the hard materialist with the weak, easily impressed sentimentalist. And so it may have been with John. His commercial instincts at war with his idealistic tendencies may have brought about a state of affairs so intolerable that death seemed preferable in comparison.

I have alluded to his habit of watching the passers-by and going into raptures over some rustic maiden. Well, possibly he at last really fell in love with one of these passing pedestrians ; and, realizing how hopeless in his case love must be, he had yielded to the promptings of hyper-sensitiveness and put an end to his existence.

But where and how ? Possibly in the old branch of the canal. Dragging, as I have said, has often been proved to be ineffectual, the body sought for having got into some hole or crevice, where it has, after lying there undisturbed for many years, been at last discovered by the merest chance ; and, granted this, no one can say for certain that John's skeleton does not lie at the bottom of the canal even now.

Although, undoubtedly many disappearances, probably the majority, are wilful disappearances, the disappearances of persons who, for various reasons, are desirous of being thought dead, I do not think John's disappearance was due to any such desire. I am inclined to trust to the instincts of his parents and friends, those who knew him best, rather than to the verdict of the police and mere outsiders, who, as the annals of crime can prove, are very frequently mistaken.

THE REV. B. SPEKE, WHOSE DISAPPEARANCE IN LONDON IN 1868 CAUSED
SUCH A SENSATION

(" *Illustrated Police News*" *Feb. 22, 1868*)

CHAPTER XII

THE CASE OF THE REV. BENJAMIN SPEKE

I N the mid-sixties of the last century the Rev. Benjamin Speke, brother of the famous African explorer, lived in Somersetshire, his parents residing with him. He had been incumbent of the parish in which he lived for eleven years, and his parishioners, one and all, loved and esteemed him. On Wednesday, January 8th, 1868, at the breakfast table, he announced his intention of going up to London that morning to attend the marriage of his most intimate friend, announcing, also, that he should return the next day. Accordingly, he drove to Chard station, and after instructing his groom to meet him with the dogcart the following evening, he took a return ticket to Waterloo and travelled up to town by the eleven o'clock express. An old colleague, with whom he had been associated in his first curacy, happened to be in this train, and the two travelled together as far as Salisbury. There the friend got out, and Mr. Speke, for the rest of the journey, had the compartment to himself. The train, due at Waterloo at 4.43, was some minutes late when it arrived, and Mr. Speke, hurriedly alighting, hailed a cab and drove at once to the house of his brother-in-law in Eccleston Square. He got there about ten minutes past five. Whilst his portmanteau was taken to his room, he remained in the hall, talking to the footman, who had been brought up in his parish, and then, telling the latter he was going to Warwick Street to buy a new hat, and afterwards to Westminster, on business, he went out, saying that he was dining with a friend at seven o'clock, and would be back in time to change. He walked to Warwick Street, called at a hatters, chose a hat, and told the shopman to be sure to send it to the address he was staying at in Eccleston Square, not later than 6.45, as he was going out at that time and should want it. He then left the shop, saying that he would pay for the hat on delivery, and, after that, vanished. On his failing to return to Eccleston Square, his brother-in-law communicated with the police, and a hue and cry was instantly raised.

Not a trace of him could be found that evening, however, and it was not until several days after his disappearance that a respectable looking man handed the police a somewhat dilapidated top hat, and told them the following story. He said he was a workman in the employ of Messrs. Maudsley &

Co., and that, at about 7.30, on the evening of January 8 he was taking a stroll through Birdcage Walk. It was all very quiet, there being hardly anyone about, and as he was walking along, thinking of nothing in particular, he noticed a hat lying on the ground. He picked it up, and thinking it might come in useful, as, although rather shabby it was still whole, he took it home with him, and, on examining it, found the name Speke on the lining. Then, of course, seeing in the papers, a few days later, that the Rev. Benjamin Speke was missing, he had come forward with the hat, to tell the police exactly when and where he found it. That was the man's story. His discovery, however, led to nothing.

Certain of the Press seemed to think it gave a distinctly sinister touch to the mystery, and perhaps it deepened the suspicion already entertained by many that Mr. Speke had met with foul play ; but that was all.

Indeed, that he had met with foul play did seem the most likely explanation of his disappearance. For what else could have happened to him ?*

A man of unchallenged integrity, exemplary in his domestic and parochial relations, of unimpaired

* *Vide* a pamphlet entitled " Mysterious Disappearances," published, anonymously, in 1868 by the author of " The Pauper, the Thief, and the Convict."

health and great physical strength, without, as far
as one knew, any financial troubles, he was suddenly
spirited away, as it were, in the early evening from
the neighbourhood of Westminster. Surely, nothing short of murder could account for it! " The
Times," deeming the disappearance worthy of a
leading article, wrote " Mr. Speke's case has
attracted more than ordinary attention from his
station in life, his profession, and the celebrity
which his name has acquired from the African
adventures and the untimely fate of his brother,"
and, continuing, remarked that it was by no means
an unusual thing for people to disappear, and that
a large percentage of those who did so turned up
again. But this remark was obviously made more
from a desire to comfort Mr. Speke's relatives and
friends than from any conviction that he would turn
up, for almost in the next line the writer adds :
" On the other hand a crime may have been committed . . . gentlemen have been murdered in
London before now ; " and in reference to the finding of the hat, while scouting the idea suggested by
various other press men that Mr. Speke had been
attacked and murdered in Birdcage Walk by a gang
of roughs, he regarded as possible, though not
probable, the theory that he may have been decoyed
into some den in Westminster (at that date the
slums between Victoria Street and Birdcage Walk

were regarded as among the very worst in London),
and there butchered and buried as the Mannings
butchered and buried Patrick O'Connor.

He, furthermore, states, and in so doing, disposes,
I think, of the last vestige of comfort he had previously meted out to Mr. Speke's relatives and
friends, that there might still be found in Westminster ruffians such as the garrotters (although,
fortunately, their garrotting activities had been cut
short), and the jail element hailing from Endell
Street,* who were capable of anything in the shape
of crime.   However, as a set-off against this depressing but, no doubt, quite true declaration, he
submitted that there was really no evidence of a
crime at all, for the finding of the hat could not be
taken as such, and, again, bringing forward the
theory that Mr. Speke was hiding, wrote, " People
are always disappearing ; sometimes under the
influence of an uncontrollable impulse bearing no
affinity to reason, sometimes under the spell of a
sudden temptation ; and sometimes out of shame
at some excess into which they may have been
betrayed. . . . We should be little surprised to
hear that the missing man has once more appeared
in the land of the living."   Though, perhaps, a
trifle more cautious and guarded in his statements,

* Then, also, one of the most notorious and dangerous of the
London slums.

the " Daily Telegraph " leader writer,* despite an assertion that he declined to express any opinion regarding the disappearance of Mr. Speke, in referring to it, could not altogether refrain from appealing to the more morbid-minded and sensation-loving of his readers. After citing several well-known cases of people who had disappeared under circumstances that created the general belief that they had been murdered, and then turned up again alive and well, he commented very severely on what he termed " the ulcerous slums of Westminster and St. Giles," designating them a positive menace to the safety of the public.

Regarding the correspondence that appeared in the Press relative to the case, little discrimination or censorship seems to have been used. The very wildest and most improbable schemes were proffered, as well as the most harrowing, and the London public was shocked to learn how many people were continually disappearing in its midst without leaving behind them the slightest clue as to their fate ; and how many had what could only be looked upon as providential escapes from robbery and, perhaps, death. Take the case of Mr. White for instance.†

Mr. White, a London clergyman, of the Chapel

* February 14th, 1868.
† See " Mysterious Disappearances."

Royal, Savoy, was walking in Trafalgar Square one morning when a man, addressing him by name, called to him from a four-wheeler. On Mr. White stopping and asking him what he wanted, he said he was a detective and requested Mr. White to get into the cab with him at once and drive to Bow Street Police Station, where he was required as a witness in the trial of some Fenians. Mr. White declined, and the man, seeing apparently that he could neither persuade nor coerce him, drove off. Later the same day, Mr. White called at Bow Street, and was informed that no one answering to his description of the man who had spoken to him was employed there, and that no such trial was in progress. Thus, Mr. White could only conclude that the stranger had had sinister designs.

On another occasion, he was accosted one autumn evening, at dusk, in the neighbourhood of Fleet Street, by a poorly dressed woman, who in very anxious tones begged him to go with her to her house and baptize her dying child. She told Mr. White that she was desperate, having been to the houses of all the clergymen in the district and found none of them at home. Impressed by her seeming earnestness Mr. White consented, and they set off together. After conducting him through the net-work of slums that, at that date, lay all around Fetter Lane, and made the locality little if anything better than St. Giles, she suddenly halted, and asking Mr. White to go on to an address which she gave him, whilst she ran to the chemist's for some medicine for the child, abruptly left him. Not knowing the neighbourhood Mr. White soon lost his way, and seeing a policeman, asked to be directed to the address the woman had given him.

" Don't go there alone, sir, whatever you do," the policeman said, " it is a shocking street, the abode of thieves and some of the worst characters in London. I don't relish going into it alone myself. So, if you like, I'll go with you and make inquiries there about the woman."

Mr. White gladly accepted the policeman's offer, and they walked through streets full of slatternly women and evil looking men (many of whom had closely cropped heads, as if but just out of prison) who, at the sight of them, exchanged meaning glances with each other, until they came to the house they were looking for, which was in a wretched and deserted-looking alley. The policeman knocked at the door, and upon asking for the woman whose child was ill was told that no such woman lived there.

" Now, sir," the policeman remarked to Mr. White, as they came away, " you'll not, I think, accuse me of exaggeration, when I tell you that you've had a very narrow escape. Had you gone into the alley alone the odds are a thousand to one you would never have have left it.   You would have simply disappeared, and nothing more would ever have been heard of you."

After reading in the correspondence already referred to some such accounts as the foregoing of Mr. White's experiences, many people came to the conclusion that Mr. Speke had met with a somewhat similar adventure, which in his case had terminated fatally.

As a variation it was suggested that Mr. Speke, finding himself pressed for time, when he left the hatter's in Warwick Street, had got into a four-wheeler, and had been driven to some lonely spot and murdered.

An advocate of this latter theory narrated an experience * that had quite recently befallen a friend of his, the nephew of a Middlesex magistrate. This young man having to see a lady home one Sunday night in November, called a cab off the rank in Tottenham Court Road, and told the cabby to drive him to Richmond Terrace, Caledonian Road.   Soon after they started, the driver pulled up, and, to his fare's astonishment, allowed a sinister-looking man, who was apparently on intimate terms with him, to mount beside him on the box.

* See article under the title of " Law and Order " in " Illustrated Times," January–February, 1868.

Then they went on again, and, on arriving at their destination, the man beside the driver descended from his perch and walked away. Having seen the young lady enter her house, the young man, whose name is not given, but whom I will call for convenience sake, Mr. M., again entered the cab, and told the driver to put him down at the corner of University Street. To his alarm, however, instead of being taken by a route that he knew, he was driven through a series of slummy, unsavoury streets, until he finally found himself in an extremely lonely spot by the Regent Park Canal. There the cab stopped and, on the cabby whistling, two men, one of whom Mr. M. recognized as the sinister-looking individual who had ridden on the box, emerged from the gloom and approached the vehicle. Mr. M., being quick-witted, took in the situation at a glance, and, springing out of the cab, successfully dodged his would-be assailants, and got safely away.

That the cabby had not applied to the young lady, whose address he knew, for his fare, but had been content to lose it, was in itself, perhaps, a sufficient proof that Mr. M.'s fears had not been unfounded, and that he had narrowly escaped being robbed and probably murdered.

And might not Mr. Speke, the narrator of the above incident argued, have had a similar adventure, and have fallen a victim, where Mr. M. had been lucky enough to escape ? In other words, whereas Mr. M. had seen his danger, Mr. Speke might have been taken completely by surprise, and consequently, before he had realized what was happening, have been set upon and overpowered, his physical strength, although great, being of little use when pitted against the combined onslaught of a whole gang of ruffians. Not a pleasant thought, this, for his family, and to harrow the feelings of his relations and the public still further, two more disappearances, that could, it was said, only be accounted for by crime, were quoted in certain other papers.

The first,* called a Regent Street Mystery, was to this effect.

A young man, twenty years of age, of the most exemplary character, beloved by his parents, popular amongst those of his own age, and without, as far as was known, a care in the world, left his home in Regent Street one morning—to be exact at 2 p.m. on July 4th, 1865—saying that he was going for a stroll and would be back in a few minutes, and was never heard of again. He took nothing with him, neither money nor clothes. Now, had he, on the spur of the moment, gone off on a visit to friends, he would surely have communicated the

* See " News of the World," February 16th, 1868.

fact, either by telegram or messenger, to his parents, to whom he was devoted, and who were devoted to him ; and, had he been staying with his friends, he would surely have written or wired to his parents to ask them to send him some wearing apparel. But he sent them no word of any sort, and when he did not return that night they informed the police, and exhaustive inquiries were at once set on foot.

All the ornamental and other waters in the London parks and commons, and all those around London, too, were dragged and wherever there were holes in them divers went down to search them ; the hospitals, jails, and even asylums were visited ; and not only were the British Army and Navy recruiting services communicated with, but also the French. Furthermore, notices appeared in all the leading papers in London and the provinces giving a detailed description of the missing youth and offering a substantial reward to anyone who could furnish any information regarding his whereabouts. However, the only result of this publicity was that the father one day received a very curious letter. It was well written, evidently by some one possessing a fair amount of education, but, though signed, contained no address. The postmark, however, showed it had been posted in London. The writer declared he was a steward on board a Mississippi steamer, and that, some few weeks after the disappearance of the son of the advertiser, he had taken a young Englishman, calling himself Bennett, about a thousand miles up the river. He suggested Bennett was the missing youth and warned the advertiser against a man who would probably call on him, pretending to have news of his son and asking for money. " Don't listen to his story," he wrote, " and, above all, don't give him a penny. You will hear from me again shortly."

The father, of course, took the letter to Scotland Yard, but the police considered it merely a hoax, and maintained the opinion they had held all along, namely, that the young man had disappeared voluntarily, and would, very probably, turn up again as soon as he had grown tired of playing truant. All the same, they advised the father to communicate with the police in New York, and inquire if there was any such boat and steward as those named in the letter. This the father of the young man did, and, in reply, was informed by Mr. Kennedy, the then head of the police in New York, who appeared to take great interest in the case, that there was no such boat on the Mississippi as that named in the letter, nor any such steward, and that all inquiries had failed to elicit any news of a young Englishman answering in the least degree to the missing youth.

Despite this failure, however, the father was convinced that the writer of the letter was *bona fide*, and that he was prevented giving any further information through intimidation.

The case was republished, apparently, for the purpose of suggesting that Mr. Speke had suffered the same fate as the father in the above-named case believed had befallen his son, that is to say, that he had been got hold of by some gang of ruffians and either kept in captivity, only to be released on ransom, or murdered off-hand.

The other case quoted in connection with the Speke case, and which originally appeared in the Scottish Press,* is as follows :

In the year 1867 a Mr. Owens, manure merchant of Edinburgh, had in his employ a foreman named William Stewart, who was a widower with three children, and about forty-five years of age. Greatly esteemed and trusted by Mr. Owens, Stewart was generally looked upon as a thoroughly steady, industrious man, typical of the best traditions of the working class of his country, a fond parent, and the least likely person to get into trouble of any kind. Well, one afternoon he came home to tea at the usual time and, after changing into his best suit of clothes, left again, and called at the house of some friends. He stayed with them, talking and

* See " Edinburgh Courant."

laughing, but quite normally, without appearing in the least degree excited, till a late hour, when he took his departure, saying it was time he went home to bed. Some one who knew him, however, saw him pass by his house and continue walking in the direction of the east pier, and, after that, he was never seen again. The river all round the east pier was searched, as was the whole town, and notices were put in various of the Scotch papers, but, in spite of the most vigorous inquiries, no clue as to his fate or whereabouts was ever found.

This case, originally, as I have said, reported in the Scottish papers, was referred to again in the London Press in February, 1868, just to show, I suppose, what opportunities for disappearances a river in a town affords ; it being still believed, despite the dragging and searching, that William Stewart, or rather William Stewart's body, was in the Firth of Forth.

Another harrowing but feasible theory put forward in the Press regarding Mr. Speke's disappearance was this : He had, it was said, a married sister whose house was in Queen's Square, Westminster, overlooking Birdcage Walk, and this lady was stated to have been out of town on January 8th. But might not Mr. Speke, not knowing or forgetting this, have called at the house after leaving the hatter's in Warwick Street, and finding no one there, and the place all shut up, have wandered into the garden and have been set upon there by some one, who had, perhaps, followed him for that very purpose. That would account for his hat being found in Birdcage Walk. But what had the ruffian or ruffians done with his body ? This question was obviously a staggerer, and the propounder of the above theory could only suggest that the body might lie buried near at hand, the police, despite their exhaustive search of the premises and their immediate vicinity, having failed to discover the improvised grave. Indeed, pretty well every hypothesis that could be put forward was put forward, and nothing that could be said or suggested to distress and harrow the feelings of Mr. Speke's friends and relations was left unsaid or unsuggested ; and yet, as the writer of " Mysterious Disappearances " remarked, out of all these theories and suggestions there was not one on which anyone would have cared to stake five shillings. If there was anything in favour of any one of them, there was also something equally, and generally more, to its discredit. Against the theory of his having been robbed—he was known to have had money on him at the time of his disappearance—and murdered, was the fact that the large reward offered for any information regarding him had not induced some one to turn Queen's evidence.

The experience of the police, who, by the way, like "The Times," held firmly to the opinion that Mr. Speke had disappeared voluntarily, was that, in the majority of cases where murder had been committed, the offer of a big reward had the desired effect; some one was eventually induced to split on his or her confederates.

And then, again, in the case of Mr. Speke's disappearance, the body not being found told against the theory of murder, since, in the event of highway robbery and its consequent unpremeditated murder, the murderer makes no attempt to hide the body. Human remains were, of course, from time to time unearthed during excavations for roadway improvements and building, that leave little if any doubt at all of their being the remains of some one for information regarding whom the offer of large rewards had been made and met with no response, but these were exceptional cases; generally speaking, money, in this, as well as in every other respect, proves effectual.

But some people argued Mr. Speke might not have been robbed at all. He might perhaps have been seized by the Fenians in mistake for some one else, and either kept a prisoner by them in some cellar or attic or killed on the spot, and, if the latter, the body might have been secretly buried and have remained in its secret burial place, undisturbed, for years.

The perfectly impartial mind had to admit that such a thing was, at least, possible ; but as it did not seem to be at all probable, the speculators eventually concluded that the hypothesis of voluntary disappearance, adopted by the police and most of the Press, was after all the most feasible.

Yet against this hypothesis was the character ascribed to Mr. Speke by his friends. If he were as fond of his parents and home, and as devoted to his parishioners as they believed him to be, a man of unblemished reputation and unchallenged integrity, thoroughly straight and upright in all his doings, and at the same time level-headed and normal, would he have gone off without giving anyone the slightest intimation as to where he was going, and have remained away without communicating with anyone ? Would he not rather, like the good and just man he was said to be, have considered the feelings of his relatives and friends before anything, and have scorned to act in such a heartless and, to say the least of it, unmannerly way towards them ?

Clearly, the voluntary disappearance theory could only hold water, on the supposition that there was something in Mr. Speke's character or disposition that even the most intimate of his friends did not suspect. Could it be that, underlying the combination of excellent qualities so apparent in him, there was hidden a tendency to weakness, and that having once yielded to animal passion he had fled, horrified at his lapse, and ashamed to face any of his old associates ?

Or, should the above be deemed unwarrantable, had he, perhaps, with the very best intentions, interfered in some brawl more disreputable than he had at first imagined, and been so disfigured that he dreaded facing his friends and parishioners ?

Or, there may have been in him, as there is in many people, a latent element of nomadism ; and his weariness of the monotony of life, and of all the people he was daily brought in contact with, becoming at length absolutely unbearable, he had succumbed and fled, whither he hardly knew, and little cared.

Yet, again, it might not have been a case of voluntary disappearance ; but perhaps through some blow or injury, or other cause, he had undergone a complete lapse of memory, and was wandering about the country imagining himself some one else. All these possibilities seemed in the eyes of the Press, as a whole, the police, and many other people besides, to be much more likely than the theory of murder, yet, against them all was the fact that no one apparently had identified him, and in view of the detailed description of him that had appeared in papers all over the country, he must have been identified had he been seen. And, yet, it was argued, one of these theories, supposing Mr. Speke had not been murdered, had not met with an accident, had not committed suicide (there had been nothing in his conduct to suggest the latter possibility; moreover, had he done so, his body would surely have been found), or was not being kept in captivity, must be right. Which was it? Lapse of memory or disappearance of his own accord?

While his family kept a discreet silence, every one else talked, and the disappearance of the Rev. Benjamin Speke formed one of the principal topics of conversation, not only in the London clubs, Mayfair and Belgravia, but in all circles of society throughout the country. Indeed, never before had a disappearance caused such a universal sensation in England, and raised so many and such unpleasant conjectures. Though society tried to assure itself that there was nothing to fear, that Mr. Speke would very probably turn up again alive, try how it would it could not help feeling that he might not, and that the fate which had befallen him might befall anyone.

Thus speculation of a none too pleasant kind was at its height when an announcement appeared in the Press one morning to the effect that the Rev. Benjamin Speke was found. What had happened was this:

Police Sergeant Soady, of the Cornwall County Constabulary, while on duty one day in the streets of Padstow, noticed a stranger who, from his costume, appeared to be a cattle driver. He was strolling about somewhat aimlessly, and Sergeant Soady, on looking more closely at him, was struck with the likeness he bore to the description sent him by the police at Hull of a man named Ayre, who was wanted for absconding from that city with a large sum of money belonging to his employers.

Approaching the stranger quite casually, Soady got into conversation with him, and finding some excuse for doing so accompanied him to his lodgings. Convinced then, when he saw the stranger without a hat, that he was the man for whom the Hull police were looking, Soady, as soon as he could do so without arousing suspicion, took leave of him and wired to Inspector Opie of Wadebridge, who immediately came to Padstow and, on seeing the stranger, expressed the same opinion as Soady, namely, that he was none other than Ayre, masquerading as a cattle driver. Consequently, the stranger was arrested and brought before Mr. H. P. Rawling, J.P., who remanded him for further examination.

The fact that a large sum of money was found on him, for which he refused to account, helped considerably to confirm the suspicion that he was Ayre. Mr. Rawling communicated with the Chief Con-

stable of Cornwall and the Superintendent of the
Police at Bodmin, and both these men came to
Padstow and examined the stranger, and, as a
result, came to the conclusion that he was not Ayre,
but that there was some mystery attached to him.

Consequently they asked Mr. Rawling to remand
him to Bodmin, and their request being granted
they travelled with him to that town.   Convinced
from the conversation they had with the stranger
during the journey that he was a gentleman
masquerading as a cattle driver, they compared him,
on arriving at Bodmin Jail, with the description
they had there of the Rev. Benjamin Speke, and at
once came to the conclusion that he actually was
the missing clergyman.

On being asked whether he was not Mr. Speke
the stranger appeared very upset, but answered in
the affirmative, expressing his shame at having
caused such a lot of trouble.   He said the sole
reason for his disappearing was that he was sure his
relatives and friends had one and all ceased to care
for him, since he became heir to some property.
This had made him so wretched and, consequently,
so unable to go on living at home and doing his
work in the parish, that he had eventually resolved
to sever himself from all who knew him and start
life afresh in America.   In reply to the Chief Constable's query as to why he had not gone to America

instead of wandering about in Cornwall, he said it was because he felt he must take a farewell of his own country before leaving it, perhaps for ever.

After some persuasion on the part of the Chief Constable and the Superintendent, he wrote to his brother-in-law, Mr. Murdock, in Eccleston Square, and Mr. Murdock, after showing the letter to the Home Secretary and going through various other formalities, came down to Bodmin, accompanied by an inspector from Scotland Yard, to take Mr. Speke back with him. At first Mr. Speke refused to go, saying that he still thought of migrating to the States, but he eventually gave way, and returned with them to London. And there the affair, as far as the public were concerned, ended.

What subsequently became of the Reverend gentleman history does not say. The case, however, is interesting, since it demonstrates into what strange situations a slight kink in the brain* may sometimes lead one ; this same kink, moreover, being either so slight or capable of being so successfully concealed, that no one would for one moment dream that it existed.

The appended is an extract from Mr. Speke's diary showing what he did after throwing away his hat in Birdcage Walk as " a blind."

* As a result of a medical examination it was decided the Rev. B. Speke was suffering from hypochondriasis.

" Went to Basingstoke same night, and next day walked to Winchester, 18 miles, thence to Bishopstoke, Southampton, Gosport and Portsmouth. Remained at Portsmouth, visiting Southsea, East Caves and various other places in the neighbourhood till Wednesday, January 29th. On Sunday, February 10th, arrived at Plymouth by steamer ; stayed in Plymouth as headquarters, till February 16th, in meantime making tour of surrounding districts and visiting, among other places, Saltash, Cotehele, Egg, Buckland, Tamerton, Riborough, Ivy Bridge, St. Germans. Attended church at St. Germans on Sunday, February 16th.

" On Monday went to Fowey, small port southwest of Cornwall. Next day to Lostwithiel, an ancient town on Fowey river, six miles distant. On the 20th arrived at county town of Bodmin, a journey of some distance. There put up at the Queen's Head, where I left my luggage, consisting of several bags, all enclosed in one large one.* The following day went to Padstow, a port on the northeast coast of Cornwall, 15 miles distant."

Here, a few hours after his arrival in Padstow, he was arrested.

* There is no explanation given as to how he came by this luggage, but presumably he bought it in London after leaving the hatter's.

CHAPTER XIII

URBAN NAPOLEON STANGER AND THE DISAPPEARANCES AT WEST HAM

IN the seventies of the last century two of the most familiar figures in St. Giles, Whitechapel, were Mr. and Mrs. Urban Napoleon Stanger.

Both were natives of Kreuznach in Germany. Marrying in 1868, they came to London two or three years later, and settled in Lever Street, which, lying between Goswell Street and the newly acquired headquarters of the Salvation Army, formed, at that time, part of the most densely populated and criminal neighbourhoods in London. Here Stanger started as a baker, and in due course acquired the reputation for being thoroughly hard working and thrifty.

As far as was known, he had no troubles of any sort, and, to the outside world at least, he appeared to be perfectly happy and content, and to be living on the best of terms with his wife, a rather stout, massively built woman with a coarse and, as some thought, rather unpleasant type of face, and a fondness for " showy " dress and cheap jewellery.

She was rather younger than he, and she was usually to be seen, at all times of the day, serving in the shop behind the counter.

They kept one maid, who, besides doing the housework, helped in the shop, an errand-boy, and a journeyman named Christian Zeutler ; but, as the two latter lived out, the actual household consisted of only Mr. and Mrs. Stanger and the maid.

Stanger, it seems, did most of the baking himself, though he was sometimes assisted by a man named Franz Felix Stumm, also a master baker. In appearance Stumm was very characteristic of a certain type of German that one cannot help suspecting may be partly Jewish. He had a long, heavy face, a long, slightly hooked nose, a short bushy beard and whiskers ; and his expression showed such a curiously harmonized mixture of stupidity, brutality and cunning that it left one wondering which of these qualities, if either, predominated.

Though a married man, he was continually at the Stangers' house, and the scandalmongers of Lever Street hinted at a rather closer intimacy between him and Mrs. Stanger than Mr. Stanger seemed to be aware of, and than was, perhaps, quite right and proper. Otherwise, he seemed to be ordinary enough, and came in for little comment. Stanger himself was a steady, industrious individual, very dull and unimaginative, and apparently interested only in making and amassing money. He had, it was said, a considerable sum stored away in the bank, and this was considered a very creditable achievement for one of his age, which was only 36. His wife, by the way, was 35, and Felix Stumm a year younger. Such, then, was the Stangers' household, or such it was supposed to be, on the 12th of November, 1881.

At five minutes to twelve that night, as Christian Zeutler was walking along Lever Street on his way home, he saw four men standing on the pavement talking, outside Stanger's shop. They were Urban Stanger, Felix Stumm, and two friends of his, Lang and Cramer. When Zeutler had passed them by, he looked round and saw Lang, Cramer and Stumm go off together, and Stanger enter his house alone.

The following day, on his arrival at the shop at about 8 a.m., Mrs. Stanger immediately asked him to go round and tell Mr. Stumm to come at once, as he was urgently wanted. Zeutler did so, and Stumm came to the shop and remained there all day. He was there the next day when Zeutler arrived, and the next day and the day after, and on or about November 26th he took up his abode in the place altogether.

All this time neither Zeutler nor anyone outside the shop saw Stanger. Frequent inquiries were

made for him, but every one, apparently, was satisfied with Mrs. Stanger's explanation that he was in
Germany, and that Stumm was merely looking
after his business during his absence.   Then, one
day, the residents in the neighbourhood got a surprise.   On passing the shop they saw the name
F. F. Stumm.   The familiar name U. N. Stanger
was gone.

This made them talk, and they talked still more
when it was discovered that Stumm was acting as
if Stanger's property were his own.   While some
believed that Stanger had, for some reason or
another, perhaps jealousy, or simply because he was
tired of her, deserted his wife, others of a more
daring imagination hazarded the supposition that
he may have been baked in his own oven.

Oddly enough, however, the police do not seem
to have taken any action in the matter, and the
first intimation the public in general received of the
affair came from private quarters.   In April, 1882,
there appeared in the Press, and on handbills and
hoardings, the following arrestive announcement:

" Fifty   pounds   reward.   Mysteriously   disappeared, since the early part of November last, from
his residence No. — Lever Street, City Road, Urban
Napoleon Stanger, master baker, native of Kreuznach, Germany.   Any person who will give information leading to his discovery will receive the

above reward.   Wendel Scherer, Private Enquiry Agent, 28 Chepstow Place, Bayswater."

It was never made known who prompted this inquiry, but it may be surmised that it was either one of Stanger's creditors or the executors of his will.

Anyhow, the advertisement created a great sensation in Whitechapel, and, owing to it, the mysterious disappearance of Mr. Stanger became a constant theme of conversation there, and in other parts of London as well. Stumm, however, continued to live in undisturbed possession of Stanger's shop, and apparently he was quite oblivious of the growing feeling of resentment which his conduct had aroused in the neighbourhood.

He was repeatedly asked what had become of Stanger, but his reply, accompanied by a shrug, was always the same :

" I don't know.   He is abroad somewhere."

And when queried as to why Stanger should absent himself thus, he invariably answered :

" He is deep in debt."

A reply that only tended to increase suspicion against him, as Stanger, it was generally believed, had been doing an excellent business and spending little.   During these inquiries Mrs. Stanger, against whom the feeling in the neighbourhood ran stronger, perhaps, than against Stumm, kept very much in the background, and eventually left the shop for private quarters in another district.

This state of things continued all through the spring and summer of 1882, and, in fact, until almost a year after Stanger's disappearance, when an announcement was made in the Press that Mrs. Stanger and Stumm had been arrested. It was hoped now that a solution to the mystery of Urban Stanger's disappearance was near at hand, and the keenest disappointment was experienced when it was discovered that there was no mention of Stanger in the charges brought against the pair.

Stumm was charged with forging and uttering a cheque for the payment of £76 15s., and, further, with conspiring together with one Elizabeth Stanger to defraud John George Geisel and William Evans of the sum of £76 15s. Geisel and Evans were executors of Urban Stanger's will, but, beyond that, there was nothing to associate the arrest in any way with Urban Stanger's disappearance.

Yet every one felt instinctively that the two events ought to have some close bearing on one another. And on the two accused persons appearing at Worship Street Police Court, some of the evidence that followed certainly did refer to the mystery, but it elucidated nothing.

Christian Zeutler merely told the tale I have already narrated, and which every one in St. Giles

136 F.F STUMM. 136
Baker
Mr ALBERT JONES
Solicitor for
THE PRISONERS
Mr FILLAN
Counsel for The Prisoners
STANGER
FRANZ FELIX STUMM
ZENTLER
EVANS
GEISSEL
WITNESSES

SOME OF THE PRINCIPAL CHARACTERS IN THE CASE OF THE MISSING BAKER OF ST. LUKE'S

(Penny Illustrated Paper. Oct. 14, 1882)

ELIZA CARTER AGED 12, WHO DISAPPEARED AT WEST HAM
JAN. 28, 1882 AND WAS NEVER SEEN AGAIN
(Penny Illustrated Paper. Feb. 18, 1882)

knew, namely that when passing along Lever Street late on the night of November 12, 1881, he had seen Stanger enter his shop alone, and that he had never set eyes on him again.

The proceedings unfolded little more. Stumm repeated his statement that he believed Stanger had gone abroad in order to hide from his many creditors ; but, on this occasion, he declared also that he had frequently lent Stanger money ; the truth of which assertion was very much questioned later on in the proceedings, when it was proved that Stanger, at the time of his disappearance, had at least four hundred pounds in the bank. This supplementary statement therefore only blackened Stumm still more in the eyes of the public, and the feeling against him was still further strengthened when the contents of Stanger's will became known.

He had left all his household furniture, effects and the entire income to be derived from realizing all his estate, real and personal, and investing the proceeds in mortgages, to his wife, conditionally that she did not marry again or cohabit or live with any other man. In fact, the proviso in this will not only seemed to suggest that Stanger had some suspicion of Stumm, but it also suggested an explanation of Stumm's having seized Stanger's shop and forged his signature to cheques and securities.

He could only have done so, of course, through

the connivance of Mrs. Stanger, and Mrs. Stanger
having, it was presumed, fallen head over ears in
love with him, aware of the clause in the will pre-
venting her coming into Stanger's money, if she
married or lived with him, had resolved to aid him
in seizing everything belonging to her husband,
hinting to him to cohabit with her afterwards.

Some even believed that Mrs. Stanger had gone
further. They believed that she had made the path
easier for Stumm by helping him to do away with
her husband, and a something in the appearance of
the defendants, as they stood side by side in the
dock, certainly seemed to favour this theory. There
was an unpleasant looking bulkiness in their build,
a sullen gloom in their eyes, which seemed incapable
of smiling, and more than a mere suggestion of
savageness about their mouths, which struck those
present in the Court as sinister, and made them feel
that it was not at all improbable that Mrs. Stanger
and Stumm knew a great deal more about Urban
Stanger's disappearance than they had admitted.
At the termination of the proceedings the accused
were committed for trial ; but subsequently, for
some unexplained reason, the charge against Mrs.
Stanger was withdrawn and Felix Stumm appeared
alone in the dock, at the Central Criminal Court, to
take his trial before Mr. Justice Hawkins for forging
a mortgage deed having relation to the property of

Urban Napoleon Stanger, missing since November 12th, 1881. Montagu Williams, Q.C., defended, and Mrs. Stanger appeared as one of the principal witnesses.

Her evidence was remarkable, as it was only too apparent to all present that she was doing her utmost to save Stumm and whitewash his character at the expense of her husband's. According to her testimony, Stanger was a spendthrift; how he actually ran through his money she did not know, for he never told her, but he would most certainly have got into serious financial straits over and over again had it not been for Felix Stumm, who continually came to the rescue and lent him large sums.

She declared that her husband did not disappear on the 12th of November, 1881, as had been stated, but either on the night of the 19th or early on the morning of the 20th. What happened on the 19th, as far as she could remember, was this :

In the morning, in answer to an urgent message from her husband, Felix Stumm came to the shop and promised to lend Stanger more money. They also made arrangements to go out together the next day, Sunday.

After tea, her husband went for a walk, and she recollected hearing him talking with several other men, about midnight, just outside the front door. He finally said good-night to them and, entering the house alone, joined her in the parlour. He appeared to be in a distinctly disagreeable and quarrelsome mood, and after they had been talking for, perhaps, half an hour, he suddenly remarked :

" I have always told you I would leave you. I will do so."

This so upset her that she went out of the room and upstairs to bed. She never saw him again.

On getting up in the morning she found he was not in the house, and believing he had carried out his threat and left her, she sent for Felix Stumm, who very kindly agreed to look after the business for her. She denied cohabiting with him and declared the forgery of her husband's signature to the securities—the deed with which Stumm was charged—had been done by her and not by the accused. She said she was in the habit of signing cheques and various documents for her husband.

This was the gist of her evidence. Under cross-examination she appeared very confused and made at least one remarkable contradiction. She stated that soon after she went up to bed on the night of November 19th her husband followed her, and after remaining with her till half-past one suddenly got up and left the room, this she now affirmed being the last time she ever saw him.

Her statement, however, did not ring true, and her voice all through her examination sounded so hollow and insincere that no one in the Court believed what she said. Many instinctively felt that she ought to have been in the dock with Stumm, to answer an even more serious charge than forgery.

As had been anticipated, the jury brought in a verdict of guilty against Stumm. White with passion, he cried out that his counsel had bungled the case shamefully, and that had the matter been properly investigated the jury would have seen that there was a conspiracy against him.

His protest, however, availed him nothing, and it was not difficult to see what was at the back of Mr. Justice Hawkins' mind when he passed the following severe sentence.

" Franz Felix Stumm," he began, " you have been convicted of a very wicked forgery, and you have not improved your position by throwing unmerited abuse upon your legal advisers. I am to punish you now for the forgery you have committed, and I take nothing into consideration, except the fact that you have committed that forgery under circumstances that have been disclosed to the jury. In all the circumstances, I feel it my duty to condemn you to be kept in penal servitude for ten years."

" Thank you," Stumm replied. " I am much obliged to you."

He was about to say more, when he was removed

from the dock by the warders on either side of him, and with his exit from the Court all public reference to the Stanger mystery may be said to have ended. At any rate, apparently, no official attempt to solve it was ever made.

If Stanger went abroad, as his wife and Stumm said they believed he did, he did not visit any of his relatives or friends in Germany, the executors of his will having procured evidence in proof of that fact ; and if he did not visit any of his relatives or friends in Germany, why did he not ?

Why did he not settle up his affairs before he went, and take, at least, some of his money with him, and why did he go without telling anyone but his wife ?

No, in this case it seems to me that public opinion was not very far wrong, and that the unfortunate Urban Stanger never left his house in Lever Street alive. What actually happened to him one cannot, of course, say, but it is quite possible there may have been something in the oven theory. Ovens have not infrequently played important rôles in great tragedies.

I cannot conclude this volume without referring, albeit very briefly, to the remarkable number of disappearances that occurred in the eighties and early nineties of the last century at West Ham.

These disappearances gave the district for many

years a very sinister name. The epidemic, for it seems to have been little else, may be said to have reached its climax with the disappearance of Eliza Carter.* Eliza Carter, a pretty little girl of twelve years of age, left her sister's house in the West Road at 10 a.m. to go to her parents, who lived close by in Church Street.

On the way she left some clothes at a laundry, and was not seen again after that till about five o'clock in the afternoon, when she stopped one of her schoolfellows in the Portway and told her she was afraid to go home because of some man.

About eleven o'clock that night she was reported to have been seen with a middle-aged woman of unprepossessing appearance, dressed in a long ulster and black frock, and after that nothing more was ever heard of her again ; but a blue dress, shorn of all its buttons, and identified as the one she had been wearing, was picked up the following day on the local football field. Rewards were offered for news of her, but in vain, and, as far as the public are concerned, her fate remains a mystery to this day.

About Easter time in the previous year a little girl named Seward,† also disappeared from her home in West Ham, and, despite the offer of a reward by the

* See " Penny Illustrated Paper," February 4th, 1882.
† See " Penny Illustrated Paper," March 25th, 1882.

Director of Criminal Investigations, nothing was ever seen or heard of her.

In April, 1882, Charles Wagner*, son of a West Ham butcher, disappeared, but in this case he was definitely proved to have met with foul play, his dead body being found under a cliff at Ramsgate.

A few weeks later there was another disappearance† in West Ham, the missing person this time being a lady of the mature age of sixty-seven.

Possessed of considerable private means, and with, as far as was known, no serious worries or troubles of any kind, she left her home in the Keogh Road on the evening of April 12, 1882, and bought some soap and candles in Stratford. The postman, milkman and various other tradesmen called at the house in the Keogh Road as usual in the morning, but received no answer to their knocks, and on the police eventually forcing an entry, as it was feared something must have happened to the old lady, it was found that she was not there. The grandfather clock was ticking away in the hall, the soap and candles which the old lady had purchased were neatly stored in the kitchen cupboard, and everything was in apple-pie order; but of the old lady herself there was no sign, and, from that day to this,

* See " Penny Illustrated Paper," April 15th, 1882.
† See " News of the World," May 7th, 1882.

her fate has remained a baffling mystery, since no clue to it of any sort was ever found.

After this West Ham enjoyed a comparative immunity for some years. There were disappearances and tragedies, but they were occasional and spasmodic. In January, 1890, however, a series or epidemic of disappearances again occurred. Three girls, all living in the same neighbourhood, disappeared, one after the other, and the fate of one only of them was ever ascertained.

The body of this one, an attractive girl of fifteen, named Amelia Jeffs, was found several weeks after she disappeared from her home, in an empty house in the Portway, facing West Ham Park; and a medical examination of her remains proved that she had been strangled, but not before she had made a desperate fight for her life. This discovery led to the supposition that the other missing girls had met with a similar fate, and it was generally supposed the crimes were committed by some sexual maniac with homicidal tendencies, some nightmarish monster that, under the cloak of a respectable exterior, prowled about the more quiet of the West Ham thoroughfares, on the look out for juvenile victims of the female sex.

One is apt to jump to the conclusion that all criminals of this class are men; indeed, Feminists, in their propaganda of the usual anti-male description, would lead us to suppose that such is the case ; but they are wrong. Some, at least, of the assassins of children have been proved to be women.

Hence the idea that Amelia Jeffs and the other girls who disappeared, but whose bodies were never found, were decoyed by a woman, must not be too lightly dismissed. Women are as susceptible to the lowest forms of mania as men.

Since 1890 there have been no more continuous disappearances in West Ham ; and, though that district has occasionally witnessed some very harrowing tragedies, it may be said to enjoy as fair a reputation now, with regard to immunity from crime and mystery, as most other districts in and around London.

People, however, still disappear. Sometimes, as in the case of the Rev. Benjamin Speke, they turn up again, and sometimes, more often perhaps, nothing more is ever seen or heard of them, and their fate remains for all time shrouded in mystery. As those who have perused these pages will have gathered, the reasons for disappearances are manifold. While some, no doubt, are entirely due to voluntary action on the part of the subject, brought about by some sudden impulse, whim, or morbid fancy, or shame of some consummate act of folly, and fear of disgrace and exposure, or desire to escape from the consequences of some even criminal act, others may be due to unforeseen accident or lapse of memory ; and others, again, to suicide and murder.*

Indeed, the by no means infrequent digging up and otherwise finding of human skeletons, with obvious marks of violence on them, demonstrate conclusively that a very large percentage of disappearances come within this last-named category.

* The White Slave Traffic is so nearly extinct in this country to-day—in my opinion, it has always been very much exaggerated—that it could only account for a few of the disappearances that are constantly occuring in our midst.